Cowgirl Come Home

THE BIG SKY MAVERICK SERIES

DEBRA SALONEN

TULE
PUBLISHING

DEDICATION

With heartfelt thanks to Jane Porter—brilliant visionary, warrior woman, gifted writer, humble saint and...best of all, friend. Jane's kindness and generosity prompted a few us to award her the title: Jane of the Giant Heart...and Great Hair. You rock, Jane. Thanks for inviting me to the Tule party.

Dear Reader,

I hope you enjoy Cowgirl, Come Home. I can't tell you how thrilled I was when Jane Porter invited me to be part of Tule Publishing's Montana Born summer series, The Big Marietta Fair. I live in a small town in the Sierra foothills of California, and the annual fair is a big deal. Dreams are made—and sometimes dashed—during the course of the fair. My heroine, Bailey Jenkins, couldn't wait to leave her hometown of Marietta, Montana, where she'd spent most of her life picking up after her reckless, larger-than-life father, OC Jenkins. She worked hard to earn the title: Fair Queen, along with a college rodeo scholarship. Unfortunately, her big break was anything but clean. Bad timing, bad luck and an excruciating choice that broke the heart of Paul Zabrinski, the sweetest boy she'd ever known, made coming home a non-option. Until fifteen years later when Bailey was out of options. And Paul Zabrinski is there to meet her plane. Gorgeous, sexy and successful, a single dad living the life she could have had if she'd stayed. What they both learn is a forever love doesn't forget, and forgiveness doesn't have a time limit.

As with every book, I turn to experts for advice. Since I haven't been a ten-year old girl in a very long time, I asked Morgan Lettice and Calli Butler to share their love of horses, riding and fair experiences to help me better understand my hero's daughter, Chloe Zabrinski. Both Calli and Morgan agreed it was pure foolishness on Chloe's part to try a dangerous trick on her horse—something neither of them would do. My thanks, too, to Donna Lettice for being such a good mom—and friend.

Writing a book in a multi-author connected series can be tricky, but the six "Big Marietta Fair" authors are consummate professionals who also love to laugh. Ladies, you made this experience a pleasure I'd repeat in a heartbeat. My thanks to Nancy Robards Thompson, Katherine Garbera, Yvonne Lindsay, Bronwyn Jameson and Barbara Ankrum, along with the fabulous Tule Publishing team!

And last, but very far from least, I confess I have a girl-crush on the coolest editor ever—with the hippest name, too—Sinclair Sawhney. Sinclair, you helped me find my writing mojo and I truly can't thank you enough!

Deb

Prologue

THE NOISE FROM the carnival midway struck Bailey Jenkins as an ironically festive backdrop for the decision being discussed at the top of the Ferris wheel. The garishly bright bulbs made Paul Zabrinski's face appear years older than seventeen. Mature. Serious. Furious.

"If you do this, Bailey Jenkins, I will hate you forever. And I'll call on my great-grandmother to curse you. She was a gypsy witch, you know."

Everyone in Marietta, Montana, knew the story of Hilda Zabrinski's supposed curse that bankrupted an unscrupulous banker who tried to screw her family out of their dry goods store. Some credited fortuitous timing of the collapse of the banks in 1929 for the man's fall from grace, but no one in the Zabrinski family doubted Hilda's powers.

"I'm doing this for both of us, Paul."

"Yeah, right. You're killing my baby because you love me so much."

The bitterness and cynicism in his tone burned. She half-expected the highly flammable white and gold ribbon stretched diagonally across her chest to burst into flames.

The past four days as Fair Queen should have been the happiest of Bailey's life. Instead, she was late. Her highly regular body failed to produce the cramps, bloating and menses she normally cursed.

Paul drove her to Bozeman yesterday to buy an over-the-counter test kit. She'd used one of the predictors right after the Fair Queen ceremony last night. The high point of her life cut short by a small blue reality check. One minute little girls were begging for autographs, the next she had to tell her boyfriend of ten months she planned to get an abortion.

"I do love you, Paul. But you're seventeen. You have your whole senior year ahead of you. I just turned eighteen in January. I'm supposed to leave for Fresno State next week. You know how much this scholarship means to me. How hard I worked for it."

They'd taken precautions. She'd been on the pill for six months…except when she'd had the flu so bad she couldn't keep water down. The chance she'd get knocked up was like one in a hundred thousand. She didn't need Paul's gypsy great-grandmother to put a curse on her—Bailey already had the worst luck on the planet.

"My parents will help."

Paul reached for her hand, but she pushed him away. His touch did things to her that robbed her of the ability to think straight. Hormones were her enemy.

"You told your folks?" she shrieked, thankful for the high-pitched screams from the teenyboppers in the carts on either side of them.

The Ferris wheel moved a space or two, jerking and rocking in a way she normally enjoyed. Now, her stomach twisted and heaved. Nerves? Pregnancy? Or a taste of the guilt she knew she'd have to live with if she went through with her plan.

"Not yet, but I know they'd let us live with them until we saved up enough money to get a place of our own. I've worked after school and on weekends at the store forever. I've got a pretty good nest egg saved up."

An image of setting up house in the Zabrinskis' basement strengthened her resolve.

"I have to do this, Paul. I'm sorry."

Her sweet, gentle, easy-going boyfriend leaned across the gap between them, his eyes narrowing. A black coldness that looked every bit as dangerous and scary as her father on a bender matched the intense fury in his tone when he said, "Oh, yeah. You're going to be sorry, Bailey. You're going to be sorry for the rest of your life."

Bailey slid to the corner of the ride, arms wrapped around her knees. Strangely, Paul's anger made her ambivalence disappear. She'd already endured two days of browbeating from her father who somehow intuitively guessed she was pregnant. The test only confirmed her fear.

"You will get rid of it. End of story," OC had shouted last night when he staggered home after one too many beers. "Your mother and I worked too hard, sacrificed too much, to let you ruin your life by getting tied down in Marietta with some snot-nosed kid who sells screwdrivers for a living."

If Paul couldn't even discuss her feelings without resorting to threats, then he was not the right person for her—or the right person to father a child. She'd lived with OC Jenkins' autocratic bullying her whole life. She wouldn't do that to her kid.

The Ferris wheel began to turn. Their basket rocked like

a baby's cradle. Nausea rose in her throat. Bailey felt Paul's fury, his barely contained urge to hurt her. She'd been hit before. Big hands, as fast as a horse's kick.

Her heart pounded painfully in her chest, her breathing shallow. As they crested another circle, she kept her gaze on the moonlit skyline of the Copper Mountains. On Monday, her mother would drive her to a clinic in Bozeman. Bailey would do what her father demanded, what Mom agreed was "probably for the best."

In a few weeks, Bailey would start college in California. Ask anybody and they'd tell you, "Marietta Fair Queen Bailey Jenkins has big plans." And a bright future didn't include getting knocked up on the eve of her grand exit.

She straightened her shoulders and lifted her chin. Life wasn't perfect. She'd known that for a long, long time. She'd have to live with this decision for the rest of her life. But that life—good or bad—wasn't going to happen in Marietta. Paul Zabrinski and his crazy curse could stay the hell in Montana because Bailey Jenkins was never coming back.

Chapter 1

Bailey Jenkins gazed out the small oval window, squinting through the double panes of airplane Plexiglas, for that trademark Montana skyline she hadn't seen in six years. That trip—her first since leaving for college had been a fly-by to give her mother a little support when Dad's diagnosis came back positive for prostate cancer.

But despite his doctor's grim predictions, Oscar "OC" Jenkins—Marietta, Montana's larger than life outdoors guide and fisherman—managed to beat a probable death sentence to continue to be a burden to Bailey's long-suffering mother, Louise. He carried on hunting, fishing, tromping through all kinds of bacteria-filled water, failing to replace a pair of worn-out boots in a timely manner, and—worse—choosing to ignore an ingrown toenail that became infected.

Until one night six months ago, when Mom crawled into bed and smelled something unpleasant. "Did a mouse die in the wall behind our bed?" she'd asked her husband of nearly forty years.

"Might be my toe. Got a bit of infection."

More than a bit. The great and powerful OC Jenkins had waited too long. Despite several rounds of antibiotics, the toe had to be amputated.

Then, rather than following his doctor's orders, OC rushed back to work. And refused to stop drinking and smoking. The infection spread. He lost another toe. And another. His appetite disappeared. He slept twenty hours a day. Depression set in.

Finally, Mom found the backbone to make an appointment with a specialist in Bozeman. The doctor wound up amputating his leg, mid-calf.

He was due home from rehab tomorrow, and once again Mom called, pleading. "I'm sorry, honey. I know you're still doctoring...and grieving, but I have to go back to work. Our bills are mounting and I don't know if...when...Oscar will be back on his feet. Come home, Bailey. Please? For me?"

"Home," Bailey murmured, her gaze on the iconic Montana skyline. The place from which she'd spent every waking day of high school crafting her escape. And when her big chance came—a scholarship at Fresno State, she'd nearly blown it. She'd let love undermine her resolve.

A crackling voice on the plane's PA reminded her to return her seat back to the upright position. Her three-hundred-pound seatmate grappled with the armrest between them, somehow managing to kick her right foot in the process.

Shards of white-hot daggers shot up her leg, making her cry out.

"Sorry 'bout that."

Sweat broke out across her lip. Her breathing went fast and shallow.

She pictured Maureen, Bailey's favorite physical therapist and friend, coaching her through the pain. "Breathe, girlfriend. Big breath. Tell the pain to take a hike."

Like I'll ever be hiking again.

A sour taste in her mouth made her poke through her purse for a stick of gum. Anything to kill the craving for a pain pill.

Bailey knew all about dependency. She'd spend her childhood making excuses for her mother's classic co-dependency on Bailey's father, who drank beer every day and polished off a fifth of Jack Daniels on weekends—a combination that made him dangerously unstable.

Bailey's need for control most likely contributed to the accident that killed her husband and left her a cripple. A cripple with a potential drug problem. Not exactly the glorious return she'd imagined when she left Marietta.

Once the majority of the other passengers were gone, Bailey stood, shouldering her small backpack—her only carry on. She'd paid extra to have her luggage go through baggage. Although her ankle throbbed like hell, she managed to walk the entire distance to the front of the plane without limping.

She couldn't make the same claim by the time she reached baggage claim. The cluster of people pressed together around the conveyor belt was enough to make Bailey plop her butt on an open bench and fish out her phone.

She'd told her mother not to make the drive from Marietta until Bailey's flight was on the ground. Bad weather in Denver had delayed her connection, and Bailey hadn't wanted to cause her mother any unnecessary stress. There will be enough of that once OC comes home from the hospital, she told herself.

How would a physical disability change OC, she wondered? Or would it? She'd met several amputees at San Joaquin Valley Rehab. Doubles. Even one quad. Some navigated the new, uncharted waters with more grace than others, but not a single person pretended their lives would carry on without change. From what Mom told her, Dad was fervently, emphatically in denial.

As OC is about anything that implies personal culpability.

"Bailey?" a man's voice asked cutting into her thoughts.

Bailey's chin shot up—and up farther. A tall man in a white Stetson, jeans, boots and blue short-sleeve cotton work shirt with the name *Paul* machine-embroidered above the chest pocket stood a foot or so away.

"It is you, isn't it?" His eyes, the color of a Montana summer sky, lit up. His tentative smile sent her heart galloping across the open prairie on the time-travel express. "Girl, you're skinny as a rail. Don't they feed you in California?" He made a face. "Oh, crap, don't tell me you're a vegan?"

"Paul Zabrinski?"

The last person she expected to see today. But when your luck sucked as bad as hers, anything was possible. "What are you doing here?"

She tapped her forehead.

"Dumb question. This is an airport. You're meeting someone. Hey, you look great. How long has it been?"

Even dumber question. She knew exactly how long it had been. Life-changing drama had a way of leaving an indelible mark.

She held out her hand, which felt stupid and forced, but

she honestly didn't have the oomph to stand and hug him—which probably wasn't the right response, either, given their history.

His smile dropped. He wasn't the boy she'd kissed till their lips were chapped. He'd added a couple of inches of height and twenty pounds that filled out his shoulders and gave his face more character. Cute? Not anymore. Now, he was handsome. His blue eyes the stuff they wrote romance novels about.

"Coming up on fifteen years in August. Hard to believe, huh? Did your mom tell you there's a new director of the Chamber of Commerce in Marietta? The fair's going to run for two weeks this year."

He chuckled in a manly way that made the woman inside her—the woman Bailey thought died with Ross—ache for a pair of strong arms around her. Even for a moment.

She pushed the foolish, pointless yearning aside. Her husband had been dead for over a year, but the tender feelings between them had been gone even longer. "No. Mom didn't tell me. We've mostly talked about Dad. And the business." *Which, apparently, is on the skids.*

Paul's sandy brows pulled together. "Tough break about your dad. I was putting the finishing touches on the handicap ramp for his wheelchair this morning when Louise asked if I could meet your plane. She's afraid to leave him alone. I guess he's been pretty depressed lately." He looked toward the thinning crowd. "Which bags are yours? I'll grab them for you."

The question sent a syringe of panic straight into her spine. She sat upright, clutching her backpack as if it held superpowers. She'd have jumped to her feet and raced back to the plane, demanding they let her in, if she could walk that far. "Did you say you're here to meet...me?"

You hate me, she didn't add.

"Your mom's been tutoring my daughter. She knew I was coming to Bozeman today to drop off the kids. Californians aren't the only ones who do carpooling, you know."

"But...how come you're not at the hardware store? Mom said you're running it now."

"The boss can take off when he wants. That's the only good part about being the boss, believe me."

Although his tone seemed a bit less idealistic than it had in high school, she doubted he was giving up on Zabrinski's Big Z Hardware. He was too stubborn, for one thing. And he'd had tons of plans once he took over from his dad. "This place is going to be more than just a hardware store when I get done with it, Bailey. You're not the only one with dreams, you know."

And, from what little news her mother had shared over the years, Zabrinski's Big Z had carved out a niche market that held its own when the big box stores moved into the area.

She was glad he'd done well for himself. "That's very generous of you, Paul. Especially considering...our history."

He removed his hat and leaned over in a mock bow. "I was seventeen and heart broke. Everything looks black and white when you're young. Funny how age and life puts things in perspective. In hindsight I'd say I overreacted with the whole curse thing," he added in a way that sounded rehearsed.

Bailey rubbed the localized pulse of pain between her eyes. "Funny. I was just thinking your curse pretty much came true."

"Oh, crap," he said. "When I heard about the accident. Your husband dying. Losing your stud horse. The thought crossed my mind that Great-grandma Hilda really did a number on you. But, Bailey, you have to know I never meant for anything horrible to happen to you. Not in a million years. I mean that."

She wished his flustered apology meant something to her. It didn't. She knew who was to blame for the disaster her life had become, and it wasn't Paul Zabrinski.

"I was kidding, Paul. Shit happens. Just ask OC. You didn't curse him, too, did you?"

His look of horror made her smile.

"I didn't think so."

She blew out a breath, exhaustion making her a little light-headed. "I came back for Mom. She's going to need help once OC gets home, and I figured free rent for a few months would give me the nest egg I need to plan my next move." Hawaii sounded kinda nice.

He pointed toward the luggage area. "Which suitcase is…?"

He did a doubletake. "No. Let me guess. The two leopard print hay bales?"

Her cheeks heated up. Ross used to give her grief about the amount of junk she lugged around on the road. "One of them is my…um…work." She needed to get in the habit of calling her jewelry making a business. Maureen had stressed the need to focus on what you *can* do, not on what you can't.

I can't ride, rope, race barrels. I can make baubles for boots and hats and purses. Big whoop.

"Your mom said you were designing western jewelry. Don't tell Chloe. She'll be bugging you for samples. We went round and round about her getting her ears pierced."

Chloe? His daughter, she presumed. "My dad wouldn't let me get my ears pierced, either. So Marsha Biggins did the deed with a potato and her mother's needle when we were fifteen. Did you give in?"

"Her mother did."

His flat, resigned tone raised questions she didn't have any right to ask.

"My ex is remarried and lives here in Bozeman. We share custody. All very civilized and the kids seem to be okay with the arrangement, but…it's not exactly what I had in mind, you know?"

He didn't wait for her answer, instead walking to the carousel to wait for her bags to complete another revolution.

Thanks to the concussion she suffered in the accident her short-term memory impeded her ability to recall what she had for breakfast, but a crystal clear memory from one of hers and Paul's conversations appeared in her head as if it were engraved on her heart. "I want what my parents have, Bailey. They fell in love in the sixth grade. We won't have that, but I know you're the one for me. My soul mate."

Hearing a seventeen-year-old kid speak with such conviction had scared her. Bailey felt barely formed at the time, open to becoming the person she was meant to be, not ready to settle into someone else's preconceived idea of who she should be. "We talked about this, Paul. I've been honest about my dreams since we first started dating. College. Pro Rodeo. A breeding program and a ranch. Where? I don't have a clue."

The fact that Paul's vision of marriage was so far removed from her frame of reference proved all the more reason why they had no chance of making a life together. At the time she believed marriage was a prison, with an abusive jailor holding the key. She'd promised herself never to make the same mistakes her mother did.

Funny thing. Promises were a lot like dreams—only as good as the person making them.

Somehow, without intending to, when she married Ross she'd returned to her roots: codependency, spousal abuse, passive-aggressive behavior…with the bonus gift: unfaithfulness.

She'd broken the heart of the cutest, sweetest boy she'd ever known and look what she had to show for it—nothing. Not a damn thing. She was back home in Montana. Broken. Defeated.

She watched Paul grab both suitcases before they could make another revolution. Her jaw went slack watching his muscles flex beneath his shirt as he lifted them effortlessly. The Paul Zabrinski she'd known in high school had been a skinny little boy compared to this man. Back then, she'd been the athlete. Now, she could barely walk without limping.

She got up when he started toward her. How did he keep himself in such great shape, she wondered. Maybe, someone in Marietta had opened a gym. She hoped so. Her ankle was getting stronger every day, but her recovery wasn't a hundred percent yet.

"Where are you parked?"

"Just across the street. Your mom gave me her Handicap Parking thingee to hang in the window of my truck. She told me your leg was still jacked up. I half-expected to see you on crutches."

Bailey lugged one strap of her backpack across her shoulder and reached around for the other. Paul dropped the bags and hurried to help.

She hated being dependent on anyone, but sometimes even the simplest things stopped her in her tracks. He guided her hand through the strap and settled the bag on her shoulders.

His fingers felt warm and capable. And this touch left an impression she swore sank all the way through her skin to the bone.

"Thank you," she said, trying not show how flustered he made her. She headed toward the exit. Slow and steady. One foot in front of the other as Maureen always preached.

The only way she'd survive her brief but necessary return to purgatory.

PAUL OPENED THE passenger door for Bailey before hoisting her oversize bags to the bed of the pickup. The luggage fees must have cost a bundle, he thought. Marietta gossips had Bailey making out like a bandit thanks to a big insurance settlement. The truly unkind had said even worse…that her marriage was over, that her husband had left her for another woman, that Bailey's professional career was on the skids even before the accident that claimed her husband's life, along with the life of their prize stud horse. He tried not to listen, but how did one break a habit of a lifetime?

"I'll get the air on for you in a minute."

Black truck. Gray interior. A late spring day with a cloudless sky and temperatures soaring to the low seventies. "Do you need help getting in?"

"I think I can do it." He could tell by the determined set of her shoulders she planned to figure out a way to climb into the lifted cab unassisted—even if she screwed up her ankle doing so.

"Oh, hell, no."

He placed his palms square against her waist, his fingers framing her lower ribs, and lifted. Her weight—or lack of it—shocked him. *Is this what California does to people? Shrinks them? Like those horrible dancing raisins?*

He had to lean in to place her on the seat—just has he would have a child. This brought his face close enough to smell the scent he would forever associate with summer nights and kissing under the stars. He didn't know the name of her perfume—or even if it was a bottled scent—only that it was Bailey Jenkins. His first love. The one he never got over, if Jen were to be believed.

Although his fingers lingered momentarily, Paul forced himself to step back and walk to the bed of the truck. He kept his mind on what needed to be done—no chitter chatter. A coping mechanism that came in handy when you were the youngest in a family of boisterous, opinionated people.

He loved his family—and missed them now that everyone had scattered. Austen to Helena, Meg to Missoula, Mia still in Cheyenne. His folks summered here and Mia's two kids came for a month around fair time, but once Halloween was over, his parents joined other snowbirds in New Mexico.

Normally, while in Marietta, Dad helped every day at the store, which was not without challenges. But his parents were staying with Mia at the moment. His poor sister was in treatment for breast cancer *and* going through a divorce. Talk about bad luck.

Paul shoved the giant suitcases into the bed of the truck and closed the tailgate. When he got in, the first thing he did was hit the AC, but Bailey reached for the power button in the door. "Could we open the windows instead?"

Paul was positive he'd never heard those words from his ex-wife's mouth. Not evva, as Chloe liked to say. "What about your hair?"

She wiggled a colorful scrunchy adorned with shimmering silver and brass beads—what he'd assumed was a bracelet—from her wrist and whipped the dark brown locks into a messy pony.

"I've missed the air in Montana."

Is fresh air the only thing you missed?

Paul knew *he* wasn't on that list. Not given the way they'd ended things.

But he meant every word of his apology. He'd learned a lot about human nature from managing Big Z's. He could see why he'd been drawn to her—she was unattainable—an ideal he could never have. And that hadn't changed. He'd agreed to pick her up as a favor to Louise—and, maybe, to satisfy an old curiosity. That was all.

As he turned to look over his shoulder to back out of the parking space, his hand accidentally brushed her shoulder. The touch did some kind of crazy loop faster than if he'd stuck a wet finger on a live wire. When he started to apologize, he noticed her color—or lack of it.

"Are you feeling okay? You don't look too hot."

She turned her chin his way, one perfect light brown brow lifted in a pure Bailey gesture that stopped his heart mid-beat. "Always a smooth talker, weren't you, Paulie?"

A nickname he hadn't heard in fifteen years. Why it should hurt even the tiniest bit baffled him?

Luckily, she didn't give him time to dwell on his crazy out-of-line thoughts. Her smile flattened and she dropped her chin to her chest. In a voice that reminded him of Chloe, she said, "I need a pain pill. Can't take them on an empty stomach. But I can make it home."

Or not. He'd been a dad long enough to spot the signs of hunger. A simple fix. Even if it meant spending a few more minutes with her.

No problem. He dealt with strangers every day. Troublesome, needy, frustrated, hardware-challenged adults who taxed his patience beyond measure. *All these years in retail were simply training to prepare me for handling Bailey Jenkins. Who knew?*

He paid the parking fee, ignoring Bailey's outstretched hand with a ten-dollar bill it. Once they were on the road, he tapped the digital dashboard to turn on the satellite radio. His favorite "station" devoted to Indie Singer/Songwriters filled the cab, easing the need to make polite conversation.

Jason Isbell's *Traveling Alone,* a song Paul had decided was written specifically for this time in his life, came on.

Paul hummed the melody. He never pictured himself as a divorced, single dad, running a business alone. Never.

As he headed toward the highway, he glanced at his passenger. Eyes closed. Asleep? Exhausted?

Depleted. That was how she appeared to him. And he felt absolutely no satisfaction in seeing how far short of her triumph she'd fallen.

If anything, he felt guilty for wishing her ill in the first place. But a seventeen-year-old boy's hurt pride knows no boundary. He remembered writing a stack of letters. Hurtful. Bitter. Hateful. *Thank God I never mailed them.*

Ten minutes later, he pulled into the parking lot of the local pizza chain he thought a California girl might like. He parked and used the controls on his door panel to close her window. The noise woke her.

"Are we home?"

"I missed lunch," he lied. "Thought we'd grab a slice of pizza on the way. Unless you think your mom will be waiting for you."

Her foggy blink told him she wasn't quite awake. "She'll be with Dad. Like usual."

A telling admission. Bailey often criticized her mother's blind devotion back when they were dating. Paul never understood what about the man inspired such loyalty.

He got out and hurried around to help. Typical Bailey, she was already standing by the time he got there. Swaying just the tiniest bit in the steady Montana breeze.

He offered his arm.

She hesitated before accepting the gesture. "Are you sure you're hungry? I could have waited. I'm trying to cut back on my pain pills. I think sitting without moving my foot was harder on my ankle than I expected. My therapist warned me but I…"

"You did it Bailey's way."

He expected to see her get her back up, but she surprised him and laughed.

"More a case of being blocked in by a human obelisk. I lost my powers to levitate a few years back."

His laugh seemed to surprise her. It sure as heck did him.

Her expression softened. Her smile one he remembered far too well and the response it triggered deep inside was nothing short of preposterous. *Oh, man.*

When she accepted his proffered arm to maneuver around a poorly placed planter-slash-light pole, her touch confirmed his initial suspicion. *Holy cow.* Bailey Jenkins was back and so were his feelings for her—or, rather, they'd never died in the first place.

He'd tried to hate her with every ounce of his being, but hate and love skated so close to the same line. The line he just crossed over. *Love.*

He'd loved her with every fiber of his being. And, now, she was back—broken and in pain. Even if he'd wanted to hate her, how could he? She needed help. She needed home. If she stuck around long enough, maybe he could convince her she was meant to be here…with him.

"YOU HAVE TO eat something, OC. The doctor won't let you leave until you have a bowel movement."

Oscar Jenkins double-fisted the thin, scratchy sheets at his side. He hated everything about this so-called hospital. The thin plastic mattress, the crappy sheets and pilled, nappy cotton blanket. But worst of all, he detested the crappy slop they tried to pass off as food.

"Honey, please. Bailey's coming. She'll be at the house when I bring you home…if you eat and…eliminate."

"Shit. Say it, Luly. For once in your life, call it like it is."

Louise Billingham Jenkins. His wife of nearly forty years blushed like the innocent she was when they first met. Sweet. Caring. Still was. Even after all this time in constant contact with him—the lowest piece of scat that ever rolled off Copper Mountain.

"Don't be coarse." She advanced on him with a spoon and a palm-sized cup of something beige. "Try the pudding. You said you liked it."

He snarled and pressed his head and shoulders into the skinny foam pillow. "Must have been the drugs."

She held the shimmery, flesh-tone glob a few inches from his lips. The tiny quake of her hand compromised his resolve. He opened his mouth, clamped down on the spoon and wouldn't let go. Louise frowned sternly, but he could tell she was fighting back a smile.

"Baby."

He covered her hand with his tenderly, before prying the handle free. The banana-flavored slop lodged in the back of his throat and nearly gagged him, but he forced it down.

"I can feed myself."

She turned away—probably so he couldn't see her smile of triumph. Louise wasn't one to gloat. Not that he'd given her many opportunities for jubilation during their years together. When he looked back at his life—and he'd had plenty of time for retrospection since his body started falling apart, he couldn't say for sure why she'd put up with all his crap for so damn long. He sure as hell wouldn't have stuck around if the shoe had been on the other foot.

I'd have lit out just like Bailey did.

His gaze fell to the flat stretch of covers where his left foot should have rested. His appetite disappeared. His mouth turned dry.

Life as he knew it was gone. And despite his pissing and moaning about the skyrocketing costs of fishing licenses and gas and idiot clients and the government's nose in his business, OC loved hunting and fishing and teaching even the dumbest flatlander how to catch a trout or two.

And, now, thanks to his cussed orneriness—and some poorly timed budget cuts at the library, he and Louise were looking at serious financial problems.

Louise had tried to keep the worst of it from him. But yesterday, she'd tearfully admitted her fears.

"We're in bad shape, Oscar. The County changed insurance companies last year and our co-pay went up. Plus, they're trying to disallow one of your surgeries. If I miss any more work, I might not even qualify for the library's policy. And with you not being able to work, our savings are pretty much gone."

"The company can't be bankrupt," he said. "Jack told me we lost a few bookings, but he's been out with clients every day—even on Sunday."

Jack Sawyer had worked for Jenkins' Fish and Game off and on for sixteen years. His wife, Marla, handled the company's payroll, bookings and website.

"Jack's good, but he's not you, Oscar. And even if he were as good as you, people don't pay big bucks to go fishing with Jack Sawyer. They want the Fish Whisperer."

OC took another bite of puke pudding to keep from sneering. The name was a joke, of course. Tossed out in Wolf's Den one night for some dumb reason. To his chagrin, the name stuck. And bookings picked up.

Apparently, the *Fish Whisperer* even had a blog—whatever that was.

Now, thanks to OC's ridiculous so-called fame, Jenkins' Fish and Game, was on the verge of declaring bankruptcy. And, to make matters worse, his daughter was coming home.

As badly as he'd screwed up his health and finances, both were small potatoes compared to the mess he'd made with Bailey. "Who'd you say is picking her up at the airport?"

"I didn't."

Louise glanced at her watch surreptitiously. Bailey's plane had landed thirty minutes earlier. Paul would have been there to meet her. A shock her daughter never would have seen coming, but not the worst she had in store.

"She hasn't been cleared to drive, has she?" Oscar asked.

"I don't know."

She took a calming breath—to prepare for the explosion to follow. He'd find out eventually, and certain news was better coming from her. "I asked Paul Zabrinski to pick her up. He had to take Chloe and Mark to their mother's. He said it was no problem."

"No problem? Woman, are you out of your mind? Bailey's probably back on the airplane by now."

Louise pulled her smart phone out of her pocket. "The next flight to Fresno isn't until tomorrow morning. She isn't going anywhere."

Oscar shook his head from side to side, slowly, as if the effort took every last ounce of his energy. No surprise since he ate barely enough to keep a fly alive. Just one of the many reasons Louise needed Bailey here.

Louise had tried everything to reignite the spark in her husband's eyes, but nothing helped. And from their phone conversations, Louise knew Bailey was skating perilously close to the edge of her own demon-filled pit of depression. The two people she loved most were giving up, and Louise would use every resource available to spark a fire. Even asking Bailey's oldest "frenemy," as the kids at the library might say, to meet her plane.

"That took balls, Luly."

She nibbled on her thumbnail…until she caught herself and shoved her hand into the pocket of her lightweight sweater. As tempting as it was to savor the small rush of pleasure Oscar's praise brought her, she needed to be frank while she had his full attention.

"Bailey won't stay in Marietta as long as she thinks Paul hates her and the whole town is judging her."

Oscar sniffed—a pale imitation of the sort of reaction he normally would have shown. "What makes you think Paul doesn't hate her? He barely makes eye contact with me when I go into the hardware store. His dad's civil enough, but I don't think young Paul and I have exchanged more than a 'hello' in fifteen years."

Louise dragged the hard plastic visitor chair closer to his bed and sat gingerly, her side tingling slightly. "Well, what do you expect? In his mind, you talked his girlfriend into having an abortion. Who's he supposed to blame?"

Her husband's big, calloused hands curled into a fist. His shoulders bunched—a sad mockery of the power that once emanated from what was reputed to be a killer right hook. "It was the right thing to do, Luly. I don't want to hear any more about it. You should have asked someone else to give her a ride."

A ride. As if that was the sole purpose of asking Paul to pick up Bailey.

Louise rocked back, her gaze dropping to her hands clenched in her lap. Her world was a nanosecond away from imploding. Diffusing a few of the land mines she and Oscar had laid so carelessly during their years of childrearing was her only chance to save them all.

She'd come to that conclusion at two a.m. two nights before. Sleeplessness—her new reality. Desperation and fear could overcome any reluctance to open a proverbial can of worms, she now realized. And this particular can was well past its expiration date.

Luckily, when Paul came to finish the new ramp she'd hired Big Z Hardware to install, he arrived alone. He and his crew had knocked out the majority of the work in a single day, but he'd run out of material for the handrail and had promised to return this morning.

A man of his word who didn't let old grievances keep

him from making money off people he hated. Although Louise knew some of the credit for mitigating the weight of the grudge he no doubt still carried was due to her efforts to help his daughter with her reading skills.

Chloe Zabrinski was a sweet kid with a diagnosed learning disability. Chloe's mom picked Louise as her daughter's tutor without asking Paul, Louise was certain. Luckily, the two had clicked. In part, because Chloe reminded Louise so much of Bailey when she was the same age.

"Paul," she'd said, approaching the tall handsome man with a confidence she didn't feel. "I was hoping to catch you before you left."

The boy had grown into a more commanding personality and presence than she would have predicted all those years back. Smart. College-educated. Innovative. He saved the family business from Big Box intrusion and turned it into a thriving, competitive business.

As strange as it sounded, Louise was proud of him. Like a mother. Or the mother-in-law she could have—should have—been to him.

He picked up a big, bulky power saw and started wrapping the cord. "I still have about half an hour of cleanup. How does the ramp look?"

She barely glanced at the new switchback tacked to the steps of her modest wood and rock home. "It's wonderful. I was sure surprised yesterday to see the owner doing the grunt labor."

"Our regular crew is a little backed up. I knew this one was on deadline. When does OC get to come home?"

"Tomorrow…if he starts eating."

Paul's lips pressed together and he gave a nod. He'd grown into such a handsome man. Every bit as strong, forceful and confident as Oscar had been at the same age. But unlike her husband, Paul didn't wear his demons on his face, in his actions and attitudes. "Heard about the leg. That's tough. Marietta's lost a colorful character."

Her back stiffened. "He's not dead yet."

"Sorry. I just meant…from what they're saying he won't be doing a lot of fishing anytime soon."

The sickness in her belly percolated. "He's been counted out before."

Stay away from that illiterate roughneck, her father had warned. *He'll bring you nothin' but grief.*

"Things will be different when Bailey gets home."

Paul dropped the heavy saw so abruptly its leading edge half-buried in the soft grass. He turned to unbuckle his tool belt. "You talked her into coming back, huh?"

A little too disinterested? A good try, but Louise didn't buy it. Never had. She'd known he wasn't over her daughter when she met his new wife. Jennifer. College girl. Pretty brown hair and green eyes. A Bailey clone. Close but…no cigar.

And eventually she divorced him and returned to Bozeman to marry a man who loved her for who she was, not who she wasn't.

"I asked." She didn't know how extensive the town's gossip tree was these days. "You knew she lost her husband in a car accident, right?"

He nodded. "Tough deal. Got hurt, too, I heard."

"Broken ankle. Opposite leg as her dad. Strange coincidence, isn't it? Luckily, she's younger and healthier. She's walking now."

His eyes showed more interest than his measured, "Oh."

"Actually, Paul, I have a problem, and I was hoping you might be able to help me out." She took a deep breath. *All he can say is no.*

"Chloe told me she and Mark are going to their mother's tomorrow. I don't know what time you usually go, but I thought, if it wasn't a huge imposition, you might pick up Bailey at the airport then drop her here on your way past?" She rushed to add, "If I'm not with Oscar, he won't eat or drink. And he torments the poor nurses so. Partly the medicine, but partly...well..."

"He's a snarly wolverine."

She bit her lip. Why contradict the person she was soliciting help from?

"Text me her arrival information. I'll let you know if the time works." He'd picked up his tools and walked to his truck before she could thank him.

She checked her phone again. Even allowing for slow baggage claim, Paul should have dropped Bailey off at the house by now. Her finger hovered over the text app a moment before she changed her mind and shoved the phone in her pocket.

What she and her daughter needed to say to each other had to be done in person. Louise's moment of reckoning was coming...in more ways than one.

Chapter 2

"So...bring me up to speed. What do I need to know about Marietta to keep from stepping in deep horse pucky?"

Bailey's question came between bites. The woman still ate like she'd come off an eight-day hunger strike. He'd always been impressed by how little Bailey cared about impressing anyone else—except when she was on the back of her horse.

"Everything's pretty much the same. A few new homes on the east side of town, a big grocery store, chain drugstore and some fast-food places."

She reached for another slice. "This is excellent. Thank you. I was supposed to have an hour and a half in Denver but then my flight out of Phoenix was late. I was starved."

He could see that.

"What about you? You're a building contractor now?"

"No. God, no. I have a crew that handles small remodels, utility sheds and decks. Mostly DIY stuff people think they can handle then find out they can't. I leave new construction to the pros."

"Business is good?"

"I can't complain." Zabrinski's Big Z's first quarter set

new records for both volume and profit. Too bad he couldn't boast about his personal life. "I'll introduce you to Jane Weiss, the new head of our Chamber of Commerce. She's from California, too."

"California's a big place."

"Hmm. Never been."

She dropped her half-eaten slice of pizza and eased back in her chair. "I'm stuffed. Thank you, Paul. I really can't thank you enough."

He'd already paid for the food before they sat down, so he closed the carry-out box lid and got up. "Am I dropping you at the house or the hospital?"

"The house. I'd like to get unpacked before OC gets home."

"In case he says something that makes you want to run away?"

She chuckled. "Maybe."

He walked slowly to accommodate Bailey's gait. "Your mom says he's mellowed."

"So have I…thanks to the drugs."

She made it sound like she was an addict, but he'd watched her cut the white tablet in half before swallowing the smallest piece.

Bailey paused at the Pizza Palace counter to thank the owner. "Your pizza is delicious. I'm impressed. Tasted like home."

Home. California.

"Where are you from?"

"Central Valley. You?"

"Outside Sacramento. We were one of the first wave of

ABCers."

Bailey nodded as if the comment made perfect sense. The two chatted a few minutes longer, then Bailey waved goodbye. "I'll be back. Thanks."

Once they were in the truck and headed toward the highway, Paul asked, "What's an ABCer?"

"Anywhere But California. A lot of small business owners have moved to other states. Ross bought a place in Nevada. My late husband."

He didn't want to ask but couldn't help himself. "You mom told me he died in a truck accident."

She nodded, but her expression didn't invite more questions.

"How bad is your foot?"

"Broken in two places. I'm now the proud owner of two steel rods and several very big screws in my foot and ankle."

He winced. "Ouch."

A red Prius cut in sharply to take the exit. Paul tapped the brakes a little harder than necessary. Bailey's torso lurched forward until the seatbelt stopped her. Paul reached out without thinking.

The back of his arm hit her mid-chest. The first boobs he ever touched. Bailey Jenkins's breasts. Still as firm and lush as his traitorous body remembered.

She reacted as if poked by a cattle prod. She shifted sideways, turning her shoulder toward him, but he could see her cheeks were kissed with red.

"Sorry."

He meant that. Yes, he wanted to touch her. But he wasn't seventeen anymore. They both had battle scars. She had barely healed wounds—both inside and out. He needed to pull from his fifteen-plus years of retail experience to sell her on a new beginning with an old friend.

They drove in silence, Bailey's gaze glued to the scenery. Every once in awhile, she'd point out something that had changed since her last visit.

Nothing she pointed out was new to him since he'd made this drive three to four times a week since Jen told him she was moving to Bozeman.

He couldn't say he'd been blindsided by her decision to break up. He'd known for months she wasn't happy. He'd just grown tired of asking, "What's wrong?" So, he stopped.

She'd left a few weeks later taking half the furniture—the new stuff—and half their savings account. He could have fought harder, but that wasn't his style. He'd tried that once with Bailey and hadn't been successful then, either. At least, this time he didn't invoke the Zabrinski family curse. Either Jen didn't inspire the same level of emotion he'd felt with Bailey or he'd grown up at little.

BAILEY DIDN'T KNOW whether to be relieved or disappointed when she spotted the outskirts of Marietta.

Together, the pizza and the pain pill had taken the edge off her anxiety about seeing her father, but the combo did nothing to lessen the sense of let down she felt about returning home this way, broken and defeated.

So not the triumphant return she'd pictured when she left fifteen years earlier waving her dreams like an American flag—all proud and self-righteous.

In the end, she'd conquered nothing, achieved nothing and had practically nothing to show for all her blood, sweat and tears.

Without conscious thought, she reached for the plastic luggage tag attached to her backpack. One side showed her contact information—Maureen's suggestion because, she'd admitted, there was an outside chance Bailey might throw a clot and die on the plane. On the other side was a photo of her beautiful Daz.

Dazzling Dandy Commander. Her eight-year-old roan stallion. The sweetest, smartest, funniest horse she'd ever known. Sturdy, fast, light on his feet and gifted in the show ring.

Ross had been the one to find him—see his potential. But Daz's training had fallen to her, and they'd bonded in a way that made her husband jealous.

Was that the real reason he moved to Nevada? A power play to see if I'd follow Daz?

And when she made it clear she wasn't giving into his emotional blackmail, Ross wiped out both their futures with one impulsive turn of the steering wheel.

"Is that your stud horse?"

She turned the tag over and sat up. "Uh-huh."

"Roan. Nice coloring."

Her throat closed up. Talking about Daz was a thousand times harder than talking about Ross. His cries still haunted her dreams, although a number of doctors had told her the concussion would have knocked her out completely and there was no way she could remember hearing anything from the accident.

They were wrong. She'd slipped in and out of consciousness, but some images were burned into her memory. Blood oozing down Ross's face. The ghostly white cast of his skin that told her he was dead. The hiss and pop of the engine. And Daz's whinny.

"He was my little boy. All twelve hundred pounds. I got him when he was four. Filled with piss and vinegar, as OC would say. So naughty, I can't even remember all the mischief he got into.

"Ross was ready to sell him. Called him un-trainable." She closed her eyes, savoring the memory. "We made a bet."

"You? Really? You wouldn't even play strip poker with me."

His joking tone made her smile. But he had a point. She never gambled. Yet, somehow she wound up marrying Ross, who would have bet on whether or not the sun was coming up the next day if he could get the right odds. In fact, the first time they met he'd bet her a kiss that he'd win his heat. When he did, he pulled her into the saddle as he rode by and kissed her amidst the raucous cheers of the crowd.

"Our bet was for sex every night for a week if he won. And an expensive box of beads if I did."

At the time, it seemed like a win-win since she enjoyed making love with her husband and the beads were a hobby she thought she might like to try.

"How'd you break him of his bad habits?"

"Jelly Bellies. His favorite was coconut. The only one he refused to touch was licorice."

"Isn't that cheating?"

She shrugged. "I stole the idea from Mom. She keeps a bag in her desk at the library. When kids are reading quietly and behaving nicely, she rewards them. When they mess around, she makes them go outside and pick up trash. When Daz misbehaved, I'd make him walk behind me in circles. Mind-numbing boredom for a smart horse. He stopped being a butt-head and smartened up real fast."

"That's brilliant. I have a horse—and a child—who could use your help."

She looked away. "My doctor says no strenuous outdoor activities for six weeks."

"Is that how long you plan to stay?"

She had no clue. "I'm taking it one day at a time."

Nothing more was said until he pulled the truck to a stop in front of the 1940s-era home, white clapboard siding with dark green shutters. Mom had painted the door a brilliant red since Bailey's last visit. A very new-looking ramp ran from the driveway to the front door, tying into the original porch.

"The ramp looks great."

"Thanks. I tested it out with a wheelchair we keep at the store. Your dad shouldn't have any trouble getting around once he's able."

Bailey wanted to hope after all this her father would cooperate and make an effort to reclaim as much of a normal life as possible, but the OC Jenkins of her childhood was a spoiled, self-indulgent drunk who never listened to anyone's advice and did things exactly the way he wanted. Period.

"Well, we'll see, won't we?"

She opened the door and carefully lowered her good foot to the ground. The ache in her ankle was back, but she'd be damned if she'd play the cripple in front of Paul.

"I can take one of those," she said, meeting him at the tailgate of the truck.

He pulled the bigger of the two out first, setting it on the sidewalk. His muscles really were quite impressive, she realized. Wishing she had some reason to touch him.

The idea unnerved her. When he suggested she let him make two trips, she didn't argue. She needed some distance, a little down time. Right now.

"Do you have the key?" Paul called out as he dashed up the ramp, the first of her giant suitcases in tow.

"I don't think Mom's ever locked the door in my entire life."

He tested the handle. Sure enough, it swung inward. He wrestled the giant, soft-sided suitcase across the threshold then dashed past her for its mate.

She'd barely stepped inside when her phone rang. *Mom.*

"Hi. We just got here."

"Wonderful. I have more good news. Oscar's doctor is letting him go home today. The discharge papers will probably take an hour or two, we'll be there in time to have dinner together."

Today?

"Great."

"You should invite Paul to join us. To thank him for picking you up."

"Really, Mom? Do you think that's a good idea? Dad's first night out of the hospital? He and I haven't seen each other in a couple of years. Maybe we should keep it family for awhile."

"Oh, of course. You're right. What was I thinking? We'll do something nice for Paul later on. I have to go. The nurse wants Oscar to shower before he leaves since we don't have that kind of equipment at home yet. See you soon, honey. I'm so glad you're here."

A few seconds later, Paul lugged her other ridiculously over-weight bag across the threshold.

"We have rocks in Montana, Bailey. You didn't have to bring your own from California."

She tried to smile, but the erratic thudding of her heart interfered with normal reactions.

Paul cocked his head. "What's up?"

She shoved her phone in her bag. "OC is being released today. They'll be here soon."

She took a step, planning to make some effort to appear the gracious hostess. Unfortunately, her ankle locked and she lunged off balance, grazing her hip on the side of her father's worn leather recliner.

Paul pivoted as precisely as Daz "heeling" in the arena. He caught her elbow and stepped in to help her regain her balance.

Close enough to smell his cologne and see the tiny strips of facial hair his razor missed. Close enough to kiss the lips that looked more familiar than they should have.

What the hell was wrong with her? This man hated her, cursed her, and she dropped into his arms like some stupid damsel in distress?

No. Good grief, no.

She jerked free and grabbed the back of the chair like a lifeline. "I'm fine. Thanks. Still finding my footing."

He started to say something then shrugged and tipped his hat. "Okay. I have to get back to the store, but I'll see you soon. Welcome home."

What surprised Bailey most is he seemed to mean it.

Chapter 3

"I T'S SO GOOD to have you home, sweetheart."

Bailey closed her eyes and returned her mother's hug. Funny how they never showed overt displays of emotion when her father was present. For the millionth time, Bailey wondered how someone as kind, sweet, gentle and loving as Mom could have wound up with a six-foot cactus for a mate.

Dad was passed out on painkillers in his bedroom.

Mom had assigned Bailey to the front guest bedroom. The small but charming three-bedroom bungalow was new to Bailey. Her parents sold the ranch and moved into town shortly after she left home.

"I'm sorry I couldn't come before, Mom. My doctor wanted me to finish my physical therapy."

Mom shrugged. "You're here now, and that's going to make such a difference."

Bailey picked up the pretty lilac print pillow sham and sat, her back against the cherry wood headboard. She put the pillow in line with her left leg then leaned forward to use her hands to lift her bad ankle to the elevated position. "Do you really think so? He barely said ten words to me since he got here. How is my presence going to do anything but give him another target?"

An image of OC target shooting from the back porch of the ranch popped into mind. Her job had been to re-set the empty beer cans on the fence after OC knocked them over. Talk about trust. "I'm not as speedy as I used to be. Can't dodge bullets worth shit."

Mom's left eyebrow cocked upward. Her stern librarian look. But she didn't say anything.

"Have you been working?" Bailey asked. Her mother loved the library almost as much as she loved her family.

"Between budget cuts and Oscar's problems, I haven't been there as much as I'd like." She filled in Bailey about all the changes at the Marietta Public Library, including a shift in leadership. "I can't wait to introduce you to Paige, my new boss. She's been very understanding about my situation."

She frowned and plucked some imaginary piece of lint from her neat gray slacks. "But I think the County is giving her a hard time about our budget. My job could be on the line."

"This thing with Dad has been going on a long time, hasn't it?"

Mom nodded. "The first toe was beyond salvation by the time I saw it, but you know how doctors are. They tried a bunch of different treatments. Oscar couldn't see any immediate results, and, of course, he didn't help matters by staying off the foot the way they wanted. The infection spread."

Bailey had discussed the challenge of caring for an unco-operative patient with Maureen. Frustration took a toll on the health care professional *and* the family.

"Even though your dad knew he had to keep his foot elevated and dry and not put any weight on it," Mom said, "if I was at work and he got antsy, he'd call Jack and order him to come get him. Put Jack between a rock and hard place."

Bailey had given the family business a lot of thought and she wasn't convinced her father's partner's motives were completely altruistic. "If OC can't go back to work, it sounds to me like Jack winds up with a pretty sweet deal."

Mom fussed with the curtain and straightened a few old copies of Montana Living magazines on the antique table beside the blue chair that used to sit in the living room at the ranch. "I don't believe for a minute Jack Sawyer wants Oscar out of the picture. Jack's no spring chicken, either. He's stepped up to keep the company going while your dad's been sick, but he's not Oscar Jenkins," she stressed. "Our regulars—the people who have been coming back year after year to fish with your dad—have cancelled and gone somewhere else because they couldn't hire the *Fish Whisperer.*'" Her air quotes demonstrated her true feelings for the phrase.

Bailey made a face. "That must have hurt. Or did Dad see it as confirmation that he really was the Fish Whisperer?"

Louise pinched the bridge of her nose. She wanted to scream. Not at her daughter, who despite Bailey's best efforts to pretend otherwise was her father's daughter. Not even at Oscar, who let his silly male ego turn him into a cripple. She wanted to scream at the unfairness of life in general.

She'd done her best to love her husband and raise a

smart, beautiful, successful child. She'd worked hard at her job, basically babysitting two generations of children while trying to teach them to love books.

She'd lived up to what was expected of a woman her age, and what had it gotten her? A staggering mountain of doctor and hospital bills, a cut in hours at work and the suggestion she might be ready to retire so they could hire someone younger, with less experience, seniority and wages.

And one other complication she wasn't ready to think about. A person could only take so much bad news.

Besides, it might be nothing, she told herself. For the millionth time.

She took a deep breath and walked to her daughter's side. She planted her hand firmly on Bailey's healthy tanned arm.

"Whatever old grievance you still nurse where your father is concerned, one thing is indisputable. Oscar Jenkins *is* the Fish Whisperer. And there will never be another like him."

"Mom, I'm here to help, but you know Dad and I have never been able to talk. Maybe things will be different since he's had to stop drinking and smoking. I'll try. That's all I can promise."

Louise took a deep breath—not too deep, she didn't want to wince—and let it out. "That's all anyone can ask, dear. I'm just glad you're here. And I know Oscar is, too."

THE NEXT MORNING, Bailey stood in the doorway of her parents' room.

Their king-size bed had been stored in the garage to make room for a fancy hospital bed. Mom had moved to the pullout couch in her "office" to avoid accidentally kicking OC's stump during the night. At the moment, she was preparing breakfast in the kitchen, blissfully unaware her husband was on the phone ordering contraband.

"Bring me a fifth of scotch and a carton of smokes. Any kind. I'm not particular."

Bailey's grip tightened on the mug in her hand. Two teaspoons of sugar and real cream. Just the way he liked it.

"Really, Dad?" she said, stepping into the room.

Even with the windows on either side of the bed open, the air smelled stale. Apparently, the nurses' effort to bathe their patient before he left the hospital had been unsuccessful.

She made a point of sniffing the air, her nose crinkling. "You stink, Dad. And now you think you're going to smoke in here? Not happening. Trust me."

OC tried to sit up but the effort seemed beyond him. Watching her once all-powerful father struggle, his skinny arms barely supporting what little weight still hung on his bony frame, made her throat close and tears rush to her eyes. But she forced herself to channel those emotions to anger.

Rule number one: never show fear. OC taught her that at a very young age.

She slammed the mug on the bedside table, not caring that mocha-colored drops cascaded like rain.

"Hey," he barked, falling sideways against his pillow. His

thin hair, oily and messy from sleep stuck up like an aged punk rocker, dull gray the predominant color. His hair had been as thick as hers and nearly onyx the last time she saw him. This ordeal had aged him more than she'd realized. Still…

"No. You do not get to set the rules around here. I came to help my mother, not you. I know what a waste of time that would be. The great OC Jenkins doesn't need anybody's help. You'll either get well or you won't. I can't make that happen, but I can make sure—damn sure—you don't take my mother down with you."

"I'll smoke if I want."

"Not in this room. Not in this house. If you want to smoke, which every doctor you've ever seen has probably advised against as long as your body is healing from surgery, you're going to have get yourself into that wheelchair and go outside.

"Mom had a nice ramp built for you. It'll get you far enough away to avoid polluting my lungs with secondhand smoke."

"This is still my house."

"Not for long."

Bailey and OC both looked toward the doorway at the sound of Louise's voice. She held a tray that wobbled unsteadily. Bailey hurried as quickly as her ankle allowed to take it from her mother's hands.

Emotion? Fear? Something else? Bad feelings made the cup of green tea she'd had with her toast roil. "Mom? Are you okay?"

Mom blinked, as if coming out of a trance. She pulled a

handful of tissues from the pocket of her apron and walked to the bed. After cleaning up Bailey's spill, she raised the head of the bed and helped OC sit, plumping the spare pillow for added back support. "You need to eat while it's hot. Chorizo and eggs. Your favorite."

She motioned for Bailey to bring the tray, which Bailey realized had legs that converted it to a mini-table. She lowered it to frame her father's skinny hips.

How could a man his size drop so much weight so fast, she wondered?

"I'm not hungry."

Her mother leaned in close and said in a fierce tone Bailey didn't recognize, "You'll eat every bite or I call the ambulance to come back for you. Your doctors were talking about feeding tubes. You promised you'd eat once you had better food."

He muttered under his breath but picked up his fork and shoveled a large bite of scrambled eggs into his mouth. Mom watched him chew, nodding encouragingly.

Bailey remembered watching her handle young readers at the library the same way. As long as they were quiet and polite they could stay. Acting up or messing around earned them one warning: "Read or go outside." Mom never backed down from a threat. Her father probably knew that.

He washed down his food with a gulp from his mug, tossing Bailey a sour look.

Succumbing to the ache in her ankle, Bailey sat on the bed as far as possible from the bump indicating her father's good foot. "What did you mean when you said, 'Not for long'?"

Mom sat in the upholstered armchair positioned beside the giant fichus. Her mother's skill with houseplants was one of the genes Bailey failed to inherit.

"Financially speaking, your father and I are in pretty rough shape, Bailey."

OC started to contradict her, but Mom shushed him. "It's bad, Oscar. There's no use pretending otherwise. You haven't worked in five months."

Bailey tried not to show her alarm. "Are you making anything from the Fish and Game?"

"A little. Jack gets paid by the hour and Marla earns a salary for bookkeeping, but we don't charge as much for Jack's tours so we don't show as much profit."

OC glared at her but kept eating.

"And all the extra hours have taken a toll. Jack's about done. He's going to finish up the bookings they have, and then he's retiring."

"Goddamn traitor. I taught him everything he knows about fly-fishing. He owes me more than a couple of months of picking up the slack."

OC shoved his tray, spilling what was left of his coffee. "I need a pain pill...and a cigarette, goddamn it."

Bailey took the tray away while her mother cleaned up the mess. She walked straight to the kitchen, ignoring the throbbing in her ankle. She needed a pain pill, too, but she'd be damned if she'd take one.

"He called somebody and told them to bring him booze and cigarettes," she said when Louise walked into the room.

"I know. Jack called me after he hung up with Oscar. That's when he told me he was quitting. Apparently, Marla is determined to buy a place in Arizona for the winter. She's been talking about it for years, and now that Jack's been working so much, they finally have the money."

How convenient. Bailey had never cared for Marla Sawyer. The woman always struck her as self-serving and narcissistic. Bailey wouldn't have put it past her to skim a little off the top of the books, either. But, she didn't say anything to her mother. If Jack was quitting, then her parents needed a new plan.

"You always said your salary filled the gap in winter when Dad wasn't leading as many trips. Has that changed?" she asked, adding OC's plate to the dishwasher.

"It helps, but even with good insurance, we've had a lot of out-of-pocket expenses." Mom touched her side, as if she had a spot of indigestion. "Our savings are just about depleted."

Bailey filled the kettle and turned on the stove. She motioned for her mother to sit at the table then joined her. "I know all about the cost of hospital bills. My surgery alone used up my entire deductible. Rehab was another eight grand. Luckily, I was able to sell the house and my truck to cover most of it."

Mom reached out and touched her hand. "How's your jewelry business?"

"Okay. The only way to make real money is to have inventory. That would mean hiring some crafters."

"I thought you made everything yourself."

The kettle started to whistle. Louise jumped to her feet with a grace Bailey envied. She filled the mug Bailey had used earlier and added a fresh tea bag. "Honey, honey?"

"Sure. Thank you." Stress, pain and grief had robbed her of an appetite. As Paul noted when he picked her up at the airport, she could stand to put on a few pounds.

"I love designing, but sitting still for long periods of time has always been my idea of torture."

Her mother chuckled. "When you were a little girl, you spent hours playing dress-up with your grandmother's old costume jewelry. I thought that was something all little girls did. Then your dad brought home a pony, and everything else fell by the wayside."

A hazy memory came to her. "I remember those. Do you still have them?"

"Of course. They're in my jewelry box. I had them professionally cleaned and appraised a couple of years ago. They're not valuable, but the jeweler told me vintage jewelry sells really well." She paused. "Do you think you could use them in your designs?"

"Maybe. Can't hurt to look? Are you sure you want to give them up?"

"I don't think Oscar and I will go out dancing any time soon."

The sadness in her mother's voice drove home the point that Bailey was going to be here longer than she thought. This was no fly-by layover. And the money issues were looking more and more complex. Bailey might need to step up her game.

"I don't suppose you know any crafty ladies looking for part-time piece work, do you?"

Mom's smile brightened for the first time. "No, but I'll post a flier at the library. I bet you'll have a dozen applicants inside a day."

Bailey blew on her tea then took a sip. "Great, but before I can train someone, I'm gonna need a place to spread out all my beads on a table sturdy enough to handle my magnifier lights."

"What about the garage? We have a card table and some folding chairs."

Bailey shook her head. "That might work temporarily, but it'll be too hot in summer and too cold in winter."

"Downstairs, then. Your dad's Man Cave."

"I heard that and the answer is no," a voice bellowed from the bedroom.

Bailey hadn't realized OC could hear them. "Why not? You're not using it. You can't go down stairs in a wheelchair."

"I'm gonna walk again. The therapist said he'd fit me with a prosthetic once my stump is healed. Leave my basement alone."

Bailey felt encouraged by the little bit of the old OC fire in his tone.

"He's going to come back from this," Mom said, lowering her voice to a whisper. "But in the meantime, we have to find a way to keep our noses above water."

"Then, tell me where to set up shop."

Mom grabbed her phone, found a number already programed in and a moment later said, "Hi. Is Paul around? This is Louise Jenkins." She listened a moment then said, "Okay, please. He has my number. Thank you."

Bailey hated the mixed feelings she got hearing Paul's name. He'd barely left her mind since dropping her off. Had she said too much? Did she appear too pathetic?

"Mom, you're not trying to set us up, are you?"

A terrible idea given their history…and the fact she'd dreamed about him last night.

"Of course, not. This is business. Paul lives and breathes all things Marietta. Besides, according to his secretary, he's having coffee with our new Chamber of Commerce lady, Jane Weiss."

Meaning Paul had moved on? *Good. That's good.* A part of her even meant it. Didn't she?

Chapter 4

"SO WHAT ARE you going to do about it?"

Paul rocked back in his chair to keep from pounding his fist on his desk. He'd returned from his coffee date with Jane, where she'd surprised him with news of her impending marriage to Sam McCullough, to be handed the phone. "It's Marla Sawyer. Again," Bev, his secretary, said, her tone as exasperated as she ever got.

"Well, Marla," he said, wishing he'd skipped that extra shot of espresso. "I'll take a look at it this weekend. When are you leaving? I'll need to put an ad in the paper."

As a renter, Marla was every landlord's worst nightmare. Paid rent when she felt like it. Complained about stupid, piddly things. Wanted perfection in a sixty-year-old farmhouse that hadn't been perfect on its best day.

But things were looking up. She'd just informed him she and Jack were moving.

"End of August. Jack will want to be here for the fair. Can't believe it's going to last two weeks. It'll cost me a fortune, but since it's our last, we might as well to do it up right."

"Your last *ever*? Does this mean you're not coming back to Marietta?"

"Oh, who knows? Jack feels some kind of loyalty to OC. Says he'll work for him again next spring if OC's able to keep the business open." She gave a snarky laugh. "Like that's going to happen. The man lost his leg, and now he's going to sit around and wallow in his sorrow till his liver gives out."

Her negativity made Paul's Café Americano curdle in his belly. He managed to pin down a firm date of departure then asked, "How are my horses?"

"As good as you'd expect with nobody riding 'em. Jack feeds 'em every day, but they're too damn wild for me. I ain't gonna get tossed off and break something just for a break in the rent."

How did this happen? Paul asked himself. How did a businessman as sharp as he was reputed to be wind up trading rent in exchange for feeding and watering—and supposedly exercising—four horses? Man, had he gotten screwed.

"I have to get back to work, Marla. Consider this your notice, then."

He made a note on his calendar and texted Bev. His next renters were going to come with references and a big deposit.

If he'd listened to Jen, he would have sold the place years ago. But the old ranch was in his blood.

A knock at the door made him look up.

Bailey.

"Well, speak of the devil."

She looked like a walking commercial for western glam—faded denim jeans, white tank with a chunky brown leather belt cocked stylishly at her hips, a saucer-size turquoise buckle that matched her pounded silver and stone necklace. The only thing missing was her hat.

"You were talking about me?"

He pointed at his phone. "Not exactly. Your old farm. You knew I bought the place, right? The last owners were from LA. Thought they wanted a summer place, for God's sake."

"Mom told me."

"Well, I've been renting it to the Sawyers, and Marla just gave notice."

She made a silent, "Oh."

"I hope they aren't expecting a good referral. Our deal included exercising my horses and apparently that chore has fallen by the wayside. Don't suppose you're up to riding, yet?"

She shook her head. A haunted look in her expression made him drop the subject.

"So what can I do for you? Good to see you survived your first night home with OC."

"Drugs are a wonderful thing. OC slept like a baby, which meant Mom and I did, too." She pointed to the extra chair opposite his desk. "Do you have a minute? I hate to bother you but I need some advice, and Mom said you were the man to ask."

He half rose, feeling stupid for not jumping to his feet in the first place. But, in all fairness, Bailey was the last person he expected to see walk into his office. *Or wanted to see.* Even having coffee with another beautiful woman hadn't been enough to erase the memory of his hot dream...he and

Bailey naked on a blanket under the bright Montana sky.

He swallowed hard. "Of course. Sit. Please. Did you walk here?"

"No. Not yet." She brushed back a thick lock of dark auburn hair and let it drop. He'd always loved her hair and was glad she hadn't cut it. "Mom dropped me off on her way to the library. A visiting nurse is at the house to help OC shower. He'll probably pass out and sleep all afternoon. No stamina whatsoever."

Paul didn't give a damn about Oscar Jenkins's medical challenges. From what he heard, OC brought about all his problems by being a bullheaded ass. "Is the ramp working out?"

"Yes. It's perfect. Thank you." She sat forward, shoulders straight. Her expression made it clear she was done talking about her father.

"I need a workshop. Nothing big. Room for three or four tables. Dad refuses to give up the basement, and Mom's afraid if I push him too hard he'll backslide into depression."

"For your jewelry business?"

"Yes. My orders have been picking up steadily. If I want to take this to the next level, I need to hire some crafters to fabricate my designs. Mom said you've got your ear to the ground when it comes to Marietta business and you might know of something that isn't even on the market yet."

"To buy or rent?"

"Rent," she said without hesitation.

Of course. Why did I ask?

"It doesn't have to be big, but I'd need Internet access. All of my sales are online at the moment."

"So, you're *not* talking retail?"

She took a deep breath, as if preparing to jump off a cliff. "I…no. Not really. It's the next logical step, but…" She looked around, not making eye contact. He knew what she was thinking. ABM—anywhere but Marietta. If she left again soon, what would that mean to his X-rated dreams?

"There are a couple of empty buildings around. I don't know if they're for sale or rent. But I know someone who would know. Jane Weiss."

"The Chamber of Commerce lady."

Her tone didn't sound thrilled.

Paul nodded. "She's a real go-getter. Did you hear about the bridal contest they sponsored this spring? The winner got their wedding and reception at the Graff, plus three nights in the honeymoon suite as a prize."

"Wow. Mom sent me a picture of the Graff. Pretty impressive."

"Put Marietta on the map. Now, she's focused on turning the Great Marietta Fair into a world-class destination. Jane is a true force of nature."

Bailey's pretty tan faded a bit. She licked her bottom lip in a sure sign of nervousness. His Bailey unnerved by meeting another woman? Impossible.

When he reached for his phone, she scooted forward to rest her hand on top of his. Her touch set off a series of wicked visuals straight out of last night's dream. His mouth went dry and he had to remind himself to breathe.

"Wait. I think I might be doing this ass-backwards, as OC likes to say. Mom was so gung-ho I completely lost sight of the fact I have no idea what I'm doing. I don't even have a budget in mind." She pulled a large, beautifully tooled western purse onto her lap and dug out a folded piece of paper. "The consultant who drew up my business plan focused on e-retail, which required practically no start-up funds."

He gave the simple operating budget for B. Dazzled Western Bling a quick glance. "Love the name."

"Thanks."

Her smile seemed bittersweet.

She re-folded her business plan and put it back in her purse. "Maybe I should just keep selling one piece at a time online until we know how things are going to work out with OC."

Paul rocked back in chair.

"Seriously?"

"What do you mean?"

He looked her up and down, his gaze lingering on her chest. *Like the horn dog I am.* "Did you make that necklace?"

"Of course."

"It's great. A little flashy and very classy. Just like you."

The color came back into her cheeks.

"Thank you. I think."

"You're thinking too damn small, Bailey. This is Montana. Big sky, big dreams. You used to know that. And you are *exactly* the reason you need a store—to model your product. My, God, Bailey, you're hot, young and gorgeous. Why hide behind the anonymity of the Internet?"

Paul's question hit Bailey like a pony kick to the gut. She had been hiding. How did he know? *Because he knows me?* Was that possible? Most days, Bailey didn't even know herself.

"I can think of a dozen ways you can open a shop on a shoestring budget. A photographer friend of mine makes poster size prints. Super cheap. Instant wall art for your shop, plus you can plaster them all over your website."

A buzzing feeling she used to get right before a race started to hum in her chest. How long had it been since she'd felt the thrill of possibility?

Before she could reply, his cell phone warbled. He looked at the name displayed and grinned. "Hey, Troy, when did you get back? What's happening? A drink? I'd love one. Can I bring an old friend?"

We're friends again? Really?

He looked at Bailey, a question in his eyes. She nodded okay.

"Great. We'll meet you in the lobby."

He listened a moment then replied, "Bailey Jenkins. She was like the last Fair Queen before that whole voting fraud scandal."

He looked at Bailey and winked—a gesture that took her straight back to their first date. "Winks are goofy. You're goofy. I don't date goofy boys," she'd told him—her upper classman superiority showing.

"I'm only goofy around you because you're so beautiful I can't think straight," he'd confessed, his sincerity winning her heart in a way the cock-of-the-walk cowboys she'd dated in the past couldn't match.

Paul let out a low, masculine chuckle that went straight to her goofy girl parts. "Yep, OC's daughter. And, nope, they don't look anything alike."

He glanced at her chest again. "In fact, she's opening a

new jewelry shop called B. Dazzled Western Bling. She can tell you all about it when we see you."

The moisture in Bailey's mouth turned to sand. Her ankle suddenly started to pulse. Mom had caught her up on all the latest Marietta gossip so Bailey was pretty sure Troy was Troy Sheenan, owner of the Graff hotel. Easily in walking distance unless you were recovering from a broken ankle.

Paul solved that problem when he grabbed his keys off the desk and stood. "Let's take my car. We can cruise down Main on our way. I'll point out a couple of empty storefronts to give you an idea what's out there."

She followed him through Big Z's—a place she remembered well from high school. Outwardly, it looked the same, and yet, the atmosphere felt different.

Better lighting, maybe? New flooring?

She put the dilemma out of her mind, focusing instead on what the hell she was doing letting Paul Zabrinski back into her life. Bad enough he occupied center stage in her dreams, was she ready to follow his Pied Piper lead down business lane?

Apparently, yes, she thought, when he opened the passenger door of the same giant black truck she rode in yesterday.

"Your ankle's better today, isn't it?"

"Much." *Liar.*

Instead of turning left to travel the two and half or so blocks down Front Street to The Graff, he turned right. They were the third in line to make another right on Fourth Street.

Bailey couldn't pass the stately spires of the Catholic Church without remembering the Midnight Mass she attended with Paul and his family her senior year.

Her parents weren't religious. Mom attended church off and on, and belonged to a women's group at St. James, but her father hadn't stepped foot in a place of worship in her lifetime to her knowledge.

"Can I ask you something? Why are you helping me? Given our past...."

His cheeks turned a ruddy shade of tan. "I like to think I grew up a little."

The blinker ticked, ticked, ticked loudly until he added, "Plus, I owe your mother a debt I can never repay. My daughter nearly failed second grade. Thanks to Louise, Chloe's reading above grade level and is doing great in school. Your mother is a saint in my book." He wiggled his eyebrows playfully. "No pun intended."

He pulled over sharply.

"Del's built a new place out by the mall. This building has been vacant for a couple of years."

The empty brick-front building that had sold auto parts when she lived in Marietta.

"I remember coming here with my dad. I wonder if it still smells like motor oil?"

"Yeah. Pretty much," he said. "This must be why I'm not a realtor." His self-deprecating grin set off a brigade of warning bells. He'd always been able to make her laugh at the dumbest things.

In the next block, he pointed out several stores that were new to her, including Copper Mountain Chocolates.

"You have to try Sage Carrigan's candy. My mom claims her single-origin chocolate bars are the best in the world, but I like the caramels with sea salt. My mouth starts to water just thinking about it. Do you want to stop?"

"Another time, thanks."

"Sure, no problem." He stepped on the gas. "And on the corner is SweetPeas. Risa Grant, the gal who owns it, is new to the area. She could probably give you all the pros and cons of opening a new business in Marietta."

He turned on First Street, and even from a block away Bailey's jaw dropped as she eyed the building she'd passed a thousand times in her youth.

"Wow. I can't believe it's the same place."

The classy facelift made her feel hopeful...and intrigued. If someone was willing pour the kind of money this restoration must have taken into a seventy-five-year-old building, maybe her old town had some life in it after all.

An hour later—after a full tour that included a peek at the gorgeous Presidential Suite, Bailey followed Paul to the parking lot, thoroughly impressed but a little overwhelmed, too.

Troy Sheenan, whom she vaguely remembered from high school, came across as committed, ambitious, connected and...miles out of her entrepreneurial league.

"The Graff is gorgeous. My dream venue. Maybe in a few years I'll be able to afford to work with precious gems. For now, I'm lucky to be able to afford Montana sapphires."

As he backed out of the parking place, Paul said, "When Troy was talking about that hunting trip OC took him and his brothers on, I thought of a place that might be perfect for you."

She checked her phone. No texts or messages. Hopefully, that meant OC was sleeping...not dead drunk.

"Okay. I could see one more before I head home."

He took Court Street to Railroad Avenue. The area predominantly had been residential during Marietta's early years but like a lot of towns she'd been in, many of the homes had been converted to businesses.

Jenkins's Fish and Game operated out of one such bungalow. OC bought the place before Bailey was born. Her parents had planned to move into town when Bailey started school, but Bailey's passion for horses kept them on the ranch.

When OC's guide business started to take off, he set up an office where sportsmen could come to discuss tour packages. And every summer, he'd hold his annual OC Jenkins' Fish Fry in the back yard.

"Here we are." Paul parked in front of the familiar gray-green clapboard building.

The two Adirondack chairs on the porch were new, but the sign hanging below the eaves was the same one her dad bought before she left for college: Jenkins's Fish and Game. Since 1972.

She looked at Paul. "OC's place? Are you crazy? He threw a hissy when Mom suggested I set up a couple of tables in the basement."

Paul shrugged. "If Jack and Marla leave, who's going to make the mortgage payment?"

"That's a very good point."

Before she could say more, her phone rang. A photo

she'd taken of her mother a few years earlier flashed on the screen.

"It's my mom. I'd better take this."

Her finger shook slightly as she slid the bar to accept the call. *Mom's really aged since I took that picture. This thing with Dad has taken a toll.*

"Hey, Mom, what's up?"

"The visiting nurse says your dad is on the warpath. I don't know what happened. I'm the only one here. Paige just stepped out and she's not answering her phone. Is there any way you can...?"

"I'm on my way home now. Paul is giving me a ride. I'll call you after I find what's going on."

By the time she ended the call, Paul had made a U-turn. "Do you want me to swing by the feed store for some tranquilizer darts?"

She tried not to smile, but wound up grinning—even if doing so made her feel guilty. "Hopefully that won't be necessary. I've got a few tricks up my sleeve."

At the recommendation of several reformed smokers she met during physical therapy, she'd purchased an electronic cigarette. "It might be time to introduce OC to his new pacifier."

Chapter 5

BAILEY COULD HEAR the roar of her father's voice before she reached the front door. Since his room was at the far end of the house, that meant all the neighbors were treated to his tirade whether they wanted it or not.

She waved a quick goodbye to Paul then walked inside.

When her mother dropped her off at Big Z's, Bailey had expected to walk away, at best, with a list of possible venues. At worst, she'd expected Paul to say, "Hey, I already hauled your ass home from the airport as a favor to your sweet mother. Isn't that enough to prove I'm a nice guy who doesn't hate your guts anymore? Now, leave me the hell alone."

Instead, he gave her two hours of his time and introduced her to one of his rich, influential friends.

She couldn't be more confused. Not to mention the fact his touch made her feel more alive than she had in a long, long time. Too bad they were so damn wrong for each other. People didn't just put their kind of history behind them and play nice again.

Didn't happen. She had the scars to prove it.

Heart racing, Bailey hurried down the hallway.

"What is all this noise about?"

She stopped abruptly to try to make sense of the scene before her. OC in his wheelchair, robe open to reveal his narrow chest covered in snowy white hair, his good leg trying to push backward while the nurse advanced toward him, a bulky plastic shell of some sort in her hands.

"Tell her to take that torture device away, Bailey. I won't wear it."

The woman in teal scrubs with a yellow and orange top looked over her shoulder at Bailey. Her silver hair put her at Bailey's mother's age, but Bailey didn't see a nametag and couldn't place her.

"The doctor wants your father to wear the boot three to four hours a day."

"When I'm dead. Not before," OC snapped.

He'd stopped pushing backwards on the wheels long enough to close his robe. From the smooth, shiny gleam of his hair, Bailey could tell he'd been bathed.

Bailey walked to the nurse.

"May I see it?"

Black webbed straps dangled from the lightweight plastic. A thick spongy padding lined the inside of it. "This thing is huge. Are you sure one size fits all?"

"The physical therapy people were supposed to fit it to him in the hospital. If he was being too ornery for them to get a good reading, that's his problem."

Bailey carried the boot to the wheelchair and held it up in front of her father's partial leg. "True. But if it's the wrong size and that impedes his progress, then it becomes your problem, right?"

The woman crossed her arms belligerently. Bailey could

tell she was ready to draw a line in the sand and die before giving an inch, so she tossed the plastic thingee on the foot of the bed and said, "Why don't we call it day? You've already accomplished so much. I'm sure you and OC are both wiped out."

"Will you call the doctor and get this squared away?"

Bailey held up her hand. "I promise."

"Okay."

The nurse glared at OC. "A nice wife *and* a nice daughter. How'd a cantankerous old coot like you get so lucky?"

"It's a blinkin' miracle."

The fact he didn't say his favorite cuss word gave her pause until the nurse chuckled with obvious satisfaction. "Well, at least, I got the no profanity rule into your thick head."

The comment made a connection in Bailey's mind.

"Mrs. Sharvis? Weren't you our school nurse back in the day?"

"That's right. My first job out of nursing school. After they stopped funding the position, I went into home health care. Never did care for hospitals and sick people that much."

"It shows," OC muttered. "Can I get some help here? I'm tired. I wanna go to sleep and I need a pain pill."

Mrs. Sharvis showed Bailey how to steady the bar above the bed so OC could shift his butt from the chair to the bed. She helped him work the remote control to elevate the lower half of the bed and find a comfortable position for his torso. Then, she covered him with a woven cotton blanket and gave him the pill he'd requested.

Bailey eyed her father's wheelchair longingly but she forced herself to walk Mrs. Sharvis to the front door.

"He's feistier than he lets on. Frankly, I think it's good medicine to get your patient sorta riled up. So, don't be alarmed if you hear us shouting at each other. His stump looks good. I think he's going to be okay."

"Really?" She agreed. Too bad she didn't hold the same degree of optimism for his business.

"We've got a great prosthetics guy. Builds every piece himself. Old school. He'll be out to see your dad in a few days. They have to shrink the stump to fit where it attaches. OC will be in pain until that toughens up, but eventually he won't even know his old foot is gone."

Bailey doubted that. Body parts didn't disappear without regret.

"Thanks for your help today. Did he ask for a cigarette?"

The woman laughed gruffly. "About fifty times. Tried to bribe me. Threatened to sue me. Even cried a few crocodile tears. Good luck with that."

Bailey told her goodbye and closed the door. She texted Louise that all was well then she went to her room to elevate her ankle and think.

She needed to get organized and make a plan. None of the places Paul showed her were right for her needs at the moment. Troy's idea of selling from a booth during the Big Marietta Fair made the most sense. But where could she work in the meantime? She needed space to create and store inventory, to package her products and to prepare attractive displays.

When she closed her eyes, the image of Jenkins's Fish

and Game popped into her mind, along with a memory she hadn't thought of in years.

In the early days of the Fish and Game, OC used the entire back half of the building for storage. Originally, the area had served as the kitchen and family room, but gradually clutter took over. Oversize nets hung askew on nails in the sheetrock. Broken rods huddled in one corner like shamed children. Several deer heads sprouted from the walls—gifts from hunters who'd snagged a ten-pointer only to be told by their wives the taxidermy beast didn't jibe with their home decor.

One stormy night, she and Paul snuck in, looking for a comfortable and dry spot to make out. The late spring rainstorm that had lasted for three days made the haymow damp, and their favorite place to park in Paul's small truck inaccessible.

"Let's break into Dad's shop," Bailey suggested. "The back door latch doesn't always catch. Dad's been saying he was going to fix it for weeks, but you know how that goes."

To their surprise, the door was unlocked.

Bailey assumed this meant her dad was on a bender and forgot to close up.

They parked around the block and ran, their wind-blown umbrellas utterly useless.

She found a couple of old beach towels some client left behind and draped them over the three square seat cushions Dad used in a boat he borrowed when someone wanted to try lake fishing.

The spiffy new flashlight Paul picked up at Big Z's had a dual-purpose feature. He used it to illuminate her way as she made their "nest," then, once their spot was prepared, it converted to a small lantern, making their area as cozy as a tent.

"Are you sure OC isn't coming back?"

"Worry wart," she'd teased, already helping Paul out of his Marietta High hoodie. "He's hunkered down at the Wolf Den, three sheets to the wind by now."

Her reassurance seemed to be the green light he needed. With practiced ease, he unzipped her rain jacket and tossed it aside. A few raindrops splashed on his face, and she licked them off.

Bailey could almost recall the taste. Crisp. Electric. Some magical elixir that made her decide she was ready to go all the way.

As a mature, pragmatic young woman of the times, she'd visited the free clinic in Bozeman and had a three-month supply of birth control pills. She even carried a few rubbers in her purse, although she'd left that in Paul's truck.

Paul hadn't asked or begged or whined, like a few of the cowboys she'd dated in the past. For that type, two dates and French kissing constituted the quit-being-a-prick-tease-and-screw-me threshold.

She admired Paul's patience. She liked him…maybe even loved him, although she had no plans to tell him that. Technically, she wasn't a virgin. On a dare, she'd stolen a half-empty bottle of booze from her dad and "partied" with the twenty-something lead singer of a country western band that was passing through town. She'd cried afterward. He'd held her until she fell asleep on the motel bed. In the morning, he was gone and she had a lot of lies to make up to cover her giant mistake. Luckily, he'd insisted on protection and the only lingering gift he'd left her was an even greater aversion to alcohol and the determination to only sleep with someone she knew and really cared for.

"I want to do it," she told Paul between kisses.

He was, hands down, the best kisser. His lips were soft and warm, but not mushy. He took his time and worked his way up to intimacy—instead of ramming his tongue down her throat first thing.

"Here?"

"Why not?"

He didn't answer but he did pull back and stare at her in a way that made her feel naked and exposed, even though she was still wearing her bra.

"You're sure this isn't about OC? Doing it here would rub his face in the fact he doesn't control you? Or some sort of Freudian crap?"

She clutched the sides of her shirt with one hand and pushed the other flat to his bare chest. "Don't be stupid. This has nothing to do with my dad."

Almost as if her words had conjured the devil, the front door banged open and OC's voice rumbled through the walls. "I swear there's a frog-gigging stick somewhere in the back room. Haven't been out for years, and you sure as hell won't find me standing around in the pouring rain on a night like this, but you can borrow it."

Bailey and Paul scrambled like cockroaches, pulling their pads, towels and Paul's sweatshirt into the gap between the sink and the u-shaped counter.

With any luck, the gigging pole was somewhere in the

opposite direction.

OC and the potential frog killer tramped through the arch doorway into the former family room.

Unlike Bailey and Paul, they turned on every light. Paul peeked around the corner while Bailey frantically buttoned her shirt. When he looked at her, his eyes were wide, his lips mouthed the word: shit.

Bailey leaned around him.

Her rain jacket hung neatly on the back of a chair. A small puddle formed below, sparking in the glare of the fluorescent light.

She curled into a ball, her heart pounding harder than when she flew across the finish line after a barrel race.

Her father had no use for kids, and even less for love. He'd make sure Bailey and Paul were publicly drawn and quartered...whatever that meant.

When she looked up, she could see Paul preparing to stand and face OC. While a part of her appreciated the heroic gesture, the kid who watched her father berate her mother in a drunken rage panicked. She grabbed his arm with both hands, pulling him against her like an anchor.

She shook her head and put one finger to her lips. "No," she mouthed.

They held each other, fear the glue that bound them tighter than sex probably would have, listening to the bullshit and banter, waiting for the moment OC turned around and spotted her coat.

"Found it," the other guy chortled. "Look out Kermit E. Frog, here I come."

Bailey braced for the worst.

She heard the two men return, something fell, a box of some kind.

"Goddamn it," OC snarled. "I gotta get in here and clean this place one of these days. Or make my daughter do it. Yeah, I like that idea."

She knew at that moment he'd spotted her jacket. The taste in her mouth turned sour. Her heart skipped every other beat as she waited for him grab her from Paul's arms.

A moment later, the light flicked off. The front door slammed with a resounding crack and she heard the deadbolt click into place.

"Holy crap that was close."

She didn't tell Paul the truth because she didn't know what just happened. Her father *chose* not to expose them? The man who routinely berated bad drivers, baffled tourists, bumbling store clerks and anyone else who didn't do things OC Jenkins's way gave her a pass? "I think we better go."

"Why? He's gone."

She looked around, her eyes nearly adjusted to the dark again. "You were right. Picking this place for our first time is a little twisted. I didn't plan it that way, but…it's not going to happen."

Paul, being Paul, shrugged. "Can I still cop a feel in my truck?"

She punched him on the arm, but she laughed, too. He always knew how to make her smile.

All these years later, Bailey sighed and relaxed, bemused by the memory.

OC never brought up that night, never asked if she'd been there. She and Paul found other places to make out.

Their first time happened in the hayloft.

She honestly couldn't remember if it was good or so-so. But she knew they got better as spring turned to summer. By the time she found out she was pregnant and they broke up, he could make her quiver like a mare in heat any time he touched her.

Groaning at the unwelcome sensation that swept through her body, she turned on her side and squeezed her eyes tight. She needed a nap, not a horny stroll down memory lane.

The last thing she had any business thinking about was a man. She'd messed up her last relationship about as badly as possible—Ross was dead, after all.

Maureen insisted Ross's death was not Bailey's fault.

She blamed "survivor's guilt" for the crushing weight Bailey couldn't shake.

"When someone close to us dies accidentally, it's human nature to spend hours, months, years thinking of all the ways we could have prevented the accident from happening. But your hands were not on the wheel, Bailey. You need to let go and move on."

As if that were possible. She might have been able to come back from losing Ross—he'd literally separated from her months before the accident. But she would never get over losing Daz. Her horse. Her baby. Her future.

She'd go on. She'd find meaningful work. She'd channel her passion for rodeo into her western art. She'd sublimate, but she'd never ride again.

Not without Daz.

LOUISE PUSHED THE book cart toward the enclave set aside for the library's younger readers. Things had changed dramatically since she first started working in the Marietta Community Library. For one thing, computers and eBooks were in hot demand by nearly all of the library's younger patrons—except for Louise's readers. The children she served loved to pick up and hold a book in their small hands.

And Louise never tired of being the one to suggest, "Have you read Thomas the Train, yet? Or, we have a new, must-read Fancy Nancy." Seeing their eyes light up more than made up for the complaints she heard from patrons who, like Margaret Houghton, the Head Librarian who hired Louise many, many years ago, preferred things to remain the same.

They never do, she thought, stopping the cart beside the first bookcase.

She'd barely finished shelving two books when Taylor Harris, the assistant librarian everyone knew had been hired to replace Margaret, stopped beside the cart.

Taylor, who hailed from Missoula, was twenty-six, ambitious and definitely positioned to move Marietta into the twenty-first century.

"Hi, Louise. Got a minute?"

Define a minute. With Taylor, whose enthusiasm often carried her off in several different directions, time became a relative thing.

"Sure."

Louise nudged the cart to one side and walked to the main counter. The library was quiet today. Margaret was in her office with the door closed, probably giving hell to someone who was urging her to step down sooner rather than later. "What's up?"

"The Marietta Friends of the Library is planning to set up a booth at the fair and they'd like us to do a couple of readings. You'll cover the kid stories...something tied into the fair, I presume. And I'll read something for the grown-ups. Maybe Zane Grey. What do you think?"

Louise consulted the large, business-type calendar on her desk before answering. She'd blocked off the dates of the Fair, August six through the nineteenth, in yellow.

Will I be well enough by then to attend?

She'd done her best to block any thought of her own health issues until Bailey got here. Now, Louise's fear consumed her every waking thought. Even her dreams were tortured by crazy images of horses running loose in the house, obnoxious tow truck drivers allowing her to get behind the wheel of a giant truck...then criticizing her for driving all over the road. She didn't know what the dreams meant but she'd awaken more exhausted than if she'd spent the night listening to her baby daughter's every breath.

"That sounds like a great idea, Taylor. I'm not the only storyteller around, though. We could make a round-robin list. You know like a ReadaThon."

"Ooh," Taylor said, a glimmer of excitement in her eyes. "What a great idea!"

Louise liked her soon-to-be new boss a lot and admired her foresight, energy and political pragmatism—something

Louise lacked. Louise hated having to beg for the crumbs to supplement their operating budget. Taylor Harris simply shrugged and found a way around the bureaucratic loggerhead.

"By the way, I bumped into Troy, and he told me he met your daughter. I didn't know she was an artist and craftsperson as well as being a top rodeo rider. I can't wait to meet her."

As a rule, Louise didn't talk about her family. Even Margaret who signed her paychecks didn't know how sick Oscar was until Louise used up the last of her vacation days taking him to the doctor.

Maybe Bailey was right and she'd done herself—and her friends—a disservice by not reaching out to let them help.

She opened the bottom drawer of her desk and pulled out the tooled leather purse Bailey sent her for Christmas. The medium brown tone made the perfect backdrop for the turquoise beads and narrow white quills Bailey had worked into a sunburst design. "She made this for me. Beautiful, isn't it?"

"Wow. That's fabulous. Does she have more?"

Louise shrugged. "I don't know how much stock she has with her—she just arrived from California, but she's talking about hiring some helpers to flesh out her inventory."

"Really?"

Taylor dashed to the community bulletin board near the library's main door. She returned a second later waving a flier. "I spotted this a few days ago. She should call the woman in charge."

The flier read: Calling all Crafters. First meeting Tuesday

night. Basement St. James." Louise didn't recognize either of the contact names.

"Thank you, Taylor. I can't wait to show Bailey."

Louise knew the best way to keep Bailey in Marietta was by getting her invested in the town, its hopes and dreams and by building a foundation for her new business.

Bailey didn't know it yet, but Louise had no intention of letting her daughter return to California. Ever. She needed Bailey here to watch over Oscar if this lump of hers turned out to be something serious.

And she'd find out soon just how serious a health problem it posed. Now that Bailey was home, Louise could make the call she'd been putting off…as soon as she found a way of breaking the news to Oscar.

Chapter 6

PAUL HAD HIS index finger on the doorbell but changed his mind at the last minute.

He hadn't seen or talked to Bailey in three days.

The first day felt right...natural. Like she probably needed some time to adjust and help her father get settled in his new reality. Just because *he* knew what *he* wanted didn't mean she was anywhere near the same page, let alone on it.

The second, he found himself thinking about her often...every five minutes or so. But he told himself not to push it. She was still healing, both physically and emotionally. Only a complete moron would show up with flowers and ask her to dinner.

Besides, he didn't give his secretary flowers often enough. She was thrilled...if a little suspicious of some new work he might have in mind for her to do.

But Day Three arrived and nothing from Bailey. Not even a text. So, when the perfect excuse to call *her* fell into his lap—or kicked down a stall, as luck would have it—he decided to act.

He listened for any kind of movement—or OC's bellowing voice, but the Jenkins's house felt too quiet to disturb. OC was either napping or not there.

On a hunch, he dashed down the steps and walked to the window he knew to be the guest bedroom. He'd been inside the house when Louise hired him to build the ramp. For a brief moment, she'd considered moving OC to the front bedroom to put him closer to the kitchen. Paul had talked her out of it.

"I guarantee he'll be more comfortable in his own bedroom. When my grandpa got sick, Mom tried moving him to our house. Between depression and Gramp's stubbornness, the man nearly wasted away before she took him back home."

From what Bailey told him, Louise had taken his advice.

With hands bracketing his eyes, he pressed his face to the screen and peered inside.

Sure enough, Bailey was stretched out on the bed, but she wasn't practicing for the role of Sleeping Beauty. She'd rigged a lighted magnifying glass to the sort of table Jen had used to deliver breakfast in bed—back when she'd aspired to be homemaker of the decade.

Clear plastic tubs filled with beads outlined the work surface. Bailey appeared to be wrapping a larger bead in fine silver wire.

He held his breath a moment, caught by the way she lifted her chin to get her focus, the tip of her tongue barely poking between her lips. His male anatomy reacted as if he were seventeen again.

"Cripes," he muttered.

Bailey looked straight at him. She froze as if he'd caught her doing something wrong then let out a sigh.

"A peeping Paul," she said, shaking her head. "Do you

do windows or should I call 911?"

Her hair was piled in a clip on top of her head. Escaped tendrils of light brown framed her face. No make-up today. Not even lipstick. But she looked as beautiful as the day she was crowned Fair Queen.

He tugged on the inseam of his jeans to adjust for his sex-deprived body then stepped sideways where the window was open. "I tried calling. Twice."

She reached across the pillow to the bedside table and picked up her hot pink phone.

"Dead," she muttered. "I've got to change my service provider. It's always roaming here. Sucks down my battery like that." She snapped her fingers then moved her tray to a flat spot on the bed.

"You could have called the house," she said, reaching for the charger cord.

"I didn't know if OC was picking up or not."

She plugged in the phone and turned to look at him. "Good point, but so far he ignores the phone completely. Claims he doesn't know anybody he wants to talk to."

She chuckled dryly. "As you can see, a debilitating illness hasn't made him any more sociable than he was in the past."

He appreciated the fact she didn't make excuses for her dad. The man was a jerk when he was sober and an ass when he was drunk. Knowing that had been the one consolation he'd clung to back in high school whenever Bailey talked about moving away. He didn't blame her wanting to leave, but he'd always hoped something would make her change her mind at the last minute.

Something happened, but even something as significant

as a pregnancy didn't change the outcome.

"I didn't ring the bell in case he was asleep."

"He is. Physical therapy wipes him out. I don't expect him to wake up until Mom gets home from work."

She cocked her head in a way that made her topknot tumble in a sexy, just-had-sex sort of way. She brushed it back carelessly. "So, what's up? Why are you here?"

"I have a horse problem. I need someone to talk me out of selling the stupid beast before my daughter comes home. I'm all out of patience, even though I know it's probably my fault Skipper's getting into trouble in the first place."

She asked him a few questions about Skipper's age, disposition, training to date, then said, "Daz went through a rough patch, too. A juvenile delinquent horse has nothing on a seventeen-year-old kid hell-bent on self-destruction."

He nodded. "That's exactly what it feels like. I remember when Austen went crazy the summer after his first year of college. Could have gone to jail but the judge gave him community service."

"What'd he do?"

"You never heard? Well, he is four years older than me. He and some friends got charged with vandalism. Drove their trucks somewhere they shouldn't and messed up the road."

"What did your parents do?"

"Tightened the strings, I guess. Set curfews all summer. Made him quit hanging around with kids they deemed 'bad influences'."

He lifted his hand, remembering one other thing. "They also made him work at Big Z's until he earned every penny of tuition for the following year.

"Dad told him, if he was going to piss away their gift, he could darn well pay for it himself."

"Well, that's probably what you're going to need to do with your horse…except for the going to college part. Work him."

She looked at the beside clock radio and exclaimed, "Wow. Later than I thought. I lose track of time when I'm working on a new piece."

She angled her body sideways on the mattress to spread a cotton dishcloth over the table. "Mom should be home any minute. I can't promise I'll be any help…my horse training days are over. But I wouldn't mind getting out of the house and stretching my legs."

"Great." He wanted to ask why she felt she couldn't train horses anymore—her most fervent passion in high school—but decided now wasn't the time. "What's happening on the B.Dazzled front?" He nodded toward her work. "Did you decide against asking OC to use his back room?"

She leaned down to take off her laced jogging shoes. "I asked. Mom thought it was a great idea. Dad said he wasn't kicking Jack to the curb. Period."

"Does he know Jack is leaving soon?"

She glanced up. "Uh-huh."

Her cutoff shorts gave him a clear look at her damaged ankle. A second scar at a forty-five degree angle intersected a deep purple scar about the width of a pencil.

A knifelike sensation arced through his belly. He'd felt the same cut and jab the time Chloe fell off the trampoline in the back yard and landed a few inches from a metal pole the gardener had set up to keep the hose from crushing Jen's flowerbed.

"Mom says I need to give OC time to process." She stuck out her tongue.

She tossed the shoes toward the closet and stood. "I should probably change."

Her long bare legs looked great to him. They brought back memories of their last summer together. She'd always led the way hiking. He never minded even when they got lost because he was happy following her trim butt and lean, tanned legs. How had he managed to block such joy and passion from his memories?

Anger, he guessed. Hurt feelings, disappointment. He refused to trivialize his feelings at the time, but life and experience helped put them in perspective.

The sound of a car pulling into the driveway made him spin around. Louise waved from the open window of her Subaru wagon. "Oh, look. Peeping Paul is back."

He blushed, feeling seventeen again.

"Dang. You people have long memories," he said, walking toward the car. "A kid with a crush on a girl gets caught looking in her window *once* and he's branded for life."

"How about all those times he wasn't caught?"

She had a point.

He opened the door for her. "Need help?"

She handed him a heavy cloth book bag that had seen better days. "Some new murder mysteries. I'm trying to get Oscar interested in reading again."

Again? Paul had no idea OC even *knew* how to read.

He held up the tattered bag sporting a faded image of

Marietta's historic library. "Here's what the Friends of the Library need to sell to raise money. Maybe with a little B. Dazzled bling on them."

Louise paused, her hand on the key. "That's a very good idea, Paul. Taylor Harris and I were talking about doing a Readathon at the fair. We could give participants a book bag and sell the leftovers."

He didn't know what a Readathon entailed but he could picture Bailey coming up with something ladies would be fighting over. "Chloe would love to be involved. She reads all the time now. Thanks to you."

Louise appeared pleased by his acknowledgement of her help. And Paul smiled when she chose the ramp over the stairs.

Bailey met them at the door. She'd kept the shorts but changed into boots. The charms and brightly colored stones dangling from the silver anklet...bootlet?...made a jingling sound when she walked.

"Dad's resting." She took her mother's purse and set it on a chair inside the door. "He had a pain pill at two. I made notes in the binder. Also, I put a pork roast in the crock-pot. There's fresh coleslaw, too. Dad always loved pulled pork sandwiches, right?"

Her mother didn't reply right away.

Was it the light or did Louise look ill? Paul couldn't decide.

"Are you two going some place?"

Paul set the library bag on the floor inside the doorway. "One of my geldings thinks he's a stud. He jumped the neighbor's fence and is causing all kinds of trouble." *No use detailing the fact my neighbor is my brother.* "I asked Bailey to help me organize an intervention."

Would Louise accept his excuse at face value or read something more into it? Would she guess Bailey had remained under his skin all these years and suddenly blossomed back to life like some dormant illness triggered by proximity?

The woman was the plague. *His* plague. And if there were a cure, he hoped it involved hot sex and a lifetime of research.

Louise looked at him a moment or two longer than necessary, and then said, "Well, good luck with that. Getting anybody—person or horse—to do what's best for them is usually a waste of effort."

Bailey touched her mother's arm. "Whoa, rough day, Mom?"

Louise shrugged and turned away. "They're all rough, dear. That's life."

Bailey looked at Paul, her eyes wide. He offered her his arm.

Once they were away from the house, Paul said, "Maybe Louise is tired. She's got a lot on her plate."

"Maybe."

Bailey climbed into Paul's SUV with considerably more grace than she managed with his big truck.

As she buckled her seatbelt she asked herself the question she'd been avoiding. *What am I doing here?*

Granted, seeing his face up against her window had set her pulse racing. But nothing about that was a good thing.

She might want a romantic relationship at some point in

the future, but certainly not now. Only a ridiculously needy and immature person would introduce a new variable into her life when she didn't have the slightest idea who she was or what she was going to do now that she couldn't be Bailey Jenkins – Cowgirl, anymore.

"Stay focused on the present, Bailey," Maureen had advised that morning when Bailey called to say she was going back to Montana. "The future can look daunting if all you see is hurdles, but each one can be mounted and overcome. I promise you that, my friend."

Maybe she'd agree to come with Paul because she was lonely and she needed to get out of the house. That wasn't so bad, was it?

She let Paul do the talking as he drove the familiar route to her childhood home. He seemed determined to be happy, and she hoped a little of his ebullience would rub off on her.

I used to be happy, wasn't I?

She looked at Paul. So handsome. Would she have been aware of his sexy maleness if they'd been together all these years or had their separation added a mystique familiarity wouldn't have held? She couldn't know. But she did take him for granted back then. Maybe because she'd been a year ahead of him in school. Like that made any difference in the real world. But in high school she'd taken a lot of flack from her classmates for dating a junior.

"When was the last time you were out here?" he asked, turning his chin to look at her. She blushed, knowing he'd caught her staring.

"To the ranch? Fifteen years ago. Dad sold the place about a month after I left. I knew he and Mom had been talking about it, still…knowing my home was in someone else's hands was a bit of a shock."

At the time, it had felt like a slap in the face. Payback for nearly screwing up her life. "How'd you wind up with it up?"

When Mom first told her Paul Zabrinski bought their old ranch, Bailey had been shocked and a little...she didn't have a name for the feeling. Hurt? Sad? Wistful? If things had been different, they might have bought it together and made a life there.

"The guy who bought it from OC was from California. Thought he wanted a summer home, but as I understand it, the economy went south and he couldn't unload either one of his places. He rented the land and abandoned the house. He didn't winterize the place so there were broken pipes, soggy sheetrock. Cosmetic stuff, which is right up my alley. I got it for a good price from the bank."

"Why this place?" she asked, hating her lack of self-control.

He appeared to think a moment then said, "Because I could."

He had the grace to look sheepish. "I have to admit there was a little sense of pay-back. Very little," he stressed. "Mostly, it was a great deal and my dad had been encouraging all of us to invest in dirt. Jen is a city girl and she flat out refused to move into the house, so I rented it to Marla and Jack. The only thing I changed were some of the corrals. I wanted a safe place for the kids to ride."

She sat forward, anxious now that they were getting close.

She couldn't see the house yet, but the large pasture to the left of the road was outlined in enough pipe and wire to hold a rhino. Someone must have added sprinklers or irrigation because the grass was a deep, vital shade of green.

Four horses were scattered in groups of two—a bay

mare and her yearling foal and two healthy-looking pintos with glossy coats and long, thick manes.

He put on his blinker when he drew up even with the high-end green powder-coated metal mailbox.

The one her family had used for as long as she lived there was a rusty but serviceable tin can that gave her the long white scar on the side of her baby finger.

When he slowed to turn into the driveway, she let out a breathless cry. "Oh, my gosh, you paved the driveway."

The Jenkins Ranch driveway had been bumpy enough to shake loose a filling or two.

"All the way to the house? Did you win the lottery and nobody told me?"

OC had complained about the state of the road for as long as Bailey could remember, but he blamed the oil sheiks in the Middle East for its condition because he couldn't afford to pave it.

Paul grinned sheepishly. "I got tired of washing my truck. It's black, you know."

As was this Escalade. He'd obviously done very well for himself. Not that she was surprised.

"You could do worse than Paul Zabrinski," her mother had said the night before Bailey's appointment. A half-hearted attempt to talk Bailey into going against her father's wishes?

Bailey hadn't replied. But in her heart of hearts, Bailey had agreed.

In a way, she'd fulfilled her mother's prediction when she married Ross. She'd done worse. Much worse.

Chapter 7

P AUL PULLED THE SUV to a shady spot beneath the
ancient cottonwood her father had threatened to cut
down every year. As much as OC hated the mess that turned
their yard white for a few weeks every summer, Mom loved
the cheery green canopy when the heat got intense.

"The place looks great, Paul," Bailey said, getting out
with an eagerness that surprised her. "I love what you did
with the barn."

The huge, classically designed structure, now painted a
pristine red with white trim, should have been featured in
some kind of Montana promotion. She especially liked the
huge, stylized Z superimposed over the closed haymow
doors. "Your logo reminds me of pictures I've seen of old
barns with advertising on them."

He walked around the car, his gaze on her not the classic
red structure. "I made this barn one of my construction
crew's first jobs after I bought the lumber yard. Had a
reporter from the Courier out to do a story on saving our
county's heritage or some such drivel. Then we held a big
Open House-slash-Barn Dance, with free hot dogs and pony
rides for the kids. Got a couple of other barn jobs from the
publicity."

Her gaze lingered on the logo, but her mind had moved to the memory of what happened behind those closed doors. Did he remember the exact location of their first kiss? *Probably not.* Only women were sappy romantics with memories like elephants.

She turned to ask him about his missing horse, but her question was cut off by the jingle of a ringtone tune she couldn't quite place.

He reached for the phone holster on his hip, like an old west sheriff going for his gun. The movement brought back the memory of them arguing over which of the actors in their favorite western, *Tombstone*, looked the most authentic.

"Val Kilmer, of course," she'd insisted. "His Doc Holliday will go down in cinematic history."

Paul, who actually seemed a bit jealous of her schoolgirl crush on the actor, swore he was going to buy a black coat like the one Kurt Russell wore, as soon as his fledgling mustache filled in.

She watched him pace with his phone to his ear. No mustache. No obvious tattoos. His dark blue Wranglers, low-heel cowboy boots and tucked in short-sleeve cotton shirt—an attractive plaid of grays and blues with an orange stripe—were the right combination of casual and successful.

He dressed much the same as he had in high school. But now, his biceps and chest filled out his shirt with a healthy maturity that made her mouth water.

Only his hand-tooled belt and pewter buckle, which resembled a Superman logo with a Z instead of an S, cried: money.

"No," Paul barked, his tone strident and unyielding.

"They signed a contract and it sticks no matter what kind of deal they think they can get in Bozeman. We aren't Bozeman and people pick us for a reason. Remind them of how many trips to the city we're saving them."

She didn't know what the contract entailed but she wouldn't have wanted to argue the point with him. Especially when he added, "If they give you any more grief, tell them my brother is a lawyer and he hasn't worked off this year's retainer yet."

After he ended the call, he ran his hand impatiently through his hair before he looked at her. "Dealing with the public never gets any easier." He shrugged. "Now, where were we?"

"We were going to see a man about a horse," she said, grinning at his blush when he caught her double entendre. Obviously, he remembered OC's code for taking a pee.

"Skipper," he said, leading the way to the barn. "That's what Chloe named him. Technically, he's her horse. I told the kids they'd each get a foal from Felicity—the mare we passed coming in."

"The little pinto by her side is your son's, then?"

He nodded. "In theory. But Mark's crazy about Legos and video games at the moment. I don't know if he'll develop a fondness for riding or not."

She wondered if that bothered him. Her father wouldn't have let a little thing like personal preference derail his intentions where his child was concerned.

"This horse isn't here to look pretty," he told her when he brought home her first pony. "You're gonna be the best cowgirl this county has ever seen, Queen Bee. It'll take work.

But you can do it."

In high school, even on cold and rainy days, she rode Charlie. Did Mom or OC ever ask what her dreams were? Did she even know?

Probably not.

"Hold on. I'm gonna let the foreman next door know we're opening the gate."

She could picture the fence line between her family's ranch and the old Armistead place. Unless something had changed, the distance was at least a mile off. "I don't think I can walk that far, Paul."

He let out a gruff snorting sound. "You and me both. That's what my quad is for, darlin'," he said sliding the barn door open with a hefty push.

She knew the endearment wasn't personal but a small squiggle of sweetness passed through her.

A couple of minutes later, he emerged from the barn driving a burly, mud-splattered all-terrain vehicle. A feedbag hung from one of the front hooks and several thick braided ropes were attached by bungee cords.

He scooted forward to make room for her directly behind him. "Hop aboard."

Paul watched to see how Bailey digested the news that she was going to have to cozy up against him for the ride. She studied the ATV for a moment then shrugged. "Haven't been on one of these in ages."

The road between the two ranches was rutted and dusty, but it appeared Austen's foreman had graded the trail since the last time Paul visited his brother's weekend estate.

"Are the Armisteads still alive?"

When Bailey leaned close enough to be heard over the engine noise, her front brushed against his back. Nice, but not quite what he'd hoped for. Admitting that made him feel about twelve.

"Mrs. Armistead died about ten years ago. John had a health scare and his kids made him move into an assisted living place in Bozeman a couple of years ago. That's when my brother bought it."

She leaned around him, holding onto his waist for balance. "Are you kidding me? Austen bought a ranch? Why?"

The sensations shooting through his body made it hard to think, let alone carry on a conversation. "Tax write-off, mostly. But then he had this…umm…thing." He didn't want to get into the political scandal that cost Austen his job. "He needed some peace and quiet. So, he's been living there off and on for a few months."

She returned to her less friendly position. Glancing out the corner of his eye he could see her hands gripping on the holds on the back fender.

"Does everyone in your family own property around here?"

"Mia's got some empty land near the river. She and Edward were going to retire there. She got the property in their divorce settlement. Meg has a cabin way the hell up and out that way." He pointed toward the Gallatin Range. He'd never been able to find the place on his own, but Meg called it her sanity spot.

The left front tire hit a rock, making the ATV buck sideways. He grabbed the handle bar to regain control.

Bailey let out a tiny yip and locked her arms around his

waist. Her warmth felt...familiar, like muscle memory. After that, he kept his eyes open for big rocks...to run over.

"Is that him?" Bailey leaned in even closer so she could direct his gaze toward a flash of brown and white. Her bosom connected with his shoulder, which triggered a reaction much lower down.

Paul eased back on the throttle as they crested a slight rise. He let the ATV roll to a stop then turned off the motor.

By focusing on the white and brown pinto forty or so feet away, he could almost talk his body out of embarrassing him in front of Bailey.

The compact little horse with four white feet and a white blaze kicked up his heels as if putting on a show for the new spectators. He snorted and tossed his mane, nearly dancing on the tips of his hooves.

"What the hell is he doing...chasing butterflies?"

Bailey snickered and rocked back. "Maybe. I've seen colts play and jump just for the fun of it."

The only place their bodies touched now was her thighs pressed against his hips. He tried to swallow and nearly choked. "Damn dust," he muttered.

"Your colt is gorgeous, Paul. Great build. Has some Arabian in him, doesn't he?"

"Uh-huh." *Brilliant conversationalist.*

"His white mane and tail remind me of Charlie." She shifted positions to sit higher on the back of the seat.

"Charlie," he repeated. The horse she'd ridden in every fair parade and rodeo during high school. "What happened to him?"

When she didn't answer right away, he slid one leg to the

ground and hopped to standing, taking care not to kick her.

Bailey's gaze was no longer on Skipper. She seemed to be staring unseeing at Copper Mountain in the distance. "I knew when I took him to Fresno State he might not be able to complete all four years, and, sure enough, the summer before my senior year, his left front knee started swelling. That's about the same time I met Ross. I could take my pick from his stable if I joined him on the circuit."

Ross. Paul had never met the man but he didn't care for him one bit. Talk about emotional blackmail. "Drop out of college and come with me and I'll give you the horse of your dreams, baby," he thought.

Bailey's self-deprecating chuckle effectively ruined his private rant.

"It didn't hurt that he looked like Hugh Jackman in a cowboy hat and could ride anything on four legs. I wasn't the only cowgirl he swept off her feet, but I was the one he wanted to marry."

Naturally. The man might be a conniving cad, but he had great taste in women.

"What'd you do with Charlie?"

"Boarded him with a friend." Her tone told him this was still a painful subject. He didn't expect her to say more, but she added, "I got a call in Plano, Texas. Charlie had stopped eating. His knees were swollen and obviously causing him pain. The vet didn't give me any choice. I couldn't let him suffer."

"That's too bad. I know how much he meant to you. You called him your life saver."

"Yep. Every time OC came home drunk, I'd hop on

Charlie's back and fly the coop. I didn't even need a bridle."

He pictured Chloe bareback on Skipper without a bridle and his blood ran cold. He offered Bailey a hand getting off the quad. "Don't tell Chloe you did that. She's a dangerous combination of horse crazy and fearless."

She put her hand in his tentatively. "I was the same way. My mother blamed her premature gray hair on me." Back in the day, she would have ignored his help and bounced off the back of the quad. "How do you plan to catch him? Can you rope?" she asked, placing her feet carefully as she got her bearing.

Seeing the changes in her—out here in what had been her natural element—unnerved him. He realized for the first time how much things had changed. It was possible the girl he'd loved with all his heart was not the same person as this Bailey Jenkins.

He leaned over the side to reach for the bag he'd strapped to one of the anchor hooks. "Not really. I'm hoping this will work. He's a bit of a pig."

"Most teenage boys are."

She took the bag from him and started toward Skipper, who was pretending to ignore them. "Hey, hey, Skip-ip-per," she sang. "I want to curry you some day. Hey, hey, Skipper, come see what's inside this bag. You'll love it, I know. Mmm...mmm."

The melody sounded faintly familiar but the words were pure Bailey.

Skipper nibbled a few blades of grass then turned their way, his reddish-brown ears cocked forward.

Bailey jiggled the feedbag, making the oats dance melodically.

Skipper's nostrils flared. He shook his head, sending his mane aflutter.

"Come here, pretty boy. I'll whisper sweet nothings in your ear and bring you nasturtiums and blue grama grass if you let me take you home."

Her tone alone would have won Paul over if he were a horse. Not surprisingly, Skipper took a couple of steps toward them. Then his gaze landed on Paul. His head lifted and his eyes rolled back. If horses could sneer, Skipper would have flipped them off before he hightailed it in the opposite direction.

Paul sighed. "Stupid horse. Good try, though. I'll call Austen's foreman and ask him to catch the little bastard."

He got back behind the wheel and waited.

Instead of joining him, Bailey headed in the opposite direction. "Stay on the ATV, Paul. He wants to come, but he can't bring himself to give you the satisfaction of caving in."

"Me? This is a power play with me?"

"You're the alpha male."

I am?

As the baby of the family, Paul had pretty much followed everyone else's lead—except at work. Maybe running the show at Big Z Hardware had rubbed off on his personal life.

His phone hummed in his shirt pocket, letting him know he had a text.

"C + M want to spend weekend w u. Y or N?"

His kids wanted to come home. The answer was a no-brainer.

He typed the letter Y and hit send. Did that make him a

pushover? Did he care? *No.* Where his kids were concerned, the only thing that mattered was their happiness.

When he pocketed the phone again, Bailey had her arms around the neck of his unpredictable young horse. Fear plunged through him like an eight-foot wave. He grabbed both handles ready to shoot across the gap between them if necessary.

His heart raced and his mouth felt so dry he could barely swallow. *Please, please, please...* He didn't have time to complete the prayer because Bailey pivoted on her good heel and started toward him.

To Paul's complete and utter shock, Skipper followed a polite step or two behind.

He knew better than to cheer so he waited and watched. She rewarded him with an appreciative smile.

"Hand me the halter...slowly...but whatever you do, don't make eye contact with Skipper."

"Serio—okay."

From his peripheral vision, he watched her fit the red nylon halter over Skipper's ears and fasten it. She petted the horse's head and neck, lavishing him with praise for being a "smart, brave boy." Then she clipped the thick braided lead to the metal ring under his chin.

He bites, Paul was tempted to say, but decided against it. *Maybe he only bites men who bring his feed.*

"Okay," she said. "Tie this off and I think he'll follow us home without a fuss."

"How do you know this? Are you the new horse whisperer?"

After securing the rope, he tried to pat Skipper and nearly lost a hunk of forearm for his effort. Disgusted and more than a little frustrated, he started the engine and made a wide circle so they were headed back on the same path.

Skipper trotted jauntily, never taking his eyes off Bailey.

"I think he's smitten," Paul said.

"He's a beautiful animal. Just rough around the edges. Your daughter should work with him every day. Lunging him, walking on a lead, daily grooming."

"I'm picking her up this afternoon. We'll stop here on our way home." He hesitated before asking, "I don't suppose you…"

She wasn't touching him at all now. Had she picked up on his earlier reaction? Or had his jest about the horse whisperer irked her?

"I'm going to a meeting of the local crafters' guild tonight. I'm hoping to convince a couple of members to give jewelry making a try."

Her business. *Duh*.

He'd completely forgotten the reason she'd come to him the other day. She'd needed help looking for a place to set up B. Dazzled Western Bling.

Damn. That wasn't like him. Jen would have been shocked. "I swear your mother nursed you at her desk in that stinking hardware store so you think it's home," his ex-wife said when she told him she wanted a divorce. "Business is all you talk about. All you dream about."

Not any more, apparently.

Lately, every dream—especially the X-rated ones—starred Bailey Jenkins.

OC DIALED THE number he hadn't called in a good month. He pushed the speakerphone button out of habit. A month ago he'd been too weak to even hold the receiver. Thank God, Bailey hadn't seen him like that.

The line rang four times before a voice said, "Jenkins's Fish and Game, Marla speaking."

Lazy bitch. What took you so long to pick up? "Marla, it's me. Is Jack around?"

"Hello, OC. Of course he's not around. It's summer in Montana. He's up in the mountains showing flatlanders where to drop a line. Probably has another three or four hours of daylight."

He'd never liked talking to Marla. The woman thought two years of junior college made her more intelligent than she was.

"Whatever you've got to say to Jack, you can say it to me, OC. I'll give him the message."

He bit back the three-word phrase he wanted to say. Although it galled him to no end, he needed Marla's cooperation to help Bailey.

"You probably heard Bailey's back in town."

"Yup."

"Well, she needs a place where she can set up her jewelry-making business. I figure the back room of the Fish and Game oughta work just fine."

Her epithet didn't surprise him. She'd always had a penchant for four-letter words. "I don't want strangers tramping through here when I'm booking trips."

"That's what the patio door is for. You'd never cross paths."

"I don't care. My answer is no."

"It's still my business. I've got a say in how it's run."

"Not really."

Her smug, self-satisfied tone made the hair on the back of OC's neck stand up.

"Jack's been keeping the Fish and Game afloat for the past few months, and we're leaving. New Mexico or Arizona. I haven't decided which."

He'd heard that claim before.

"I haven't taken any new bookings for after August first. You're welcome to take over if you're back on your feet...excuse me...*foot*, by then."

The vitriol in her tone made his skin crawl. "That's your idea of helping out a friend? Leaving while I'm still flat on my back?"

Marla chortled. "You're no friend of mine, OC. My husband has a blind spot where you're concerned. Thinks you hung the freakin' moon or something. But, you're a drunk—a mean drunk, who wouldn't have a business if it weren't for Jack Sawyer."

OC didn't argue with her. Not when there was some truth to her claim. But that didn't keep him from wishing he had the strength to get out of bed and march into his shop to bodily throw her ass out the door.

Obviously relishing her chance to give OC what she thought he deserved, Marla told him, "Jack's nearly killed himself with exhaustion trying to be two people. And the whole time he's carting those flatlander chumps from fishing hole to fishing hole, do you know what he has to listen to? Them complaining because he's not the Fish Whisperer.

"For some reason, they're convinced the great and powerful OC Jenkins would have taken them to a special, secret stretch of river. Jack doesn't complain, but it has to hurt when he walks the same stinkin' streams as you did. There's no secret spot, is there, OC?"

The only gift his father ever gave him was the ability to read rivers and streams. OC could *see* where the water cut a little deeper and the big fish liked to hide until he coaxed them to the surface with a specially tied fly.

Not that he'd ever tell her that. *Obnoxious cow.*

"Well, hell, Marla, if you're in such a goddamn hurry to leave, why don't you get the fuck out of there today? I'll tell Bailey she can have the whole damn house to set up her business. She can sell jewelry in the front part and make the shit in the back. Sounds like a damn fine idea to me."

Marla sputtered. "What? You can't…" She stopped.

Something clattered to the floor. He hoped it wasn't the overpriced computer she talked him into buying.

A second later, she was back on the line. "Okay, OC, if that's how you want it, fine. I'll leave the key on the counter. I don't know what you'll tell the people who are booked through August, but I guess that's not my problem anymore."

She hung up before he could tell her to take a flying leap. The irritating sound of an open line made him swing at the phone. It shot across the nightstand, along with all stupid doctoring crap people thought he might need: tissues, water bottle, pill bottles, a mystery novel he couldn't stay focused on long enough to read.

"God damn it all to hell."

A movement in the doorway made him bite off the more colorful cuss words that were forming in his head. Louise didn't abide swearing in the library or her house.

"That went well."

She took her sweet time walking across the room, her gaze never leaving him.

"I always said that woman had a screw loose. Now, it's popped clean off."

Louise laughed, but her expression turned serious a moment later. "Marla has been acting a bit strange lately. I attributed it to being overworked."

Half the time when he'd show up at the shop she was playing some kind of candy game on the computer.

Louise set the phone in place and slowly re-organized the other crap.

When it came to the small amber plastic pill container, she hesitated. "I tried to re-fill this prescription this morning and the clerk said our insurance wouldn't cover it."

"God damn stupid bureaucrats."

"Maybe. Or maybe Marla didn't pay the company's health insurance premiums."

OC didn't like the ominous tone in her voice. The need for a drink got stronger. "Why wouldn't she? She and Jack are on the same policy."

"Are they?"

He didn't know.

He'd been in a bad way for a couple of months before

his first surgery. Fact was he'd gone off the deep end after Bailey's accident. He didn't give a rat's ass about his dead son-in-law. Ross seemed like a cock of the walk—a big talker who expected Bailey to do all the heavy lifting.

Like me and Louise?

"I need a cigarette. Hand me that fake electric thing, will you?"

The device Bailey had given him had fallen off the table, too. Louise had to bend over again. This time when she straightened, she grabbed the edge of the open drawer for balance.

"What's the matter with you?"

She didn't answer. She didn't meet his gaze, either.

"I need to call the bank. You haven't been getting a pay check from the Fish and Game, but Marla's supposed to be paying the mortgage on the building."

"And all the utilities, insurance and taxes."

She pulled her cell phone out of the pocket of her loose sweater. As she scrolled around looking for something, she told him, "The other day I saw a special on printer paper. I tried to use the company debit card and it was declined. Forty-six dollars."

She looked at him, her expression serious. "I meant to call Marla and see if our pin got changed but I forgot."

He turned on the fake cigarette and put it to his lips. Bailey said it vaporized liquid nicotine so he got his fix. Placebo or not, he didn't care. Just the act of holding it and taking a drag calmed his nerves and helped him think straight.

Louise punched in the number then held the phone to

her ear to wait.

"We have money in savings," he said. "We'll be okay."

Louise shook her head. "Mostly gone. Co-pays, out-of-pocket, food, lights, gas—"

Her list stopped as she listened. "Yes. Hello. This is Louise Jenkins. Can you tell me the balance on our loan? Yes, the Fish and Game. Oh, he's doing well, thanks. I'll tell him you asked."

She smiled at OC, but her expression seemed oddly muted. Something wasn't right, and he didn't think it had anything to do with their banking issues.

Her eyes opened wide. "Excuse me? When was the last payment? March? And you've had nothing since?"

Holy shit. Marla stopped making the mortgage payment on the Fish and Game? What the hell was she thinking?

As soon as Louise re-pocketed her phone, OC reached for the landline. "Is that dumb bitch trying to screw us out of everything we worked our asses off for all these years? I'm not calling her. I'm calling the police."

Louise covered his hand with hers. "Marla's not smart enough to plan our downfall. But she is an opportunist. March is probably the last month you were still going into the office. Before that, you signed off on the books, didn't you?"

He couldn't remember for sure. Between the pain pills he'd borrowed from Jack and the booze, most of this past spring was a fog.

"If she didn't pay our bills, what'd she do with the money?"

"Bought a home in New Mexico, I'm guessing."

The pit in the bottom of his stomach instantly filled with piranhas and his left foot began to throb—even though it wasn't attached to his leg any more.

PAUL PUT SKIPPER in the pasture with the other horses and returned the tack to the storage room. He was on his way to the SUV where Bailey was waiting, when a late model extended cab four-wheel drive pulled in.

He'd have recognized the truck right away even without the colorful Jenkins's Fish and Game logo on the door.

Normally, Jack Sawyer was behind the wheel, but not today. Marla eased off the gas pedal as soon as she spotted him.

Crap. The last thing he wanted was a confrontation with his renter. He picked up his pace and trotted to the SUV.

"Paul," Marla bellowed stomping on the brakes so the truck's rear end broke loose and skidded sideways, raising a ridge of blacktop at the same time. "I was just going to call you."

"Lucky me," he muttered under his breath.

Bailey apparently had lowered the windows to avoid overheating. Her low chuckle told him she'd overheard his snide remark.

"What do you need, Marla?"

"I need you to let me out of my lease a couple of months early."

He glanced at Bailey. "But you just gave notice."

Marla lifted her arm and pointed at Bailey. "Tell that to

her asshole daddy. OC fired me, and I know Jack won't tolerate that, so we'll be leaving sooner rather than later. To hell with the fair. They probably have fairs in New Mexico."

Paul had no words. Jack Sawyer had been OC's right-hand man for as long as Paul could remember. "When do you plan to be out?"

"Soon as we can get packed. A week, maybe?"

Paul looked at the house. He'd only been inside a couple of times to make small repairs, but he'd had to turn sideways in places to get past all the clutter.

"Good luck with that," he muttered softly.

Bailey let out a soft chuckle. Not low enough to escape detection by Marla, apparently.

The woman, who was a foot shorter than Paul, hopped to the running board of the SUV so she could face Bailey at the same level. "You think that's funny, Miss Queen Bee? Well, you won't be laughing when your dad's company goes into receivership."

"What are you talking about, Marla?"

"Jenkins's Fish and Game is falling apart. Jack and I have done everything we can, but people believe all that crap I put in the travel magazines about OC being the *Fish Whisperer*. They call to book a guide and they want OC, even though Jack's every bit as a good."

Bailey's expression said she didn't believe that for a minute.

"OC's a surly drunk who brought all his current problems down on himself." Marla zeroed her laser squint on him. "Isn't that what you told your brother a few weeks ago? You were in Grey's. I was at the table right behind you."

Paul felt Bailey's gaze on him. "Might be true, but that doesn't mean you should kick a man when he's down."

Marla turned her back on him to address Bailey. She half leaned in as if ready to climb through the window. "Is that what you think, Queen Bee? That we're picking on your poor old daddy? Jack's been working double time all these months and the great OC Jenkins couldn't even be bothered to say thank you."

"Oh, for god's sake, Marla," Bailey snapped. "We all know OC's no saint. But the man's been in and out of the hospital for months, doped up on pain meds and fighting a major infection. Now, he's dealing with an amputation. Is it too much to expect a little compassion? Or, at the very least, could you cut him some slack until he's back on his feet?"

"No. I can't. He just called and instead of asking how's everything going, he demanded that I clean out the back room so you can set up shop. Just like that. No warning. Just 'Move your shit, Marla,' the Queen Bee is back in town and she needs your space."

Marla's foot slipped and she had to grab the window to keep from falling. "Well, guess what? You want that space so bad, you can have it all because I quit."

The stricken look on Bailey's face hit Paul mid-gut. He nudged Marla just enough to make her jump down from the runner.

"I didn't ask him to boot you out, Marla." She looked at Paul, her frustration clear. "OC's worse than a bull in a china shop. He's a matador with a red cape waving the whole herd inside."

Paul walked around the car and got in. Through Bailey's

open window, he told Marla, "I'll take a look at your lease tomorrow. But, for the record, I think renting the back half of the Fish and Game to Bailey is a great idea. Good luck when Jack hears what you've done."

She turned in a huff and marched back to her truck, which was still idling. When she stepped on the gas and let out the clutch, the husky back tires churned up a plate-size divot of blacktop.

Paul got out, grabbed his phone and took a photo of the damage.

When he got back in, he told Bailey, "That woman has been a pain in my ass since the day she moved in. This—" He held up his phone. "—is coming out of her deposit."

They drove back to Marietta in silence, for the most part. He turned on the radio but his mind couldn't focus on the lyrics.

"It sucks when people attack people you love, doesn't it?" he asking, recalling how frustrated and upset his family had been when Austen's scandal broke.

"I quit making excuses for OC when I was ten."

"Still…he's your dad."

She turned her face toward the window.

"Yeah, and some things never change. I married my father—a self-destructive egoist—and became my mother—the co-dependent little woman. When I dared to leave him, he killed himself and the horse I loved like a child."

The bleak despair in her tone nearly made him pull over. He recognized that spiritless despondency in her voice—he'd heard it fifteen years ago when she told him she had no choice but to go through with the abortion.

Her phone beeped and vibrated on the seat between them.

She picked it up. "Mom." She closed her eyes and let her head fall against the seat's built-in headrest. "I guess it's time to circle the wagons."

Paul stepped on the gas. "It sounds to me like you need a forensic accountant, and I happen to know the best."

Chapter 8

"WHERE DO WE even begin?" Bailey asked her mother the following morning.

They stood shoulder-to-shoulder looking across the floor-to-ceiling stacks of boxes, plastic bins and general clutter that filled the back half of Jenkins's Fish and Game.

The former kitchen looked pristine by comparison, but Bailey had peeked into a few of the oak cabinets and found everything from empty Jack Daniels bottles to ten-year-old cancelled checks.

Marla Sawyer was a pack rat with hoarder tendencies.

"Toss all her crap on the lawn," OC bellowed from the doorway between the office and the back rooms.

To Bailey's profound relief, his wheelchair fit through the main entrance. She hadn't realized the city had required him to install a handicap ramp and bathroom when he converted the home to a business. The first lucky break of the day.

"Some of this stuff might be ours," Louise said, picking up a stack of mail that looked fairly new. It had been sitting under a coffee cup skimmed with green mold.

After Marla's bombshell the day before, her father seemed more like the OC she remembered from her childhood—the strong, brusque, determined businessman, not the angry drunk of her teen-age years.

She'd returned home from her trip to the ranch with Paul to learn her parents had decided on a plan that started with Bailey and Louise going to the office to retrieve the computer, checkbook and any easily transportable files.

Their evening at the kitchen table had been an eye-opener. She'd known within minutes of opening the company's accounting program just how serious a matter this was.

She'd texted Paul, "Need big guns." He could take the innuendo any way he wanted.

Paul had texted her back with a time to meet: 9:45.

She glanced at the yellow enamel clock above the sink. "Hey, that used to be in our kitchen." She reached for the lined tablet she'd brought from home to keep track of inventory. "Old clocks are highly collectible. Maybe there are other antiques of value around here."

"Oscar always loved old stuff," Louise said. "The garage should be full of things he bought at auctions or stumbled across up in the mountains."

"Yeah, and you're not gonna touch that. I'm gonna get into restoring stuff one of these days."

Bailey clamped her hands on her hips and pivoted to face him. "Guess what, Dad? One of these days is here. Now."

She pointed at his leg. "Even with a prosthesis, you aren't going to be hiking nine miles a day anymore. Your new job is going to be figuring out how to sell all this crap on eBay."

She'd called Maureen earlier—too early for California—
to ask for advice on how to handle her dad's rehabilitation
now that they were facing a financial crisis. "OC's only been
out of rehab for a week. Is that too early to get tough with
him?"

"There's a time for sympathy and TLC," Maureen told
her. "But at some point, the patient has to push through the
pain and make life happen again. Your dad isn't going to get
back in the game by sitting around feeling sorry for himself."

"I'll do it. How hard can it be? Where's my e-cig? Louise,
where'd you put it?"

Bailey bit down on a smile. A small victory but still a win.

She'd gotten him out of the house and focused on the
future—a more realistic future. He might be able to lead
short fishing excursions again some day, but until then, he
had to find a way to be productive and regain some control
of his life.

Mom stepped out of the public bathroom. "At least,
Marla kept the public areas neat and tidy. We can be thankful
for that."

She'd just helped OC turn on his cigarette when someone knocked on the closed screen. "Anyone here?"

A spunky little thrill she had no business feeling moved
up and down Bailey's spine the moment she heard Paul's
voice.

*No. Don't go there. It's too soon. We have too much history be-
tween us.* But the truth was she hadn't stopped thinking about
him since she got home.

"Hey, everyone. I brought you a present. Sheri Fast, the
best forensic accountant in Montana." He opened the door

for a tall, lanky blond with a French twist, a gray pencil skirt, four-inch pumps and a tailored white shirt.

Holy mother. That's an accountant?

Bailey blushed, realizing how sexist her observation sounded. To make up for the gaff, she purposefully marched across the room—ankle be damned—to greet the woman. "Hello. I'm Bailey. These are my parents, OC and Louise Jenkins. Thank you for coming so quickly."

"My name says it all." Her manicured hand felt cool, her shake firm and businesslike. "When it comes to embezzlement, time is of the essence."

Louise led the woman to Marla's desk with the computer and high-end monitor they'd brought back this morning. "We don't know for a fact Marla's been stealing, but—"

"Of course, she has," OC said, interrupting. "The company's broke. Our business savings has been cleaned out. And every room in this place is stuffed full of shit. Doesn't take a rocket scientist to know somebody had her hands in the cookie jar."

The accountant set her Louis Vuitton briefcase beside the desk. "Opportunistic thieves are the easiest to catch," she said, sitting with the sort of big city grace Bailey envied. "Unfortunately, they also provide the biggest challenge when it comes to obtaining restitution."

"Why is that?" Bailey asked.

The woman slipped on a pair of tortoise shell readers that transformed her face into some Hollywood porn producer's ideal image of an accountant.

Bailey looked at Paul to see if he was drooling. Strangely, he was looking at Bailey.

"Because by the time they get caught they've already spent the money. It's all about immediate gratification."

Bailey pictured the big truck Marla had been driving the day before and her stomach soured.

Paul cleared his throat to get their attention. "Um…speaking from experience here, I suggest we all step away and let Sheri do her thing."

He started toward the back rooms but stopped abruptly. "Holy smokes. We're gonna need a bigger dumpster."

Even OC chuckled, which made Bailey so grateful she almost kissed Paul. Luckily, he'd started poking into boxes. "What is all this stuff? This looks like an OCD version of Hoarders."

"I have no idea. We haven't gotten that far."

"As long as it's not body parts, you'll be okay."

She gave a little laugh that suddenly took on a life of its own. "You…crack…me up." She braced herself using his shoulder until the fit of laughter passed. "Sorry," she said, wiping the tears from her eyes. "It was either laugh or freak out."

She took a deep breath and squared her shoulders. "Okay. Here's the plan. One box at a time. Anything of value can go in one pile. Anything with a receipt might be returnable so that goes in another pile. Pure crap we'll bag for the dump. Or recycling."

"Playing Devil's Advocate here, what if Marla shows up demanding all her shit back?"

Bailey picked up the box cutter she'd brought from home. "She can pay me now or pay me later—after she gets out of jail."

"Sounds like fun. Can I help?"

Yes. Please. Thank you. Her neediness made her scowl. "Don't you have a business to run?"

"Took the day off. I have to pick up the kids this afternoon. And I promised to take Sheri to lunch, but other than that, I'm all yours."

Bailey looked at the armada of boxes and decided she couldn't afford to be picky. Volunteer help was free help. She snatched up a box and shoved it into his arms.

"Have at it. With any luck we'll be done by...Christmas."

Paul laughed. Now, this, he thought, was the Bailey he remembered from high school. The girl who made up her mind to become Fair Queen and didn't let anything or anyone stop her from her goal.

A moment later, Louise opened the patio door and called out, "We're leaving, honey. Oscar's appointment is in ten minutes. I'll pick up some trash bags on my way back."

To Paul, she said, "Thank you, again, Paul. We are forever in your debt."

"Forever's a long time. I'm happy to help."

Her smile struck him as strained. He wondered again if this whole mess was making her ill.

"Is your mom okay?" he asked after Louise was out of earshot.

Bailey tipped a cascade of packing peanuts into a garbage can. "She'd better be. Without her, Dad would fall apart—worse than he already has."

She examined the contents of the box, her top teeth worrying her bottom lip. Paul's groin tightened. How could someone dressed in cut-off shorts, scuffed cowboy boots and an oversize men's western shirt tied at the waist look so damn sexy?

She carried a stack of paperback books to the counter. They appeared to be six copies of the same title.

As she flattened the cardboard box, she added, "It's kinda weird. I used to think OC was the strong one and Mom was a wimp. Now, she stands up to him, and he actually does what she tells him." When she shook head, the navy bandana she'd used to tie back her hair slipped.

He curled his fingers into a fist to keep from reaching out to fix it.

"Believe me," she said cheerfully. "I never thought I'd see the day."

Me, neither. I never thought I'd see the day when I was lusting after Bailey Jenkins. Again.

Twenty or so boxes later, Paul stretched and let out a long, well-earned groan. "This sucks. I'm now an official member of the I Hate Marla Sawyer Club."

"Told 'ya," Bailey said, her tone far too chipper for someone dealing with an overabundance of junk.

She bent over and touched the ground, stretching in a yoga pose. Her shorts fit like workout pants, showing what she'd always called her saddle butt. He called it perfection. Just round enough to fill in her jeans, firm enough to show she was an athlete.

His male anatomy stirred. Again.

"Is it lunch time, yet?" Sheri called from the outer room.

"Hell, yes."

Paul kicked the four-foot by six-foot box he'd started to open. It didn't budge. "Are you coming with us, Bailey? It's on me."

She blew out a weary sigh. "Thanks, but the locksmith won't be here until four. OC thinks somebody needs to keep an eye on things in case Marla comes back."

From the doorway, Sheri Fast said, "Very good point. I've copied the majority of the files to a thumb drive, but I'm only about halfway through the initial eval."

"Are any of these purchases showing up?" Bailey had been giving Sheri every invoice she ran across.

Sheri nodded. "Believe it or not, yes. She used an email addy linked to the business website to order everything you gave me. Whether she thought that would make the purchases appear more legitimate is anybody's guess."

"Can you print a list?"

"After lunch. I'm famished." She looked at Paul. "Is your brother joining us?"

Paul caught Bailey's unmistakable look of surprise. *She thought Sheri and I had something going on, but Sheri only has one Zabrinski on the brain—Austen.*

As he escorted the beautiful accountant to his truck, he considered the idea of spelling out his feelings to Bailey. "I still have feelings for you and I'd like to explore those feelings as adults, not wet-behind-the-ears kids."

Kids. Shit. He was picking up his kids today. Did he want to risk introducing Chloe and Mark to Bailey only to have her take off a month or two down the road? Hell, no. His kids had been privy to enough of his mistakes without adding an affair with Bailey Jenkins to the list.

★

"USELESS," OC MUTTERED, his arms shaking from the effort of getting into his bed with only minimal help from Louise.

No. Worse than useless. He'd become a goddamn burden. He had to be driven everywhere. His wife had to load and unload his stinking wheelchair.

He didn't know where she found the strength. She'd lost weight these past few months. His fault, too.

So had he, but he'd started with more. A lot more. Belly fat, mostly. From too many beers. Way too much whiskey.

Sugar and empty calories, Nurse Sharvis said, every time he asked for a bottle. More than anything, he did it to get under her skin. But there'd been a few weeks—a month, maybe—where he'd dreamed of booze, tasted it on his tongue, craved the smooth bite in the back of his throat.

Now, he didn't yearn for the taste so much, but what he wouldn't give for a temporary escape from this shit-hole reality he'd created.

"Nobody to blame but me," he said softly, hating the prickling sensation behind his eyes. Tears for God's sake. Like a worthless crybaby.

His pa would have laughed his ass off seeing OC like this. The man was as unsentimental as a fence post—and about as friendly. The only time OC ever saw him smile was when he hooked a trout.

Watching the dance between fisherman and fish—his father's skill and experience paired with the fish's need to escape, to live, to procreate—was the only good memory Oscar retained of his childhood.

By fifteen, he was working nearly fulltime, catching classes as he could. He officially dropped out of school when the principal found him asleep on the front step of school, the best shelter he'd been able to find, and assumed the smell of whiskey on his shirt came from OC's drinking, not his old man, who had flung a bottle at his son when he kicked him out.

Pride had kept him from telling the truth. Pride nearly cost him life, too. He'd tried to hide the severity of his infection from Louise, foolishly treating his sore toe with some snake oil Marla recommended. By the time Louise identified the smell of rotting flesh, the infection had spread.

"Goddamn fool."

He closed his eyes, worn out by the day's effort. Not even two in the afternoon and he needed a nap, like a baby.

Baby.

The word always brought back the memory of Bailey telling him she was pregnant. "Paul thinks we should get married and have the baby. He said we could live with his folks until we can afford a place of our own."

OC had blown up, of course. All his hopes and dreams for his daughter's success and happiness blown to smithereens by some horny little boy's sperm.

He knew Paul Zabrinski and didn't have anything against the kid—except he was a kid. Still in high school. And he knew what small towns were like. Bailey might be Fair Queen this week but once word got out, she'd be a loser—just like her dad.

So, he'd shared his opinion.

"You terrorized our daughter," Louise said later. "She asked for our advice and you called her a slut."

He didn't remember that, but he had been drinking. And

whatever kind of relationship he'd thought he'd been building with Bailey was gone.

So much so that when her husband was killed and she needed help, she called her mother, not him. "Just you, Mom. I can't handle OC right now."

He'd died a little that day. And to kill the pain, he'd turned to his old friends, Jim Beam and Jack Daniels. At some point in the night, he tripped and fell and screwed up his toes—the ones that eventually turned black and needed to be amputated.

A gruff cough made his eyelids bounce open. Jack Sawyer. OC hadn't seen Jack in over a month. They'd been friends once. Closer than most brothers. How could an honest man screw over a friend the way Jack did and still come calling?

"You alone?" OC asked. Your wife isn't welcome here, he could have added but didn't.

"Yep. Can I come in?"

"Sure. I could use some help pulling this big ol' knife outta my back."

Jack's mouth pulled to the right—the way it always did when he was upset about something, but he clutched the brown paper sack he was carrying to his middle like it might protect him from whatever OC could throw at him. He sat on the edge of the chair, the sack making a crunching noise as his fingers squeezed and released it.

"Things are getting outta hand here, OC. Marla's always been high-strung. Seems like lately she's gone over the edge a bit. But we can still make it right between us." He held up the sack like a peace offering. "I brought you a bottle."

OC's mouth went dry, and a nest of meat bees took up buzzing in his chest. "You think a bottle of booze is going to make up for ruining my business and sending me and my wife to the Poor House?"

Jack ran a hand through his lank, brownish-gray hair. He'd started growing out his sideburns, OC noticed, to make up for the thinning spot on his crown.

"Oh, come on, OC. It's not that bad. Marla said she borrowed a few bucks to pay off some bills, but nothing big. She can fix it. Hell, she would have had the accounts all back to normal by the time we left for New Mexico if you hadn't gotten in her face about letting Bailey move in."

Jack reached for OC's water glass. He picked it up, leaned over to pour the contents into Louise's big leafy fichus, and then set the glass on the bedside table.

A second later, OC heard the "crack" he knew all too well—a plastic screw top breaking free of its seal. As Jack poured a few glugs into the glass, the tangy aroma permeated OC's senses.

"Guess we'll have to share a cup, huh? Won't be the first time. Do you remember when we were up on—?"

OC reached out and grabbed the bottle from Jack's hands. He threw it with as much force as he could muster—an embarrassing lob that failed to hit the wall. The sack landed on the carpet, half out of the bag.

Breathing hard from the effort, OC leaned sideways so he could look Jack in the eye. "I don't remember shit. Most of the time I was drunk or hung-over. Made for easy pickings for you and your wife, didn't I?"

Jack's hurt appeared genuine enough. OC wanted to

believe he knew nothing of Marla's embezzlement, but not admitting and not knowing weren't the same thing.

"You drive a new pick-up, Jack. Mine's ten years old. You have three new rods. You showed them to me the last time you stopped by—a month or so ago. Your wife told my wife you're buying a place in New Mexico. It never crossed your mind to question all that abundance?"

Jack picked up the glass and gulped down about half. He held up the glass, staring into the amber liquid. "I figured it was my turn. I've been working like a dog. Ten...twelve...even fourteen hours a day. If that don't earn me the right to buy a truck, I don't know what does."

OC didn't have a response, which was just as well because Jack sprang to his feet and tossed what was left of the booze in OC's face. If OC had been talking, he probably would have ingested some and that might have been all it took to get him hooked again.

OC used the edge of the sheet to wipe off the liquid. The smell nearly gagged him. But even dunking the corner of the blanket in the plastic water pitcher that followed him home from the hospital didn't clean it up completely.

He dropped back on his pillow. He didn't have enough energy to try to get out of bed and take a shower, but, hopefully, Nurse Sharvis would arrive before the smell drove him out of his mind.

"HONEY, WOULD YOU mind running home to check on your dad? Nurse Sharvis just called. She has a family emergency and can't come today."

Mom's voice sounded as frustrated as Bailey felt. Going through boxes of other people's junk was not what she came home to do. If she hoped to gain any traction in sales at the Marietta Fair, she needed product to sell.

"Sure, Mom. Paul and the accountant should be back from lunch any minute. He'll probably keep an eye on the place until I get back."

She'd wanted to go to lunch with them. Normal people, doing normal things. But, even if she hadn't been worried about Marla showing up, Bailey knew she had to keep her distance from Paul.

Broken people had no business glomming onto healthy, happy, normal people.

As if on cue, a man's voice called, "We're baaack."

Try though she might, Bailey couldn't tamp down the squiggle of excitement that darted through her chest. She hoped it wasn't what she thought it was...that old feeling she didn't want to call love.

"If that Arnold Schwarzenegger imitation was for my benefit, you should know he hasn't been governor for a couple of years."

Paul laughed as he walked into the back room. "Hey, look at the progress. Way to go, Bailey."

She straightened, arching her back to relieve the tension of bending over. "Really? I was just thinking these boxes were multiplying like Tribbles."

"Tribbles. I forgot you were a cowgirl Trekkie. Believe it or not, my kids are huge Star Trek fans. We have the whole TV series on DVD."

"We brought you lunch," Sheri Fast said, holding a To-Go box from the Main Street Diner.

Bailey recognized the eco-friendly packaging. "That's nice of you. Thanks."

"Paul changed his mind about twelve times before settling on the Chinese Chicken salad. God, I hope you like it," she said, rolling her eyes in a friendly, girlfriend-he's-got-it-bad air.

Bailey couldn't help but laugh—especially when she spotted Paul's blush.

"Four, at most," he insisted.

Bailey's mouth watered when she opened the lid and inspected the fresh greens and a plethora of yummy toppings. A small plastic container of dressing was tucked into one corner of the box. "This looks like enough for two people. I should take it home to share with OC. His nurse had to cancel."

"Do you need me to drive you?"

Distance. Distance.

"Thanks, but I managed to make it over here in Dad's truck this morning. Doesn't have power brakes, but I drove slowly."

She grabbed her purse and the salad and headed toward the door. "I'll be back in an hour, if that's okay?"

Paul picked up a broom and held it in front of him like a sword. "I will defend this place to my death, m'lady."

"Please don't. I haven't found a single bit of junk worth it. Just threaten to call the Sheriff, and Marla will run away."

He frowned. "And people think I micromanage."

She drove slowly—in part, enjoying the freedom of

being behind the wheel again. She'd missed driving almost as much as she missed riding. She understood what her father was going through better than he knew. Being dependent on other people for the smallest little thing was humiliating and depressing.

Maybe his new prosthetic leg will help, she thought.

She wasn't sure which was worse—the old, bitter drunk OC or the new, defeated and humbled OC?

Bless you, Paul Zabrinski, she thought as she walked up the ramp. Her father wasn't the only one who couldn't handle stairs well. Especially after a long morning of being on her feet.

The front door was unlocked, as usual. She dropped her purse on a chair and set the take-out container on the kitchen counter. Humming under her breath, she took two plates from the cabinet and divided the lush greens evenly.

Her mouth watered as she drizzled the aromatic dressing over the mosaic of large hunks of chicken and crunchy Chinese noodles. She grabbed a cloth napkin and fork before starting down the hallway.

Her humming lodged sideways in her throat the moment she caught a whiff of an unfamiliar—yet too familiar—smell. Booze.

"Dad?"

She hurried into the master bedroom, equal parts fear and dread making her hands shake. She was so focused on the unmoving body on the bed she tripped over something on the floor. Pieces of lettuce fell like green rain, but she managed to recover her balance.

She looked down. A distinctive brown paper sack. An

amber pint bottle.

Her stomach clenched. Tears sprang to her eyes. Disappointment pressed heavy on her chest, making it hard to speak.

"Oh, Dad, how could you? You heard the doctors. You drink, you die. Is that what you want? Then why the hell did I spend the whole morning trying to fix this mess you made? Why, OC? Why?"

Her father came to on the bed, either passed out or sleeping. He opened his eyes and looked at her. His eyes weren't bloodshot and rummy. He didn't appear drunk, but he'd had an entire lifetime to practice faking sobriety.

Her fingers clenched the plate. It took every ounce of self-control she possessed not to dump the salad on his lap and storm off. The only thing stopping her was the knowledge either she or her mother would have to clean up the mess.

"I should have known you couldn't do it," she said, setting the plate on his bedside table.

"Where's the nurse?"

"Cancelled."

"Your mother?"

"At work. Everybody is doing what needs to be done to dig you out of this hole. Everybody but you, apparently. Who brought the bottle?" she asked, but stopped him before he could answer. "Never mind. I don't care. I'm done."

"What do you mean?"

"I picked up after you for most of my life. Helped Mom clean up your messes. Apologized for your drunken ugliness. I made it my job to show this town the Jenkins name wasn't the punch line of a bad joke."

She shook her head, anger intricately entwined with disappointment. "I don't have it in me to fight the good fight again. If you're going to drink, I'm leaving—only this time I'm taking Mom with me before you kill her, too."

He didn't say a word when she walked away.

But, then, what could he say? Drunks made promises they couldn't keep. She knew that. Why had she thought for a minute he'd changed?

OC HAD KNOWN pain before. The ache of infection eating away on his flesh was nothing compared to the burning cut of his daughter's words, the sizzling acid of seeing complete and utter disappointment in her eyes.

Like the principal who judged without giving OC a chance to defend himself, Bailey had condemned him, too. But unlike the school administrator, Bailey had good reason to think the worst. He'd ruined her childhood.

He liked to think there'd been a few good parts. He'd worked from pre-dawn to dark every summer to be able to afford to keep the horse she loved and the ranch she called home. He'd done that for her. But his demons had undermined his good intentions. When the drink got hold of him, he'd turn into somebody he recognized but didn't like. His father.

His hand shook when he reached for the phone. He couldn't tell if Bailey was still in the house—packing her bags, maybe—or crying her eyes out. He wanted to go to her, to tell her, "I didn't so much as taste the stuff." But he couldn't reach the wheelchair.

He could reach what was left in Jack's glass.

His mouth turned desert dry. His finger shook as he punched in the number he knew by heart.

"Marietta Library. Louise speaking."

"Come home, Luly. I need you. Please," he added. A word he didn't use often enough.

AT THE RATE her heart was beating, Louise feared she'd have a heart attack before she got home. Although Bailey said she'd check on her dad, Oscar's truck wasn't in the driveway. A take-out container and full plate of salad sat on the kitchen counter.

She hurried down the hallway to the bedroom. "I'm here. Taylor came back just before you called. What happened?"

She could tell by the way his hands gestured as he spoke how upset he was. His words tumbled over each other. He pointed to the floor. A bottle in a sack. God, she'd seen a million of them. In the bathroom. On the backseat of her car. Under a hay bale in the barn. This one looked nearly full. In the past, she only found the empties.

"Who brought this?"

"Jack." He sat up a little straighter. "I didn't take a drink. He did. And he threw what was left in the glass at me. I need a shower."

She could see the truth in his eyes. She knew him under

the influence. Lately, she'd gotten to know him sober. She could tell the difference. But Bailey…her poor, fragile daughter probably could not.

"Yes, you do. You stink."

She helped him into the wheelchair. He was getting stronger, at last. A week ago she would have had to lift him onto the white plastic shower bench. Today, he did it himself. He washed his hair and used the hand-held adapter to rinse away the bubbles. By the time he called out to tell her he was done, she had the sheets changed.

"I don't want to go back to bed. I want to find Bailey."

Louise shook her head. "You can't. I told Taylor I'd be right back. Today's story day for the preschoolers."

"I could drop you off…" He looked at his stump, naked and exposed. His leg was healing but it wouldn't support the effort required to drive a car—even an automatic.

"When was your last pain pill?"

"I don't remember."

"Eat your lunch, take your pill and rest." When he started to protest, she added, "I'll call Paul. He'll know where to find her. We can go together when I get off work. I promise."

She crossed her fingers behind her back. She'd call Paul, but Bailey could be anywhere. She had credit cards and her father's truck. She could be on her way back to California for all Louise knew.

Unconsciously, she put her hand on the lump.

"What's wrong with your side?"

The eagle eyes of a hunter. "Nothing."

"Don't lie to me, Luly. I've seen you poke at that spot

before. Tell me what's wrong."

She closed her eyes and took a deep breath. "I found a lump."

"What kind of lump?"

"I don't know. It's bigger than a plum but smaller than a peach." She'd decided this while shopping in the produce aisle the other day.

"Sh...show me."

She unfastened the waistband of her skirt to release her soft cotton top. She carefully pulled up the fabric. In the past couple of days, she'd noticed an increased sensitivity around the spot.

Oscar placed his hands on her hips and pulled her a step closer, then positioned her to take advantage of the sunlight coming from the window. "How long have you had this?" His voice held the gruff tone of fear.

"A month. Maybe a little longer."

"Oh, good God. Why didn't you tell me?"

She looked at him, conveying an answer too obvious for words.

"Of course. Because of me." He let go of her and sat back in his wheelchair. "Call the doctor. Make an appointment. Whatever it is, we'll get through it."

Then he opened his arms and she went—same as she had since that day forty odd years earlier when he admitted he couldn't read. He was her heart. Good or bad. Healthy or sick. Bailey didn't understand. Louise had lost count of the times Bailey had begged her to leave him. "Why, Mama? Why do you stay?" Louise couldn't explain why she couldn't leave her center of being, any more than she could explain why the sun came up every day.

"I know we will," she said, feeling a sense of hope she'd thought was lost forever. Oscar Clark Jenkins was back.

Thank God.

Chapter 9

Paul finished tightening the last screw before reaching for his phone. A generic, uninspiring ringtone. Not the Carrie Underwood song he was hoping for.

"Oh, hi, Louise. I thought you might be Bailey. She said she'd be back by two. It's nearly three. Is everything okay?"

"No. It's not." When she finished explaining what she believed happened, she added, "I looked Oscar in the eye, and I can swear to you, Paul, he did not drink."

"But Bailey assumed the worst." *Why wouldn't she, given her history with her father?*

"Oscar and I need to go out for awhile. Might even be overnight. Oscar's afraid she'll leave town before he has a chance to explain."

The poor woman's tone sounded so bleak, Paul almost groaned. He looked at the door knob he'd just finished re-keying. A part of him wanted to lock up and walk away for good.

What did he have invested? A few hours of his time? And all for what? The vague, problematic, probably ridiculous chance of reconciliation with his first love? If he left now, who'd know? It wasn't as if he'd broadcast his intention to the world.

Accept for the observant Sheri and his impossibly intuitive brother who'd both commented on Paul's burgeoning relationship with Bailey.

At lunch today, Sheri had laid it out straight. "I can see why Austen called Bailey your Kryptonite. She's beautiful and wounded. What man can resist that combination?"

Paul gathered up the packaging from his locks and walked inside. Sheri appeared to be packing up her briefcase.

"I take it Bailey's not answering her phone?" he asked Louise. He'd tried Bailey's number half a dozen times himself but his calls went straight to voicemail.

"No. I left a message, but she hasn't called back. OC feels awful. But he doesn't blame her for assuming the worst."

The comment took Paul by surprise. The OC Jenkins he knew always blamed the other person for whatever fights or unpleasantness came his way.

"Has she reconnected with any old friends since she got back?"

"Only you."

Neither spoke for a moment, then Louise asked, "Is there any hideout or special place you remember her running to back in high school?"

"She mentioned laying low in the haymow when her dad was on a rant. But surely she wouldn't go to the ranch with Marla and Jack around?"

"Probably not. Unless she heard the same rumor I did. Taylor told me they were seen packing up a great big U-Haul truck last night. OC didn't see what Jack was driving, but he remembered hearing a truck engine." She let out a small choking sound. "Oh, my word. Of course. Jack's last stop on the way out of town was to get Oscar drunk. I bet Marla put him up to it. She knows as well as anyone what would happen if Bailey came home and found her father drinking."

Paul knew, too. The dirty trick made him change his mind about walking away. Paul didn't care about OC, but Bailey didn't deserve that kind of underhandedness.

"I'll swing by the ranch on my way back from Bozeman." He paused then added, "By the way, I re-keyed all the doors. You can cancel your locksmith. I'll give the new keys to Bailey if I find her."

"You're a saint, Paul," she said, her tone somber and filled with emotion. "I don't know what our family would have done without you."

A saint? Hardly. I'm the guy who put a curse on your daughter. Apparently, it extended to the whole family. Who knew?

BAILEY PULLED INTO the long, beautifully paved driveway with a small squiggle of trepidation. You didn't grow up the child of an alcoholic to willingly court discourse. But a line had been crossed. Jack and Marla knew how fragile her dad's recovery was and one of them decided to help him screw up.

Nobody deserved those kinds of so-called friends.

She glanced at the black face of her cell phone on the bench seat beside her. Dead. Her car phone charger had burned up in the accident and when she bought a new phone she couldn't afford the added expense. But, now, she regretted not replacing it. If Marla went cuckoo or Jack did something stupid, nobody would know where to find her—

or her body.

Plus, she felt terrible about running off and abandoning Paul at Jenkins's Fish and Game. Was he still there waiting for the locksmith? God, she hoped not. She owed him a huge apology.

Unfortunately, Bailey wasn't her father's daughter for nothing! The shock of finding OC drunk made her so infuriated—and hurt, she'd stormed out of the house and hopped in the truck. Her plan? To put as much distance between her and her father as possible.

She was nearly to the Montana border before her anger solidified into resolve.

"Am I going to let his demons chase me away again?" she'd asked aloud. "Hell, no."

One of the things about seeing your dreams crushed and everything you worked so hard for disappear is you walked—or limped—away with perspective. She couldn't fix her father and she was done trying. Just like she was done running away.

What she could do was help fix the mess Marla and Jack had created for them, and she planned to spell that out to the Sawyers in person. And as soon as Paul's fancy accountant proved there were misdoings, she'd call the sheriff.

The moment she aimed the steering wheel toward the house, she realized she was too late. No car. No truck. Only a yard full of junk—a broken table, a faded umbrella, a riding lawn mower with grass growing in a crack on the seat.

She got out, pocketed the key—a habit from living anywhere *but* Montana—and walked to the house. The kitchen door was unlocked. Typical. She put her head in and looked around. A filthy, chaotic mess. Exactly what you'd expect if someone moved out in a hurry.

"Can you say guilty and soon to be charged?" she muttered under her breath.

She didn't need to go inside. She might have walked in to use the phone but remembered her mother saying Marla had gone to cell phone only to save money.

She turned away and started back to the truck when she spotted the colt kicking up his heels in the pasture. The other horses had shown her little interest when she pulled in, but Skipper raced back and forth as if vying for her attention.

Her ankle felt surprisingly okay considering she'd been driving for two hours. In fact, she needed to move around, so instead of hopping back in the truck, she walked across the open staging area between the house and barn.

Many a night she'd been the one driving their truck and trailer home from an event. Her ribbons, belt buckles or trophies on the floor beside her father's feet while he slumped passed out on the seat beside her.

She'd learned fast how to back up a horse trailer without taking out the power pole or a hunk of fence. She'd learned how to hose out the floorboards if OC threw up, too.

She walked to the side pasture where Paul put the colt the day before. From a plastic bin, she filled a two-cup measurer with oats and dumped the grain into the trough. Naturally, Skipper had disappeared as soon as she headed in his direction. *Typical teenage boy.*

She pressed two fingers against her bottom lip and blew hard. The shrill whistle never failed to bring Daz running.

She closed her eyes and listened. Seconds later, the thunder of hooves made her smile. The horse rounded the corner of the barn as if his tail was on fire then slammed on the brakes when he saw her standing an arm's length from the fence.

He tossed his head and did a little turf dance, but the flaring of his nostrils told her he smelled the grain.

"Yummy. Yummy," she said, keeping her tone light. "No strings. I don't want to ride you, groom you or give you a shot. Nothing. I just want to smell you. And maybe touch you. May I do that?"

She let him settle into the feed before extending her hand. She moved cautiously.

"So, how was your day? Mine kinda sucked." His ear flickered but he didn't lift his head. "My folks have been bled dry by a friend they trusted. I can't set up shop to make jewelry until I unload a dumpster full of crap. And, oh yeah, my dad is drinking again."

His eyes came level with hers. If Skipper had been Daz, she would have seen a hint of wisdom that may have given her some insight, or, at the very least, a bit of peace. Instead, she saw the dispassionate query of a stranger, asking, "Why are you telling me this, lady? I don't even know you. Why should I care about your problems?"

"So, true," Bailey said out loud, starting to laugh. "That's it in a nutshell, isn't it?"

She gave Skipper a quick scratch on his white blaze then headed back to her truck. She'd just reached for the door handle when the sound of a car engine caught her ear. Her heart rate sped up. Jack and Marla?

A second later, she caught sight of a familiar black SUV. It veered her way the moment the driver spotted her.

Paul.

An instant later, she made out two children in the back seat.

"WELL, WHATTAYAKNOW? SHE'S here," Paul murmured out loud.

"Whose truck?" Mark asked.

"Probably belongs to the lady standing beside it," Chloe answered. "Duh."

Paul heard Mark slug her bare arm. "I didn't see her, okay?"

"Because you were playing your stupid game. That's all you do anymore."

"Kids. Please. Bailey's an old friend. She's back in town helping her parents. Her mother is Mrs. Jenkins, Chloe."

"Really?" Chloe slipped out of her seatbelt to press her face to the window. "She's pretty."

She is. And now was probably not the best time to introduce her to his children.

"Stay in the car, please. Louise asked me to find out why she's not answering her phone. As soon as I'm done talking to her, we're going to feed the horses and check out the house to see how big a mess the Sawyers left." He'd already explained that part of their stop.

He put on the emergency brake but left the engine running. The day had heated up and his spoiled children would complain non-stop if he turned off the air-conditioning.

"Bailey," he called hurrying toward her. "Are you okay? Your mom was worried when she couldn't reach you."

She brushed back a lock of hair that had slipped free of her fancy, pink and purple clip. He realized he was starting to be able to identify her B. Dazzled style and it wasn't even on the market. Him—a man known for his discerning taste in screwdrivers.

"My phone died and I don't have a car charger. I told you I'd be right back and then never showed. I'm really sorry."

"No problem. Sheri held down the fort while I went to Big Z's and got the stuff to change your locks. I couldn't wait for your locksmith because I had to pick up my kids." He handed her his phone. "Your mom's worried."

Their hands touched during the exchange. That stupid zing he tried his best to ignore shot straight up his arm and exploded through his body. *Damn.*

He stuck his hand in the pocket of his jeans. "The kids and I are here to feed the animals and check on the house. Did you look inside?"

She answered him while punching in a number. "The door's open. I think they're gone."

"Rumor has it they tossed everything they could carry into a U-Haul. Your mom thinks their last stop on their way out of town was to see OC."

She put the phone to her ear. "I figured that's where the booze came from."

"Marla's parting gift of nastiness."

She hit end then said, "No answer at the house. Let me

try her cell."

Paul turned at the sound of his car door opening. "Dad, it's boring in here. I'm hungry," Chloe called.

"We'll pick up pizza on the way home."

"Not pizza," she wailed. "Mom bought pizza last night for the babysitter to make. Frozen. Gag."

He noticed Bailey's grin before she pursed her lips and whispered another message into the phone. Apparently, her mother wasn't picking up, either.

She handed him back the phone. "I have a sack of snacks in the truck. Had to stop for a bottle of water and they don't take credit card charges for under ten dollars. I got all of OC's favorites."

A telling admission considering she was mad at him.

"Louise says he didn't actually take a drink. He threw the bottle across the room and Jack tossed his glass in OC's face after they argued."

He saw the change in her face. Relief? Sadness? Skepticism? He couldn't be sure. "Maybe they're at the Sheriff's office filing charges. Sheri said Marla left a very obvious paper trail and will be going to jail."

"Dad."

The three syllable variety.

"I need to use the bathroom."

"Oh, crap," he muttered, adding softly, "no pun intended." To his daughter, he asked, "Number One or Number Two?"

"That is nobody's business but my own. I just need to go. Now," Chloe added in a tone that sounded exactly like Jen.

He didn't need to look at Bailey to know she was stifling a grin. "Fine. I suppose technically the house has been abandoned, so... Bailey says the house is open. There's a bathroom right off the kitchen."

The car door opened and slammed. Paul watched his lithe ballerina-slash-bronco rider sprint across the blacktop to the rear patio area. "Those people were pigs," Paul said, taking in enough junk to require a dumpster.

"Hoarder pigs."

"I don't think there is such a thing."

Paul looked down. He hadn't even heard Mark get out. "Hey, Mark, this is my friend, Bailey."

Bailey smiled. "Hi. I like your T-shirt. I'm a Loki fan, too."

Paul had to look a second time to figure out what she was talking about. Mark's T-shirt—one Paul had never seen before—sported a cartoon figure reclining on a throne with the caption: Chillin' like a Villain.

His son eyed her suspiciously. "My mom does, too, but that's because she likes the guy who plays him in the movie."

"Tom Hiddleson. Me, too."

Mark rolled his eyes. "Girls are weird."

"Mark..." Paul started to reprimand him, but Bailey interrupted.

"You're right. It's what makes us interesting."

Mark shrugged the way eight-year-old boys did. "When are we going?"

"After we feed the horses. You want to help? Give the horses a couple of flakes of hay."

His son gave him a patented "get-real" look and walked

back to the car. Paul could have gone after him, argued for five minutes then forced him to do the chores, but that would have effectively ruined the rest of their evening. The resounding slam of the car door made him look at Bailey and say, "His mother and I don't agree on how to discipline them, so they pretty much get away with anything and everything."

"I'm the last person who should give you advice, but I have trained a few horses and I learned the hard way, giving in is merely delaying the pain."

She rubbed her elbow. "My first thoroughbred. Most obnoxious animal I ever met. Thought she was a princess. She even convinced me she was fragile and ladylike...until she threw me over the fence. My elbow grazed a tree."

"Broken?"

She shrugged. "Didn't have insurance at the time. The pain went away after about a year."

Rough and tough—that's how he'd defined Bailey...until he got to know her.

"I'll help you feed," she said. "It's the least I can do to repay you for wasting your whole day at the Fish and Game."

He followed her toward the barn, his gaze never leaving the rocking hip motion of her cut-offs. *God, I have it bad.*

"It's gross inside that house, Dad," Chloe called, bursting from the back door as if exposed to a pandemic virus. "I'm not going to work in there. No way."

Paul stifled a sigh. Parenting was a thankless job most of the time. Especially when your partner traded up. "Well, come help feed the horses." He waited for her to catch up and then asked, "Don't you need to start getting ready for the Fair?"

"Yeah. I told Mom last week, but she said that was your problem."

Jen's lack of interest in horsemanship, shows, 4-H, anything having to do with the ranch was emblematic of the deep divide in their marriage. "Well, you're in luck. This is Bailey Jenkins, one of the last Fair Queens of Marietta."

Bailey's blush triggered a rush of tender feelings that he tried to cover by grabbing a flake of hay.

Chloe stopped dead in her tracks. "*OMG.* You rode your horse in the parade instead of standing on the float."

Bailey shrugged. "My horse, Charlie, was the reason I won Fair Queen. It didn't seem right...or *fair*...to exclude him just so I could wear a fancy formal that would have looked dumb on me anyway."

He remembered how proud he'd been of her standing up for her beliefs. He'd envied her guts.

They shared a smile for a second or two. Long enough for Chloe to notice.

"So...did you two like...um...date in high school? You did, didn't you? Did you go steady? Did you kiss?"

Paul groaned. Before he could answer, Bailey said, "Your dad was my first love. But I was too young to know how special he was. We broke up when I went away to college."

Wow. Frank. Honest. A bit more information than I would have shared, but... He could see Chloe reassessing her opinion of Bailey. Kids appreciated being told the truth.

"Hey, kiddo, go check on Skipper, then we're outa here."

He watched Bailey's face as Chloe trotted off. Mostly

unreadable, but was that a hint of poignancy? Did she see herself at that time in her life? There are worse role models than Bailey Jenkins, he told himself.

On impulse, he said, "Since pizza's off the table, it looks like we're going to barbecue tonight. Would you like to join us? We have a pool."

"A pool," she repeated, her tone wistful. "I did water aerobics every day until my insurance dried up."

He watched her weigh the pros and cons of his invitation. For some reason, Chloe's frustrated sounding, "Dad, Skipper's being a butthead," seemed to tip the scales.

"That sounds nice. What can I bring?"

"Dessert," Mark yelled from the SUV.

Paul rolled his eyes. "Ears like the freaking CIA."

Bailey's laugh made him wish the kids were anywhere but here. He wanted to kiss her so badly he actually turned and walked away to resist the temptation. "Mark. Out of the car. We need to check out the house and see what kind of work has to be done to get it ready to rent. Bring the iPad."

Chapter 10

A CCEPTING AN INVITATION to dinner might have been a mistake, but Bailey didn't want to be alone. Nor was she ready to hash things out with her parents. She wanted to swim and hang out with Paul and meet his kids. She was curious about his life. Was that wrong? Somehow the lines between right and wrong, smart and foolish, blurred when she was with Paul. Always had.

She watched Paul cajole his son out of the truck. Paul's easy-going manner seemed stretched a little thin when it came to dealing with his kids, but once the youngster was walking at his side, Paul ruffed his hair and said something that made the little boy laugh. A twinge of poignancy made her breath catch. Obviously Paul's life was rich and full. A wildly disparate comparison to hers. She envied him. *Is this what life would have been like if I'd stayed?*

A gust of emotion swept through her. Bailey blinked away the tears that threatened to form.

Focus on the now.

Maureen's advice. Sound advice.

She turned and headed back the way she'd come. Even from a distance she could see Skipper giving Chloe a bad time. Ears flattened. Tail swishing. A danger to himself and others, as her father would say. OC had been her first teacher. He'd taught her to read animals the way he read a river.

"My first pony was the meanest thing on the planet when we got her," she said stepping beside Chloe, who was perched on the top rung of the fence, obviously trying to work up the nerve to get into the pen. "Mean."

"What'd you do?"

"Same thing you're doing. I sat on the fence and watched her. I was scared to get down. Any time I'd get close she'd kick or bite."

Chloe's blue eyes went wide.

Would Paul's and my child have had blue eyes?

Bailey forced the thought away. *Focus.* "Finally, my dad took pity on me and showed me how to win her over. Eventually, she followed me everywhere like a big puppy."

"Really? How?" The eagerness in Chloe's voice touched a part of Bailey she thought died in the accident—that intangible connection between young girls and horses.

"First, bring a bribe when you first show up. Carrots. Apples. Sugar cubes. Whatever your horse likes."

Chloe frowned a moment since, obviously, she hadn't brought any of those items with her. "What about grass?" She hopped down and raced to a patch of headed out grass at the base of a light pole. "Skipper loves grass," she said triumphantly when she returned.

Bailey looked over her shoulder. Skipper's ears were cocked forward, his nostrils hopping. "You're right. He does. You know your horse."

Chloe's smile brightened.

When Skipper came to the fence, his mouth practically watering, Bailey told her, "Once you have *his* attention, you need to give him *your* complete attention. Be aware of his body language and look for signs that something is off or not quite right."

"What kind of signs?"

"A horse can't speak, but he can tell you everything you need to know if you take the time to watch and listen."

"I don't understand."

Bailey grinned. The exact response she'd given OC. She leaned close and said softly, "That's because you want this to be easy. I certainly did. The last thing I wanted was to have to spend a lot of time getting to know my horse and trying to figure out what he was thinking." She rolled her eyes. "What a pain, right?"

Chloe nodded. "I just want to ride him."

"Of course you do. Who wouldn't? He's beautiful. He's strong and fast and riding him can help you forget about everything that's going on around you. All the stuff you don't have any control over."

Chloe's expression changed. Bailey knew in that moment how difficult her parents' divorce had been for Chloe. "Yeah. How'd you know?"

Bailey shrugged. "Why do you think I spent most of my time on the back of my horse? Charlie was my best friend. I could tell him anything and I knew it would never come back to bite me in the butt." She rubbed her behind, which made Chloe laugh.

"Skipper bit me on the butt once. I didn't dare tell Dad. I thought he might sell him."

"Dad's are like that. They get a little crazy when something bad happens to their daughters." Bailey's voice caught in her throat. An awareness she'd successfully kept at bay crept into view. OC loved her. She'd always known that. Life and his personal demons had conspired against them, but he'd always been there for her…the best he could.

"Did your horse ever hurt you?"

"No. Charlie and I were a team. He protected me from myself. If I wanted to try a new trick and I wasn't ready for it or was doing something wrong, he'd simply freeze and that was it. Talk about horse sense. I can't tell you how many times he kept me from getting hurt."

Chloe heaved a big sigh. "Skipper and I aren't like that at all."

She sounded so broken-hearted, so close to giving up, Bailey made a rash decision. She opened the gate and walked into the pasture. "Trust develops over time. It's not a magic pill you can take. You can't will Skipper to love you. You have to earn his trust and you start by showing him you're in charge."

Skipper didn't run. After their meeting in the field and their little bonding over oats this afternoon, Bailey had a faint sense of him. The horse was young and undisciplined but not mean. When she walked up to him, he butted her with his head, playfully. She talked to him while giving Chloe a lesson at the same time.

"You're a good boy at heart, aren't you, Skipper? You're a little bored right now, though. No friends your age. Your mom and dad have a new baby to keep their attention. The girlfriend you jumped the fence for is long gone. You go days on end with nobody to ride you. Boring. Boring. Boring."

She scratched his neck in a place that always made Daz toss his head.

Skipper tossed his head as if agreeing with her statement.

Chloe clapped. "Me, too. It's so frustrating. Dad won't let me ride my bike out here, and Mom hates horses. Animals in general. She says her life is too full for pets. And Dad's so busy with the store I hate to ask him to drive me when he gets home."

Bailey never had that problem. Every day after school, the bus would drop her at the end of her driveway and she'd hop on Charlie's back. Bareback. No helmet. No bridle. Nobody around in case she fell off and got hurt. Sounded crazy today, but at the time she'd felt happy and lucky. She'd had a great childhood. Had she ever told her parents that?

It wasn't too late, she reminded herself.

"Hand me the lead. I'll show you a few grooming tricks that will lead straight to his heart."

Paul opened the upstairs window to air out the mostly empty room. The south-facing window gave him a bird's eye view of the barn and paddocks. He could see Chloe and Bailey brushing Skipper. At one point, Bailey set her brush aside and showed Chloe how to do something, her hand over Chloe's. A motherly gesture. His breath caught in his throat and tears prickled across the bridge of his nose. Powerful emotions he had no business thinking bounced around in his head. *Chloe should have been our daughter, Bailey. You could be teaching our daughter how to ride. How does that make you feel? Are you sorry? Why didn't you let us try? How can I feel the things I feel and still resent what you did?*

"What else, Dad?"

Paul spun around. "Huh? Oh. In this room?" He gave the place a cursory inspection. A rickety chair with a broken leg leaned against the wall like a traveler who'd come to the end of the line. Dust bunnies and general debris. "There's a hole in the wall I don't remember seeing. Write down: Bailey's room sheetrock patch and paint."

Mark looked up from the iPad. "This was Bailey's room? How do you know that?"

"I told you. She was my girlfriend in high school."

"You came into her room?"

"A few times." *When her parents were gone.*

"Did you play Minecraft together?"

"We did our homework." *And made out until our lips were numb.*

He checked his phone for the time and saw a text from Jen. "Your mom wants to know if you and Chloe would mind spending a few extra days with me this week. Andrew has something to attend in Denver and she wants to go along to shop for your DisneyWorld trip."

Mark cocked his head in a way that was pure Jen. Both were planners with a strong sense of time. Mark hated to be late and normally abhorred last minute changes. "Can I go to the Summer Park's program with Ben?"

Ben Knight, his best friend in Marietta. The two were passionate Mindcraft devotees.

"Sure, if the program has room for you. I'll call Ben's mom when we get home."

"You'll forget. Text her now."

The kid had a point. Helping Jane with the fair had stretched him thinner than usual. Plus, he now had a house to clean up and rent *and* he had to figure out what to do about his feelings for Bailey. He'd invited her to dinner and she was bonding with his daughter at this very minute. Maybe it was time to admit the boat carrying that decision already set sail.

Chapter 11

BAILEY ADJUSTED THE strap of the cloth grocery bag on her shoulder and pushed the doorbell, bumblebees raising a ruckus in her mid-section.

She'd checked the address twice. Right number. Right house. But she still couldn't quite believe it.

She'd never been inside, but when they were dating, she and Paul had cruised down Bramble Lane debating about which house they'd buy when they were rich and famous.

"This one," they'd said simultaneously, on more than one occasion.

Two stories, skinny lap siding with brick accents, a porch that begged you to sit there every evening as the neighborhood settled down. This wasn't the biggest or showiest house on the street, but she liked how it seemed lovingly coddled by older trees and full, green hedges.

Although she could hear the chime echoing inside the house, nobody came to greet her.

Out back, she guessed.

She held tight to the handrail going down the steps. The entire porch had been replaced by new, manufactured "wood." Winding her way past a skateboard, a girl's bike and some kind of motorized scooter, she reached the privacy fence gate. A post-it note fluttered in the late afternoon breeze.

"Come in," it urged, in hot pink ink with five odd-shaped hearts forming an arch.

She was tempted to snatch it up and press it to her chest but didn't. She opened the gate and walked into a world unlike anything she'd been expecting.

"Hey," a high-pitched voice called from the large, rectangular pool. "You're here."

Chloe abandoned her orca-shaped raft and rolled into the water. Once her head re-emerged, she yelled, "Da…ad, your girlfriend's here."

Bailey waved but didn't walk any closer, still trying to take in the unexpected landscaping.

Somehow—at tremendous cost, she guessed—he'd built a year-round pool right up against the back patio of the house. The roof reminded her of something she would have seen at the Louvre—a pyramid with solar panels and skylights and retractable doors that opened a wide expanse to the elements. Presumably, the panels could be closed in the winter.

"Wow. This is really something," she said when Paul vaulted over the back porch in a pair of board shorts and a black tank. "Four seasons of swimming, huh?"

He tried to look modest but she could tell he was proud. "Thanks to the power of solar energy. You recognized the place, right? I couldn't believe my luck when it came on the market. I made an offer without consulting Jen."

He winced elaborately. "You can imagine how well that went over. She'd been working with an architect—an overpriced ninny from Bozeman—to design a new home on one of the lots south-west of the river."

Bailey knew about the development but she hadn't seen it. To her taste, downtown Marietta was the only place to live, if you couldn't afford a ranch.

"The house was in pretty rough shape, so I got it for a song. Jen remodeled the inside, and I designed the pool. What do you think?"

"It's amazing."

He looked proud and pleased. "Like I told Jen, if you're going to have a pool in Montana, you better build a cover or those couple of summer months will go by much too fast."

Jen.

Bailey couldn't help but wonder about the woman Paul loved enough to marry and give two beautiful children. She hoped to learn more from the house Jen decorated and made her own.

"I knew you'd done well for yourself. Mom said the Chamber of Commerce voted you Businessman of the Year a while back."

"Big Z's was neck and neck with the Wolf Den. Voting was this close." He held up his thumb and index finger about two inches apart.

She laughed with a joy she'd forgotten she knew existed. Yes, life sucked at the moment, but she made her shoulders relax. Maureen insisted down time was key to recovery. "It's okay to let go once in awhile, Bailey. Have fun. Your body will thank you for it."

"Can I get you a drink? A glass of wine? Iced tea?"

"Tea sounds good."

He took the carryall from her and led the way to the rear porch. "Any news on your folks?"

"Mom left a note on the table. And once my phone was charged I listened to her voice mails. She's adamant that Dad didn't drink. I don't know if she's trying to convince me or herself."

"Where are they?"

"Not a clue."

She stepped carefully on the flagstone path. She felt silly wearing boots with a swimming suit, but her ankle wasn't strong enough to handle flip-flops. Luckily, her ivory cover-up wasn't wrinkled too badly from being stuffed in a suitcase.

"Wow," Chloe said sliding to a stop opposite a few feet away. "You look different. Where'd you get that awesome belt?"

Bailey's gaze dropped. The belt had been a last minute addition to off-set the boots.

"And look at the bling on your boots. O.M.G. That is the coolest ankle bracelet evva. I love it." When she looked at Bailey, her blue eyes sparkled with honest excitement.

"Thank you. I made them. Both."

Chloe dashed closer. "Wow. That buckle is so awesome. It looks like Skipper. What kind of stone is the eye?"

Paul bent over for a look, too.

"Montana sapphire. I met a woman at a rodeo whose family has been digging them for years. My late husband bought the stone for a ring, but after he died, I decided to make it part of a tribute to my horse, Daz."

"Does he have blue eyes?"

"No. Dark brown. He died a little over a year ago." Bailey's heart thudded hard against her chest, but she got the words out with barely a stumble.

Chloe's bottom lip quivered, and her eyes filled with tears. "That is so sad. I don't know what I'd do if Skipper passed away. Was he old?"

Paul wormed his way between them with a plate of nachos he must have had on the nearby grill to keep warm. "Take this to the table, please, sweetheart. There's pop in the outside fridge if you want one. Just one before supper, though."

A moment later, he popped the top on a can and poured the contents into a frozen mug. "Here," he said holding its handle out to Bailey. "To heck with tea. Root beer used to be your favorite."

The fact he remembered made her ridiculously happy. Her fingers closed around the icy handle and she took a huge gulp. Ignoring the foam mustache she knew clung to her upper lip, she burped loudly and said, "Ahh. I needed that."

PAUL WATCHED FOUR hours slip by as if they were minutes. A part of him couldn't believe Bailey Jenkins—*his* Bailey Jenkins—was playing Marco Polo in his pool with his children. What she lacked in speed and maneuverability she more than made up for with ruthless competitiveness. Both kids were laughing and breathing hard by the time they all took a break.

At first glance, she looked the same as she had at eighteen, but a closer study showed the truth. Her body had matured. Her breasts filled out the demure, navy blue and white stripe two-piece—even if her ribs were a bit too pronounced and her hip bones could have used a bit more padding, in his opinion.

But the biggest change wasn't physical. This Bailey enjoyed playing with his kids. The old Bailey never had time for children. The teenage Bailey wouldn't have asked Chloe and Mark clever, revealing questions over dinner...then listened, truly listened, when they answered.

Later, when they gathered around the stone fire pit for dessert, Mark asked the question he and Chloe had probably discussed privately at length. "What happened to your foot?"

The children had been skeptical when Bailey produced marshmallows, graham crackers and Hershey bars for dessert. It wasn't that they'd never eaten s'mores, they simply couldn't conceive of roasting marshmallows over glowing embers of broken glass.

"Car wreck. My foot got pinned under the front end of our truck. I was lucky."

"What do you mean?"

"They had to use those big hydraulic Jaws of Life to get me out. But I only had a concussion and a broken ankle."

Only. Paul had to work to keep from cringing.

"Were you driving?"

"Were you wearing a seatbelt?"

"No...and yes. I was in the passenger side. One of the Highway Patrol officers told me my seat belt saved my life."

The tremor in her voice told him the memory still brought her pain. So, Paul cut off Mark before his morbid curiosity—typical of eight-year-old boys—asked for details about blood and missing body parts. "Where are the rest of the candy bars?"

"Mark," Chloe cried. "You didn't? Oh, my God, you are such a pig."

His son's lips were ringed by a suspicious brown outline, but he fervently denied the charge until Bailey hauled him onto her lap and ticked him until he confessed.

"Okay. Okay. I did it. I ate the last of the chocolate. So sue me."

Bailey put him down. "Not necessary. A perfectly roasted marshy doesn't need chocolate."

She pushed a white square onto a skewer and leaned forward, resting her elbows on her knees. Her loose off-white cover-up slipped from one shoulder.

Paul had forgotten how lovely her natural skin tone was. But he remembered viscerally how smooth and silky her skin felt when he rubbed her with baby oil doctored with Mercurochrome—an old wives' tale recipe for a deep brown tan.

A minute later, she lifted the golden brown treat to her lips and blew.

His groin reacted.

"Nothing beats a sticky, gooey marshmallow straight off the fire." She pinched a hunk and pulled the bite toward her lips, strings of glistening white sugar trailing behind. With a flourish, she spun the filaments onto the bite and lowered it into her open mouth.

Chloe clapped and grabbed another marshmallow to try for herself.

Mark squinted at Paul. "What's wrong, Dad? You look like you swallowed a marshmallow whole."

Outed by an eight-year-old. Damn.

Paul jumped to his feet, gathering the empty wrappers and used napkins. He carried the mess to a nearby trash can then said, "Bath time, kiddos. Your mother gave me hel— heck last week for not making you wash your hair after swimming. She says it's going to turn green."

He made a mad scientist gesture that brought a grin to Bailey's lips. Her sticky sweet lips.

"Scoot, you two. I left bottles of anti-chlorine shampoo in each of your showers."

Mark and Chloe took off with a minimal amount of grumbling. He could see they were worn out. The best part of owning a pool, in his opinion.

Bailey waited until both kids were gone before getting to her feet. She didn't want to intrude on their nightly family rituals. She picked up the children's half-empty water glasses and followed Paul into the kitchen. The place had all the bells and whistles any TV chef might expect: granite countertops, polished chrome appliances, hardwood flooring and dark golden oak cabinets. The recessed lights in the ceiling turned the butterscotch walls a warm, inviting color.

"Your home is beautiful, Paul. Could be right off the pages of a decorating magazine, and yet it seems perfectly functional at the same time." She pulled out one of the chrome stools tucked under the island and sat.

He wiped a spill on the gorgeous marble countertop before her elbow connected with it then tossed the rag into a big, white, apron-front sink.

Was it possible to have sink envy, she wondered?

She'd wasted so much time designing a dream kitchen to fit in Ross's log cabin. A kitchen not unlike this one, with windows behind the sink overlooking the backyard.

"Jen spent more money on this room than the rest of the remodeling combined. I told her we wouldn't be able to afford food to cook by the time she was done." He carried the bag of leftover marshmallows to a walk-in pantry about the size of her mother's guest room.

He returned a moment later, a liter-size green bottle of imported water in hand. She recognized the label but rarely splurged on the pricey brand.

"Although compared to the cost of our divorce, the kitchen was a real bargain," Paul told her, grabbing a couple of glasses from a cabinet with beveled glass panels.

His cynicism made her uncomfortable. Was she ready to talk exes?

Given the fact hers was dead...not really.

He unscrewed the cap with a powerful twist and poured two glasses of the fizzy water. "My new go-to drink, instead of beer. Chloe's class stared a recycling campaign. When I loaded all the bags of crushed cans into the truck, it looked like a flaming alcoholic lived here." He held out his glass. "Cheers."

She touched the lip of her glass to his and looked into his eyes. Friendly, yes. Interested, too. The kind of interest a part of her desperately wanted to explore. Too bad the thinking part of her brain knew better than to start something she couldn't finish. She hadn't talked to OC yet. Could she trust him or not? Was she staying or going? At the moment, she honestly couldn't say—and the subtle tug on her heartstrings she felt when she was around Paul wasn't helping.

She slipped off the stool. "Excuse me. I'm going to try Mom's phone again."

Coward. She walked to the dining table where she'd left her purse hanging over the back of her chair.

She carried her phone outdoors and took a seat by the fire pit. The flame had been shut off but the night was warm enough without a fire.

She could understand the attraction of these click-to-start units, but they didn't compare to the romance of a wood campfire like the one she and Paul made love beside that last summer. They'd lied to their parents and spent an entire weekend hiking, fishing and camping alone. They'd shared a single sleeping bag. She'd never experienced sex as pure and delicious—lust combined with the stamina and abandon of youth.

Her breasts tightened and her nipples puckered inside the cups of her mostly dry swimsuit. The still damp crotch of her bottoms felt unnaturally warm and moist.

She couldn't remember the last time she had sex—aside from the occasional self-pleasure that usually left her a sobbing wreck.

"You need to get laid," Maureen told Bailey at their last physical therapy session. "Sex is a great healer. So is forgiveness. Once you dump that heavy burden you're carrying around, you'll be able to run and ride again."

Run? Maybe. She'd been walking a lot the past few days and her ankle felt much stronger. But, ride? She couldn't picture it. She'd told herself her riding days were over. But she had to admit, she'd enjoyed helping Chloe bond with her horse this afternoon. She'd missed the smells, the feel, the connection more than she'd thought possible.

Before she could call up her mother's cell phone number, Bailey's phone rang. Mom's image appeared on the screen.

Bailey sat on the chaise and crossed her legs. "Hi. Are you home?"

An awkward pause—as if someone fumbled the phone—made her sit up. "Mom?"

"No. It's me," OC said. "She's asleep. They gave her something."

They? Bailey's pulse jumped.

"Luly has a lump on her side. I made her call the doctor. He saw her right away and sent us to Bozeman."

"T...to the hospital?"

"Yeah. Took six hours to get a room. Can you believe that? The surgeon's going to do something in the morning."

"What time?"

"Nine. But you know how that goes."

"Wh...what do they think it is? Cancer?" Her voice cracked in a broken whisper.

"Not sure. One of the doctors thought it might be some kind of infection. Endimidercondriac or something."

"Endometriosis?"

"That sounds like it. Could be leftover from her gallbladder surgery."

"Her gallbladder? But that was last year." Bailey's last trip home before Ross and Daz died.

"I know. I don't get it. But, she says it doesn't hurt."

Oh, Mom. Do you ever complain? "Do you need me to come pick you up?"

"No. The nurse made a bed for me on the couch. I got my pills. I'll be fine. But I know your mother wants to see you before she goes in."

"Of course. I'll be there first thing. Text me if you need anything from home."

"I…" He paused. "I'm sorry about today. You were right to think the worst. They say you have to hit rock bottom before you can start to climb out of the pit. I'm climbing, Queen Bee. And this time I'm gonna make it. You'll see."

He ended the call before she could get her emotions under control to reply. Did she dare hope? He'd made promises before. Did OC's problems even matter now? Her mother—the glue that had been holding them all together—was sick, dealing with a potentially serious disease.

Dad isn't the only one who has to step up.

She got to her feet and walked inside. Her expression must have conveyed her distress. Before she could say a word, Paul cleared the distance between them. "What's wrong? Your dad?"

"Mom. She's in the hospital in Bozeman. They've scheduled her for surgery in the morning. Some kind of l…lump." She shared what little OC told her. "If it's cancer, they'll discuss a protocol. If it's not—please, God—they'll remove it and release her."

"How big a lump?"

"I…I don't know. She never told me. All this time. I can't believe it. I don't know whether to cry or scream."

He took her in arms. "Whichever makes you feel better."

She closed her eyes and for a moment she felt...home. Was this what it was like to know somebody had your back?

I could have had this. But she chose to leave. And she knew why. *Because, bottom line, she was Bailey Jenkins, and Paul Zabrinski always deserved better.*

That hadn't changed.

She started to pull away, but Paul tightened his hold. "Don't run away, cowgirl. Not tonight."

"I have to leave early in the morning."

"I know. I wish I could drive you, but..."

"You have the kids. And a business to run. A life. I appreciate all the help you've given me. In fact, I feel a little guilty about it. I...I feel like I need to give a little back. What would you think about me driving Chloe to the ranch every day to spend an hour or two with Skipper? I can't do it tomorrow, of course, but maybe the next day. If Mom's okay."

"Are you serious? That would be fabulous. Chloe has talked about nothing else all day. She's determined to get him in good enough shape to participate in the fair. I've been racking my brain trying to figure out a way to make that happen." He frowned. "But what about B. Dazzled Bling? You haven't changed your mind about setting up shop here, have you?"

She moved back a step. She could barely think when he was holding her. "I changed my mind so many times today I was starting to feel like a politician."

"Like Austen," Paul put in. "He's a pretty unhappy politician at the moment and probably wouldn't recommend it as a career choice."

She vaguely remembered Paul's older brother and wasn't curious enough to ask for details. Instead, she admitted, "I'll admit, I considered throwing my suitcases in the back of Dad's truck and leaving. The thought of watching OC implode again..." Her throat tightened. She forced a swallow and straightened her shoulders. "But then I decided, no. I'm done letting OC's issues determine my future. I don't know if Marietta is the right place for me—business-wise, but if I leave, it won't be because my father fell off the wagon."

"Good for you."

"But before I commit to a lease and a full-fledged store, I need to figure out whether or not there's a retail market here for my product. And I need to find artisans to work with my designs. I can use the back rooms at the Fish and Game for now, but until we hear from Sheri Fast, we don't know if the bank will work with us to get back on our feet. And how fast that happens will depend in part on Mom."

"Are you sure you want to take on coaching Chloe, too?"

"If you'd asked me yesterday, I'd have said no, but I really liked working with her today. She's a quick study, bright and passionate about her horse. She reminds me of myself at that age."

"Me, too." He rolled his eyes and made a face. "I mean, she reminds me of you. Did I ever tell you the first time I saw you? You were Chloe's age, riding in a fair parade with your dad. You had a big smile on your face and you waved right at me. I told Austen, 'That's the girl I'm going to marry some day.'"

"Really? You said that? How come you never told me?"

His blush made her want to wrap her arms around him and start something she couldn't finish so she stood perfectly still and waited for him to say, "Because I knew you'd ask me what Austen said."

"Oh." She hesitated. "I was only a kid. What'd he have against me?"

"Not you. Your dad. He said I could do better than the daughter of the town drunk."

Nothing she hadn't heard before but it still hurt, oddly enough.

He pulled her into his arms again. "My brother was an opinionated ass. Still is. I'm sorry."

Then he kissed her. And her lips remembered the feel of him…as if she and Paul had never been apart.

"YOU SHOULD HAVE let her come pick you up."

OC was so startled by Louise's voice, her phone jumped out of his fingers and landed on his lap—the only good thing about being in a wheelchair. "I thought you were asleep."

"I nodded off for a minute. I'm sleepy but worried about you. You're too big for that couch. You'll roll off in the night and re-injure your leg. If your stump gets infected, it'll be months before you can be fitted for a prosthesis."

He leaned over and grabbed his stump—whoever would have pictured OC Jenkins with a stump? Dead before thirty, maybe, but cut off below the knee? Never. The craziness of the situation made him laugh. "You know what everyone at rehab asks me?"

She shook her head back and forth in a laconic way that told him the drugs were taking effect.

"Do I have diabetes? I say, 'No. I lost my leg the old-fashioned way: booze and orneriness.'"

Her pretty lips curled up in a smile—the smile that saved his life so many years before.

"Is Bailey coming tomorrow?"

"Of course. She wouldn't miss a chance to scold you the same way she's been harping on my case all these years. 'Bout time you got a piece of the action."

"Defense mechanism," Louise muttered.

"Huh? What's that?"

"You heard me. She yells at you because she loves you so much and she wishes she didn't. You disappointed her."

"Yeah, well, she did her share of letting me down, too. Got pregnant. Dropped out of college to marry a goddamn cowboy. She was too smart and ambitious to mess up like that."

Like the way I messed up.

She lifted her hand, wanly. OC rolled closer to the bed. The nurses had moved a table and extra chair so he had room to maneuver. He wasn't very coordinated, but he planned to get better. And he would walk again. As soon as possible.

He reached out to take her hand in both of his own, then leaned close to kiss her fingers. He couldn't imagine life without his rock.

The thought terrified him in a way losing his leg never had. Physical pain was part of life. His father taught him that lesson, hands on. But emotional pain scared the bejesus out of him and made his mouth turn dry. A drink would have been nice, but that option was off the table.

"Go to sleep, dear. I'll be right here."

Her breathing evened out and her grip lessened. When he was sure she was asleep, he rolled to the skinny little couch under the window. Someone had set up sheets and a pillow. He locked the brake on his chair, removed the left armrest and levered himself onto the couch using his good leg and upper body strength.

He had a long way to go, but he'd be damned if he was giving up. He was a husband and a father whose family needed him.

Chapter 12

"HE'S DOING BETTER, isn't he, Bailey? Look how he turns when I shift my weight in the saddle."

Bailey caught herself unconsciously shifting her weight on the top rail of the fence and nearly fell off. Damn. Not a good thing. "You're both amazing. But keep your focus on him, Chloe. Remember what happened the first time you rode him."

A lazy horse ready to be done with all the rules and riding in a circle simply lowered his head and gave a small buck that sent unsuspecting Chloe airborne. Luckily, only her pride was bruised.

"Skipper's still in the testing phase, Chloe. If he senses your attention is elsewhere..."

"I know. Sorry."

They'd only been at this for two weeks, but Chloe's and Skipper's progress surprised them both. Bailey had never considered herself a teacher, but she guessed a really motivated student made all the difference. For two hours every morning, Chloe did anything Bailey asked—right down to mucking out the horse stall.

They'd covered the care and feeding of her horse the first day.

"Caring for your horse is your most basic expression of love. You want him safe and healthy, his hooves clean, his coat shiny. The same way your mom and dad feed and clothe you and provide a clean, cozy house."

"How come you don't have any kids?"

Bailey had known the question would probably come up so she had her answer ready. "Daz was my boy. I loved him like a child."

To Bailey's surprise, she'd found herself talking about Daz a lot during these sessions. She'd been afraid the pain would be too great to bear, but Skipper wasn't anything like Daz, and Chloe was such a sweet kid and so eager to learn, Bailey found she was too busy teaching to feel sad.

"Don't saw the bit, sweetie. Nice even pressure. Squeeze with your knees and don't forget your posture."

Bailey watched for each correction then said, "Nice. Ten more trips around then we have to go."

"No…" Chloe protested. "Please? Half an hour longer?"

"Maybe tomorrow. I have to meet with the Dazzling Minions this morning."

She could hardly believe it. She'd hired four local crafters who were not only happy to make jewelry from her designs, they were thrilled to be working for her. Apparently, they liked what they saw on her Etsy page and were eager to be part of her team.

"I have a team," she murmured softly. "Amazing."

Thanks to the Minions, Bailey had stock. Added to what she'd brought from California, she had enough earrings, necklaces and bracelets, boot bangles, hat bands and belts to risk signing up for a booth at the Great Marietta Fair.

Paul had used his connections to secure her the last indoor booth in Exhibit Hall-A.

She hadn't seen him much since their kiss, except in passing. She'd thought about him a lot and dreamt about him more than she wanted to admit, but between his commitments to the fair and her juggling both parents' doctors' appointments and setting up a workspace in the back of the old Fish and Game building, they were lucky to catch a minute alone.

Probably a good thing, she told herself. She looked at the next few weeks as an experiment. Would her jewelry sell? Was her brand unique enough to warrant opening a retail store in Marietta? Would her dad stay committed to his recovery? Every setback, physical or emotional—like the possibility he and Mom would have to declare bankruptcy— set Bailey on edge. She wasn't sure how long she could live with the fear of his falling off the wagon. Thankfully, her mother's diagnosis and prognosis were straightforward and good.

One less thing to worry about.

"My mom said she wants to meet you," Chloe said when her circle brought her close to Bailey. "Apparently, Dad told her all about you."

Bailey watched the back of Chloe's pink T-shirt bounce with the rhythmic trot. *All about me? Great.*

"Great," she said, faking perkiness she didn't feel. "Is she coming to the fair?"

"The fair? Mom? Are you kidding me?" Chloe's bark of laughter made Skipper side-step abruptly. If she hadn't been paying attention, she would have been left in mid-air like a cartoon character, but she managed to keep her seat. She immediately patted Skipper's neck and spoke to him too softly for Bailey to hear.

"Good job, Chloe. Now, bring him in," Bailey said. "I'll meet you at the gate."

PAUL CHECKED HIS watch. He had ten minutes to make it to the Main Street Diner. His brother commanded this lunch date via text: *"Meet MSD today noon. B there."*

Normally, that wouldn't be a challenge since Big Z's was only a few blocks away from the popular café. Unfortunately, today was a full scale disaster and it wasn't even noon.

He'd pulled his remodeling crew off a job to help Jane Weiss put out fires—so to speak—at the fairgrounds. Turning the Big Marietta Fair into a two-week event was turning out to be more complex than anybody figured.

Unfortunately, the homeowner expected the job done yesterday. She was not happy. Not that Paul blamed her. If he'd had his head on business instead of lusting after Bailey, this might not have happened.

If that explained the ass-chewing Austen had in mind, he'd take it. Although Paul doubted Austen had the slightest idea what was going on at Big Z's. Other than acting as Big Z's attorney of record, his brother had nothing to do with Paul's business.

Before pulling out of the parking lot, he texted Chloe to tell her where he'd be.

For the past two weeks, she'd spent every morning on

Skipper's back, working with her new riding coach—Bailey Jenkins. It had only been a matter of time before his family found out about Bailey's re-involvement in his life. And, although Paul could truthfully say nothing had happened between him and Bailey beyond that first, tentative kiss, he'd be lying if he said he wasn't bound and determined to convince her to stay in Marietta and give their relationship a second chance.

And the last thing he needed or wanted was his brother sticking his nose in Paul's business. Besides, it's not like the golden boy had all that much to brag about lately. His career was on hold, his reputation in the dumper and, if Paul understood correctly, Austen had dumped Sheri Fast—or was dumped. Paul hadn't found time to ask.

Of course, exiting the store proved easier said than done. Mrs. Hayes stopped him in Aisle 8 and asked if they carried surgical tape.

Surgical tape? In a hardware store?

He led her to the flashy new display of patterned duct tape. But on his way there, he interrupted two summer hires—students whose names he couldn't remember—in a lip lock by the paint mixer.

Something to deal with later.

Normally, such inappropriate workplace behavior would earn them a stern reprimand, but how could he get in their faces about inappropriate behavior when he wanted to be inappropriate with Bailey so bad it hurt?

Literally.

He woke up every morning hard as he had in high school.

He lucked out finding a parking place right beside his brother's Land Rover. Even if he didn't know Austen's ride, the vanity plates were a dead giveaway: ZLAWMN.

Paul's eyes had barely adjusted to the difference in light before he heard Austen call, "Over here, little brother."

Little brother. Good grief.

Paul slid into the window booth across from Austen. "Hi. What's up? I'm swamped at work. I really shouldn't be here."

Austen stared at him with eyes narrowed, not missing a thing. "From what I hear, there are a lot of things you shouldn't be doing."

"What's that mean? I'm busy. I don't have time for your big brother lawyer mind games. What was so important you had to pull me outta Big Z's today?"

Austen took a pull from his ice tea. "Dad's orders. He's worried about you. Mom would be, too, but she's too busy taking care of our sister. You remember Mia, right? Bald woman. Looks like me only skinnier."

Paul's stomach cramped. He hated thinking about what Mia was going through. He felt helpless. Worse than helpless. He adored his sister and, normally, she was the person he'd turn to for advice where his love life was concerned. Of course, he couldn't call her now. His problems were insignificant compared to her health issues.

So, when they talked last, and she asked what was happening, he felt compelled to make the crazy mess that landed in Bailey's lap sound like a funny plot in a sitcom.

He didn't mention the strong connection he still felt for Bailey or the compassion he had for OC. Which probably explained why their conversations felt stilted and awkward.

"I talked to Mia last week. She said she feels like crap, but otherwise is doing fine."

"She lied. The chemo is turning her inside out." Austen made a growling sound. "I'd string that piece of shit ex-husband of hers up by his nuts if he had any."

Paul didn't point out Mia's ex had been Austen's college roommate and best friend at one time. He knew the line between love and hate could shift slowly like tectonic plates or suddenly quake and split, creating all kinds of long-lasting damage.

"Mom and Dad are frazzled from taking care of the kids. They're all coming for the fair. Mom was hoping you'd help, but, as unbelievable as it sounds, you're involved with Bailey Jenkins."

"I picked her up at the airport when her mother asked. You would have said yes, too. Louise saved Chloe when she was floundering."

"That was months ago. What about hiring one of the most expensive accountants in the state? Sheri doesn't work pro bono, you know."

He'd received her bill and paid it. He'd consider asking for restitution from what the family recovered from Marla and Jack…if they got anything.

"The truth is, I haven't spoken with Bailey in days. I hear about her every day because she volunteered to work with Chloe and her horse. Jen refuses to have anything to do with the ranch and I've been too busy to take her out to ride regularly. Bailey is doing me a huge favor." He leaned across the table and lowered his voice. He didn't want the gossip mill to create any more havoc than it already had. "She's not the same person she was when she left. She's hurt and hurting but trying to move on with her life. Surely, even you can appreciate that kind of gumption."

Austen didn't appear convinced, but he eschewed his comment because a waitress Paul hadn't seen before walked up to take their order. He wasn't hungry but he ordered his usual bison burger with sweet potato fries. Mark's favorite.

Speaking of kids... He checked his phone. Nothing from Mrs. Knight, the mother of Mark's best friend, Ben, who'd offered to take both boys to a day-long summer recreation camp.

"Have you talked to Sheri lately?" Paul hadn't heard the outcome of the audit, nor had he read about any charges being filed against Marla Sawyer.

"Not really."

"What's that mean?"

If his brother had a conscience—a question often debated among his siblings, the slight ruddy hue that appeared in his cheeks might have indicated a blush. "You saw her but didn't speak?"

"We bumped into each other at a gala fundraiser at the Edgewater the weekend before last. We'd both had rough weeks and drank a little too much. So, we did what unattached consenting adults sometimes do when they're attracted to each other."

"You had sex," Paul exclaimed.

Too loudly.

Heads turned.

Austen snarled. "There was a suite available. We grabbed

it.'"

"What else did you grab?"

"Shut up. Sheri's great. Unfortunately, as you announced in church when you were six, 'Austen's not nice.'"

A family story Paul had heard a thousand times growing up. Apparently, the entire church heard and laughed, which made Austen, who was turning eleven a few days later, shout a very bad word and storm away...thereby proving Paul's point.

"I'm a better judge of character now."

"Are you? What do you think is going to happen with Bailey? She's suddenly going to decide that Montana isn't as bad as she thought and settle down here for good?"

Yes. He saw that scenario unfold in his dreams—in a dozen various incarnations—every night. He wouldn't admit that to his big brother, though. "No."

"Good. Because I've got news for you, brother, Bailey Jenkins is a user. As soon as her feet are on the ground and she's got a grubstake, she'll leave. Just like before. And you'll be a heart broken puppy again."

Before Paul could tell him where to shove his absurd prediction, their waitress arrived with their food. Paul settled for mouthing a less satisfying, "F-you."

Austen snickered and turned on the charm to coax extra ranch dressing for his French fries—a culinary favorite no one in the family understood.

They ate in silence, the hum and energy of the diner adding to the underlying tension Paul always felt in Austen's presence. One didn't get to Austen's level in the game of cutthroat politics without a lion's share of ego and the drive to impose your will on the people closest to you.

Paul chewed a bite of the delicious burger, but when it came time to swallow, he had to reach for his glass of tea. His throat felt tight, his stomach tense.

Damn you, Austen. I wish I'd never agreed to have lunch with you.

Too late. The seed of doubt had been planted. Was Bailey using him? Again?

"OH, GOOD. LOOKS like my mom is here. That must mean her check-up was good."

Chloe chewed on her fingernail—a habit her mother hated—as the old truck pulled into the driveway behind the little house that housed Bailey's father's fishing business. She'd ridden her bike here from the Big Z this morning.

Now or never.

Mark was supposed to go to the ranch with her today, but he'd jumped ship the minute Ben Knight invited him to play Mindcraft at some stupid Day Camp. That was all he cared about. He didn't care that Daddy liked Bailey. A lot. Chloe saw the mushy looks they gave each other. That night at their house, she even peeked out the window and saw them kiss. And not an old friends' kind of kiss. The real thing. Like on TV.

A few weeks earlier, Chloe overheard her mother tell a friend that her ex was a great guy but absolutely hopeless when it came to women.

"Paul's sweet, but that business owns his a-s-s. No woman wants to play second fiddle to a hardware store. I tried, but, trust me, the effort that went into being Mrs. Big Z was not worth the money."

Chloe knew from what happened to Cinderella that having a stepmother who married your dad for his money was not a good idea. That's why she decided Bailey would be perfect for him.

Anybody who liked horses couldn't be too high maintenance. She drove an old truck. Plus, they wouldn't have to date for years and years before getting married because they'd already dated in high school.

And Chloe was going to need a stepmother sooner rather than later if what Mark overheard was true.

Andrew, their step-dad, was up for a promotion, which would involve moving to Atlanta, Georgia. A state about a million miles away from Montana.

No, thank you.

Her horse was here. Her best friend lived here. Her dad was here. Chloe loved Montana. Even the winters.

But Chloe knew her dad didn't trust himself to be a full-time single parent. That's what he told Chloe and Mark when they asked to stay with him full-time and visit their mother every other weekend—instead of the other way around.

"I'm at the store too much. Kids need a mom to be there after school and stuff."

Like that happened. Chloe loved her mother, but Andrew's work required a lot of parties and fundraising events that took up most of her mom's time.

If I can find Daddy a girlfriend...or a wife, Chloe thought, *maybe he'd keep us.*

And who better than Bailey?

"Um...can I ask you something?"

Bailey turned off the key and dropped it in the ashtray on the dash. "Sure. What?"

"Would you...um...date with my dad?"

"'Date' him?"

"Yeah. You like him, don't you?"

The look on Bailey's face said she was trying not to laugh because she didn't want to hurt Chloe's feelings. "Yes. I like your dad. He's a great guy. But...relationships are tricky."

"My dad says the only way you're guaranteed to fail is if you fail to try."

Bailey blinked. "That's...that's true. If I wanted to get involved with your dad, how would you suggest I do it?"

"Ask him to the Fair."

"On a date."

"Yeah. On the first night, Mark and I always go with Grandma and Grandpa Z and our cousins. My aunt's been sick lately and she might not be able to come, but the kids will be here. Uncle Austen is flying to Wyoming to pick them up."

"Austen's a pilot?"

Chloe nodded. "Daddy is, too, but he likes riding horses better."

"Oh."

"So? Will you? Ask him out? Please."

Bailey thought a long time. Like a minute, at least. "Why now?"

Chloe wasn't expecting that question. She decided to go with the truth. "Because he doesn't have anybody. And I don't think that's right."

Bailey took a big breath and let it out. "I'll be working at the B. Dazzled Western Bling booth at the fair anyway, so…I could ask. Maybe we could get a corn dog together or something."

Chloe had to force herself not to jump up and down in the seat. "He's having lunch at the Main Street Diner today. If you hurry, I'm sure you can catch him."

"What if he turns me down?"

Chloe made a swishing motion with her hand. "He won't. I heard Mommy tell Grandpa Z on the phone that Daddy has it bad for you. Sometimes, bad is a good thing. You know?" She opened the door and hopped to the ground. "I have to go to Amber's. See you later."

She dashed to her bike and pushed it through the gate. She'd been brave enough to ask, and Bailey said yes. Sooo much better than going up a level in dumb ol' Minecraft, she thought, humming her favorite song from *Frozen* as she pedaled toward Amber's. She couldn't wait to share this news with her BFF.

Chapter 13

BAILEY PACED, FRETTED and stalled after Chloe left. But, eventually, her grumbling stomach convinced her to call for a take-out order from the Main Street Diner.

If she *happened* to bump into Paul and circumstances warranted, she *might* consider bringing up the subject—or at least telling him his children were worried about his lack of a social life.

"What's one lousy date?" she muttered, climbing into her dad's truck.

We can walk through the Fair like the old friends we are. Grab a couple of corn dogs. Maybe, watch a show.

She'd seen the completed line-up of events but hadn't paid close attention since she expected to be working in her booth the whole time.

But the Dazzling Minions had their own ideas.

"Here," Tonya, the bossiest, said earlier that morning when she popped in to pick up more seed pearls. "The girls and I came up with a schedule. You'll still have to put in a lot of hours, girlfriend, but you won't end up losing your foot like your dad did."

Bailey's ankle continued to improve, but she still dealt with some swelling after a long day at the shop.

"Oh, and, by the way," Anne added. "Our kids are going to pass out fliers to advertise our sale prices and some giveaways. It'll cost you a few ride tickets, but if you buy them in advance, they're cheaper."

Bailey glanced at her phone on the seat beside her.

Maybe she'd have time to run to the Fairgrounds Office on her way back. She might pick up tickets, some for Chloe and Mark, too.

Chloe. A grin formed on her lips. Paul's daughter was something else. In a good way. Self-assured in a way Bailey never was. *Probably helps to have a normal father in your corner.*

She felt a little guilty harping on the negative when her father had been trying so hard in recent weeks. He seemed to accept the fact the only way he was going to get better was by learning to work with his doctors and physical therapists.

When he called to tell her he had a new leg, she asked, "How's it look?"

"Not pretty. Good thing I never went in for wearing shorts."

She slipped into a parking spot one over from the handicap stall. "Rock star," she called, sliding from the seat.

The aroma of burgers on the grill made her mouth water. She'd developed a peculiar addiction to buffalo meat thanks to Paul Zabrinski.

Who, to her surprise, was seated at a window booth.

She smiled and waved.

He nodded. No smile.

Was he mad at her? Or was the pensive look on Paul's face due to the man in the expensive suit sitting across from him?

Austen?

Had to be, she decided. She only had a vague recollection of Paul's older brother since he left for college before she and Paul started dating. But everybody in Marietta *knew* Austen.

His name had been in the Courier every week since he was MVP in at least three sports. All the girls wanted to date him, although he never had a steady that Bailey could remember. He gave the class speech at graduation. She knew that for a fact because she'd been selected as one of the four freshman girls to pass out programs at the door.

She'd listened closely because he had the audacity to buck the system, showing up with his longish hair artfully tousled, a movie-star goatee and bare ankles, hinting that he was wearing shorts under his gown.

At the time, Bailey had been impressed.

Now, not so much. She'd met more than her share of promoters, lawyers and wealthy stockmen over the years. And one thing she knew for certain was money did not automatically signify class.

More nervous than she had been when she left the house, she walked slowly and deliberately, trying not to limp.

Show no weakness. She couldn't remember if the adage applied to wild animals *and* lawyers, or just lawyers.

Thank goodness I called in an order. She could pick it up and run. No need to bring up the ridiculous idea of going on a date. *No harm, no foul.*

She went straight to the cash register, not looking right or left. "Bailey Jenkins. To-go," she told the young woman behind the till.

The girl—about sixteen working her first summer job, Bailey guessed—spun about and dashed to the kitchen window, where a clothesline of white orders were strung.

"Ironically appropriate, don't you agree? A To-Go order. Your modus operandi, no?"

She turned, her purse clutched to her belly—bling side out, as if the glitter might magically ward off the attack she sensed coming. "I beg your pardon?"

Austen had changed since the cocky kid at the school podium. More than the expensive suit and cover-model haircut, his style shouted, "Warning: rich, influential, angry man with agenda. Look out."

He leaned in. Not so his words were kept between them. No. In fact, he spoke loudly, with succinct clarity so the entire jury of her peers could hear. "It's not *my* pardon you need to beg, Bailey. It's my brother's."

His cologne hit her olfactory memory center like a tsunami. Ross wore Bleu de Chanel, too. What was the chance?

Feelings she'd kept in a locked box burst forth, her mind instantly awash in pain and nightmarish fear. The beautiful smell forever juxtaposed against the bitter mix of blood, gasoline and deployed air bags.

Austen went on, either not noticing her reaction or misinterpreting it. "And my parents'," he said. "You killed their first grandchild, after all."

"God damn it, Austen," Paul shouted, shoving his brother with enough force to make Austen take two steps back. "I told you to leave Bailey alone. This is not your business."

"You're my brother. You fucking up your life a second

time is too my business. But more importantly, I'm not going to let Bailey Jenkins do another number on Mom and Dad. They have enough on their plates without worrying about you being let down when your pretty little cowgirl gets a wild hair and takes off again."

Austen looked at Bailey, his eyes as cold and dispassionate as a wolf about to attack. "And that's what you do, isn't it? Suck a man dry then take off?"

Bailey was aware of the noise level in the diner dropping as people turned to watch the real life drama play out.

She'd been in this situation so many times as a kid, she knew exactly how to hide her feelings and do what needed to be done to salvage a tiny morsel of pride. She slid a twenty across the glass countertop, picked up her to-go sack and said, "Keep it."

She couldn't afford the gesture, but money was the least of her worries at the moment. Not making matters worse by punching Austen in the face was her first concern.

She pivoted on her good ankle and headed toward the door, chin high, sunglasses in place. She paused beside Paul, who looked ready to tackle his brother.

"Don't bother," she said. "Chloe asked me to invite you to the Fair. She thought you needed a girlfriend. Tell her I changed my mind." She looked at Austen. "I'm good at that."

Then she left before she could change her mind again and kiss the look of disappointment and anguish off Paul's face.

Paul gave the door the shove he wanted to give his brother. "Bailey. Wait. Please."

She had the truck door open by the time he reached her. For a woman with a bad ankle, she moved pretty fast.

"You heard your brother. I leave. It's what I do."

"Yeah. I know. I was there, remember."

Instead of climbing in, she set her purse and food bag on the bench seat then turned, hands on her hips.

"I left, Paul. I had to." She took a step closer, probably knowing full well the entire café was watching. "Am I disappointed you shared my private, painful decision with the whole town? Yes. You're not the man I thought you were." Her eyes narrowed with disappointment and disgust.

"I was seventeen. Heart broke and bitter. I turned to my family, who, naturally, took my side. What did you expect? Do I wish I'd been a better person back then? Fuck, yes. But I wasn't. I'm not perfect, now, either. But I am sorry." He meant that. More than she could ever know.

She shrugged, as if his apology wasn't worth the air it took to say the words.

He grabbed her arm, probably more forcefully than he should have. "That's all in the past, Bailey. We are not our families. You're not a drunk. I'm not one of the Great Zabrinskis."

"The what?"

He glanced toward the café, half-expecting to see Austen gloating in the doorway. "Meg, Austen and Mia used to call themselves that. It was a family thing. They made it clear I would never be good enough to be one of them."

"Ouch." She touched his hand, setting off the usual sparks through his body. "How come you never mentioned this when we were dating?"

"Once they were all off at college, I pretended I was an only child. The fact your siblings think you're a loser is not the kind of thing you say to impress the girl you're crazy about."

She pried up his fingers. "True. I get that. But family is family. And yours obviously hates me."

He stuck his hands in his pockets to keep from doing something stupid, like kissing her. "Not all of them. Meg was on your side from Day One. Mia's worried about me. Austen...he's going through a lot right now. He always set ridiculously high goals for himself and met them, but a few months ago one of his heroes threw Austen under the proverbial bus and...let's just say Austen hates everybody right now, himself included."

She nodded as though that was something she could understand.

"Is your offer still open? For a date to the fair? My answer is yes."

Before she could reply, a car sped into the handicap parking spot. The Subaru wagon had a blue wheelchair sign hanging in the window, but neither door opened. Instead, the passenger side window rolled down and OC Jenkins made a "come here" motion with his hand. "Paul Zabrinski. Just the man I'm looking for. You still got your pilot's license?"

"Dad? What's going on?" Bailey hurried to the window. "Why do you need a plane?"

"That crazy bitch, Marla, shot Jack. He told her he was done running and wanted to go home. So, she shot him in the back at a laundromat in Reno."

"Reno? I thought they were moving to New Mexico?"

OC tossed up his hands. "She's a thief, a killer and a liar."

"Jack's dead?" Paul asked.

"Dying. He asked for me. If I don't get there soon, it'll be too late. He was my friend for thirty years. I owe him a chance to make peace. I'll pay you whatever it costs as soon as I'm back to work."

Paul wanted to help, but he couldn't just up and leave...or could he?

"Hang on a second." He walked to the door of the restaurant and hollered, "Austen Zabrinski, get your ass out here. Our family owes the Jenkins an apology, and this is how it's going down."

Two hours later, Paul, OC and an obviously reluctant Bailey were airborne. He'd waved goodbye to Mark and Chloe standing on his porch, Bailey's mother beside them.

Leaving Louise in charge was a no-brainer. The kids were in perfect hands. Choosing Austen as his stand-in at Big Z's might have been a stretch, but his brother graduated at the top of his class from Harvard. He'd rise to the occasion.

As for the Great Marietta Fair, Paul was confident Jane Weiss could boss his crew without Paul's micromanaging fingers in the pie.

With any luck, they'd be back in town tomorrow afternoon.

His family's Cessna wasn't a white horse, but Paul felt like a hero. Sort of.

OC had insisted Bailey accompany them. Something

about needing help remembering his meds so he didn't reach for a bottle of booze by mistake.

Paul was sure the man's not-so-subtle blackmail didn't fool anybody. OC wasn't thrilled about being stuck in a little plane for God knows how long with the person he once threatened to hike to Coffin Lake at gunpoint so he could dump his body well away from Marietta.

Sure, OC had been drunk at the time, but seventeen-year-old Paul had slept with a hunting knife under his pillow for a week before his mother confiscated it.

Paul had always felt relaxed and at home in the air. Jen claimed that was why he didn't fly more often. "You're addicted to drama. Big Z's is like your personal soap opera. When things get boring, you fire half the staff and bring in new characters."

"I do not," he'd denied. "That only happened once when half of them failed a drug test. What was I supposed to do?"

She'd waved aside his question. "I'm not wasting my breath trying to tell the great and powerful Paul Zabrinski how to run his store. Just don't kid yourself. You'd be a basket case without the drama."

In a way, she was right, but not for the reasons she thought: ego, power or distraction. The store was home to him. Growing up, he often felt overlooked by his busy family. His sisters alternately adored him or ignored him. Austen accepted Paul's adoration as befitting a hotshot big brother but gave little if any attention in return.

On the days his mother dropped him at Zabrinski's Hardware—before it became Big Z's—so she could do her weekly shopping in peace, Paul explored. He watched and learned. And he knew he'd take over from his father some day.

The same way he'd known he would learn to fly the first time Grandpa took him for a ride in his old mail plane.

"When did you learn to fly?" Bailey asked, leaning forward and sideways. She'd chosen to sit directly behind the co-pilot's seat. OC wanted to sit in the back so he could sleep, but the logistics proved impossible. Of the two, Bailey was more nimble.

"I took lessons in college. It was cheaper. Everybody in my family has their pilot's license—even Mom, but none of them can teach worth shit. We formed a consortium awhile back and went together to buy this bird." Since then, he'd bought Mia's share to help her pay for her divorce and Meg's share so she could use the money to fund some kind of wolf-related study project.

The plane hit a pocket and made a stomach-lurching drop. Bailey gave a little gasp. Her big, badass father moaned.

Paul glanced sideways. Sure enough, the larger-than-life, watch-out-Big-Foot-here-I-come OC Jenkins was afraid to fly. And the tinge of gray in his cheeks made Paul glad he had a supply of barf bags.

To spare the old man's dignity, Paul pointed to the pouch in the door and said, "Your pain meds might not work so well at cruising altitude. There's a barf bag just in case. No shame. Happens to the best of us."

OC gave him a look through narrowed eyes that told Paul nothing. But he fumbled for a sack and held it on his lap for the rest of the trip, which, luckily, didn't include any more turbulence.

OC'S HANDS WERE shaking on his walker by the time he reached Jack's floor. He couldn't complain about the flight or his pilot. Young Zabrinski did a good job piloting the plane. He didn't even make moon pie eyes at Bailey the whole time—even though OC picked up on some kind of undercurrent between the two.

He'd made up his mind not to think about what they might be doing back at the hotel. Bailey was a big girl, and she more than deserved a little happiness, if that's what Paul Zabrinski was offering.

Whether or not Paul could deliver was another thing outside of OC's control.

"Excuse me, ma'am. I was told I'd find my friend, Jack Sawyer, on this floor. Could you point me in the right direction?"

OC hated the walker. He hated looking handicapped. But the darn thing got him help when he needed it.

A Hispanic woman in a bright purple uniform—when did nurses stop wearing white, he wondered—burst from behind what looked like the helm of the Starship Enterprise. "You must be OC. He's been asking for you. We're all curious what OC stands for."

"Depends on who you ask. My wife would tell you Oscar Clark. Most of the bar owners in town would say Obnoxious Customer."

"Oh," she said, kindly, patting his hand. "I don't believe that." She directed him to an open door a few steps away. "Mr. Sawyer is resting at the moment. He's been in and out of consciousness. More out than in, lately, but I know he'll be very happy to see you."

OC followed her into the room. His second stinking night as a visitor in a stinking hospital. Welcome to old age, he thought bitterly.

He and Jack used to joke about how they'd die.

"I plan to be thigh deep in spring melt with a twenty-pounder on the hook," Jack once told him.

Hooked up to more bells and whistles than either of them ever saw wasn't even close, OC thought, pausing in the doorway to observe the body in the bed. Tall and gangly as ever, but something about hospital beds made even the heartiest person look half-shrunk.

The nurse brought him a chair and positioned it close enough that OC could speak without feeling like he was shouting. They had some things to say to each other. Not good-bye. That was a given. OC wasn't leaving until Jack stopped breathing. He knew if their positions were reversed Jack would have done the same.

He felt a vibration near his hip. Bailey had insisted on him taking Louise's cell phone so they could keep in touch.

He appreciated that she and Paul had given him this time alone with his friend. Louise wanted to come along, but her doctor couldn't be reached for permission to fly.

The last thing Jack would have wanted was to cause Louise and OC any more pain. So, she'd stayed behind to watch after Paul's children and keep an eye on that fancy-dressed brother of his.

He held the phone out far enough to read the screen. *Take a pain pill now.*

He snickered. The text came from a number he didn't recognize but the tone was Louise's. His wife was getting to be near as bossy as his daughter always had been. *Stop drinking, Dad. Quit smoking, Dad. Get off the floor, Dad.*

Back then, he'd ignored their pleas and thumbed his nose at sane and polite behavior. But look where going rogue got him.

He massaged the fleshy part of his leg above his stump as he felt the pain starting to radiate outward. Louise knew him better than he knew himself.

He poured water from the plastic pitcher beside Jack's bed into a paper cup and took one of the green pills. The blue ones were to help him shit the rock hard stools produced by the green pills.

He sighed and closed his eyes a moment, worn out. A sound made him look up. Jack's eyes were open, blinking.

Was he trying to figure out where he was and how the hell he got there? OC knew the feeling well.

He reached out and put his hand on Jack's forearm. They weren't touchy-feely kind of men, but each was the closest thing to a brother either had.

Jack's chin turned. Slowly. The drugs appeared to keeping a thick layer between the patient and his world.

"OC," Jack said, his voice scratchy, barely audible. "You dead, too?"

OC let out a gruff hoot. "Not yet. Neither are you."

Jack's eyes closed. "Will be soon."

A peculiar smile formed on his cracked, dry lips.

"Whatcha thinking, pal?"

"Marla never did have any patience. If she'd waited a few months, she wouldn't have had to shoot me. I'd have keeled over from the cancer."

OC squeezed his hand. "You knew?"

Jack nodded. "For a few months. My coughing was scaring the fish. Doc said the X-ray of my lungs looked like Swiss cheese."

"You didn't tell anybody? Even Marla?"

"Couldn't see the point." His head moved a tiny bit. "Like you always said. No fixin' stupid."

OC flashed to the many nights he and Jack wound up at the Wolf Den lamenting about the silly, hopeless flatlanders they'd spent the day trying to turn into sportsmen. His mouth could almost taste the whiskey.

"Louise thought maybe Marla's embezzling was because you needed the money for treatment. She was sure you were headed to Mexico for some kind of witch doctor cure."

Jack smiled for the first time. "Your wife is the kindest woman I ever knew. Tell her I said so."

A little cough escalated to a full-body engagement that took on the nature of an epileptic fit. A nurse—an older black woman dressed in lime green—came in. She raised the bed a few inches and helped Jack take a sip of water through a straw. She fiddled with something on one of the tubes leading from a clear sack to Jack's arm.

She gave OC a kind, encouraging smile before she left.

"Goddam cancer sticks," Jack muttered. "Bailey was right. Sorta pisses you off, don't it?"

OC laughed again. "Remember when she was a little girl and she'd hide our smokes?"

Jack smiled. "Stopped up the can once."

OC bit his lip, the memory as clear as if it happened earlier that day. Bailey was nine or ten. She found a brand new carton of cigs OC left on the counter at Fish and Game.

They figured it must have taken her an hour to open every pack, break them into pieces and flush down the toilet.

When OC and Jack got back from a long day on the mountain, OC was the first to use the toilet. Since it was a particularly smelly job, he flushed before standing up to zip. The monumental backup chased him—pants around his ankles—into the main office.

Jack laughed so hard he fell to his knees, holding his gut as he rolled, well away from the mess. Despite his best effort to stay mad, OC couldn't help but join in. The two laughed until they cried.

"I'm gonna miss that girl. Best of both you and Louise."

"What are you talking about? There ain't no good in me."

Jack turned his head to look at OC. His expression stern. "You saved my life, Oscar. I'd have wound up being a bum on the street if you hadn't snatched me outta the gutter and taught me how to fish. All the mistakes…I made those myself. Those are on me. Not you. I'm only sorry I didn't do something to stop Marla sooner. I always knew she was poison. I let her ruin things between us, and for that I—."

OC gripped Jack's arm hard. "No. We're good, Jack. Always have been."

A tear slipped from the corner of Jack's eyes. His labored

breathing eased slightly, his muscles relaxed. The monitor showed his heartbeat slower but still steady.

Sleep took him fast. OC could only hope death did the same. But, for as long as this process took, he'd be here, keeping watch. His best friend in the world would not die alone.

Chapter 14

BAILEY STOOD AT the window of their hotel looking toward the desert. Twilight was a funny thing on the vast openness. The Sierras to her right cast long shadows spreading out like the aftermath of a wildfire. Highways packed with car lights crisscrossed what once, not long ago, had been barren land.

Somewhere four hours south of here was the ranch Ross bought for them. She'd only seen it in photos. She'd resisted, protested, ignored and, finally, disconnected herself from Ross's plan. Only now did she really understand why.

I could never live in this dry, barren landscape.

She was Montana born. Since returning home, she'd slowly started to feel alive again, re-connected to her mountains, to the green and the heartbreakingly blue sky. She'd spent the past fifteen years trying to outrun something that was bone deep inside her.

"Sorry about the room," Paul said, exiting the bathroom.

She turned. "What do you mean? It's fine." Fourteenth floor of a casino. Functional. Sparse. The kind of room designed to make people eager to go gamble.

He put out his hands in a your-guess-is-as-good-as-mine gesture. "You wanted two rooms. They only had one."

She shrugged. "That was when I thought OC was going to be with us. I hate to think of him sitting up all night at Jack's bedside, but he's going to do what he's going to do. Always has."

She walked to the closest bed and sat, glad to get off her feet. She used the spare pillow to elevate her foot. "There are two beds. We're grown-ups."

"How's your ankle?"

Sitting in the cramped backseat of the plane hadn't been the most comfortable, but she really couldn't complain. "It's okay. You're an amazing pilot. Smoothest flight in a small plane I've ever been on."

He walked to the minibar in the étagère across from the foot of her bed. "We got lucky. Great weather. I wasn't sure your dad was going to be able to hold it together the whole way, but he did."

"He's a tough old coot."

She'd come to appreciate that fact more and more the past few weeks.

He cracked open a beer. "Want anything?"

"No, thanks. I'm still full from lunch. Dinner. The bibimbab or whatever it was called."

She'd left her To-Go box with Mom, not certain how her stomach would handle the flight. So, as soon as they had a room and dropped off their bags, she started looking for a restaurant, but Paul surprised her by insisting they hop back in the rental car and head to the closest Korean barbecue.

"My secret weakness," he said as she called out directions via an app on his phone. "Jen wasn't an adventurous eater, and her tastes have rubbed off on the kids. But I'm holding onto the hope they'll come to the hot side eventually."

She'd enjoyed every bite. She'd enjoyed the company, too.

Had Austen's public airing of their dirty laundry somehow liberated them from the past? Wouldn't that be some sort of poetic justice, she thought glancing at the clock radio on the table between the two beds.

Seventy-thirty's too early to go to bed.

Paul must have been thinking the same thing because he asked, "Do you like to gamble?"

"I gambled every time I got on a twelve-hundred pound horse. Figured that was enough excitement for a lifetime."

"Good point."

He dropped into a chair at the tiny round table and kicked up his booted feet.

He flicked on the TV and cruised up and down the menu of stations. "Movie?"

"Sure." Bailey settled her tote bag on her lap and switched on the bedside lamp.

Over the years of being on the road with rodeo, she'd learned how to travel light and still carry everything she needed to work on jewelry. Well, not everything. She couldn't do big wire wrapped stones or intricate solders, but she could finish a few more pieces for the fair.

"Action-adventure? I've been meaning to watch this, but it looked too violent for the kids."

"Anything you want. I've become pretty adept at working and watching whatever's on. Ross couldn't be in a room with a TV without turning it on. In some fleabag motel in

West Texas, he watched a Three Stooges marathon until I thought I was going to turn into one of them."

"You'd make a cute Curly."

She looked up. "Really? I was leaning toward Moe."

"Naw. Curly. He was a sweetheart." He hit mute. "Did you know his brother, Shemp, started out in the role but quit, and Curly took his place?"

"I did not know that. Thank you," she teased. "Now, I have even more Three Stooges trivia crowding the limited space in my brain."

He laughed and turned off the TV. "I'm too wound up from the flight to watch something. Wanna go for a walk?" He looked at her foot, resting on the extra pillow. "Oh, dumb idea. Sorry."

His blush touched her. He was a kind person. Not once during today's flight had he asked, "What's in it for me?" She hadn't asked herself that question, either, but now that they were alone in a hotel room, it seemed a bit disingenuous to pretend there wasn't a large elephant ambling around.

"I went to the diner today to ask you out on a date, remember?"

He pressed his hand to his face, peeking between two fingers. "I know. I'm still waiting for you to forgive me for having the world's biggest jackass for a brother."

She set her work aside and curled her legs under her. "As much as I hate to admit it, your brother is right about one thing. I ran away. From you, your parents, my family, my life. I told myself I was running *to* something, but my freshman year was a disaster."

He moved to the foot of the bed and sat, hunching forward, elbows on knees. "How?"

"I went from a big fish in a small pond to a guppy surrounded by a lot of local kids who knew each other and were a lot cooler than some hick girl from Montana. I cried every day for a month. I would have left, but I couldn't afford to ship Charlie home."

She looked at him and admitted, "And I had nobody to talk to about what I was feeling. You were my best friend. And you weren't speaking to me...even if I had been brave enough to call."

He polished off the last of his beer and tossed the empty can into the garbage can. "I didn't leave the house except to go to school and work at the store for four months. When Meg came home for Christmas, she told me I was an idiot who had his whole life ahead of him."

"She sounds smart. Did I ever meet her?"

"I don't think so. She went straight from her BS to her master's and doctorate. She teaches and does research on wolves, and was involved in their re-introduction to Yellowstone."

"Wow. That is so cool."

He nodded. "Not all the ranchers around here would agree with you, believe me."

Bailey made a face. "When she was home, did you tell her about me?"

"She'd heard about the abortion from Mom. Meg's the only one I told about the curse."

"What did she say?"

He was quiet a moment then answered, "She called me a brat for trying to invoke some ridiculous, unsubstantiated hocus-pocus drivel simply because I didn't get my way."

He gave a wry laugh. "If I remember correctly, her exact words were, 'Life isn't fair, little brother. Just ask the wolves.'"

Bailey didn't say anything for a moment. "Ross always dreamed about living off the grid. I think he saw himself as some old west cowboy bucking the system. Just him, his horses, and, maybe, me." *As an afterthought.* "At the end of his last season, he had enough money and enough interest in Daz to line up some investors. He bought a place a couple of hundred miles south of here...without telling me."

"Ooh. Bad idea. I speak from experience."

"I refused to even go look at it. He left Daz with me and said he'd be back as soon as the fencing was done." She found out later he picked up some gal from the circuit on his way through Bakersfield. "I'm sure he expected me to be a wreck without him. Instead, I got busy making and selling jewelry."

She fiddled with the turquoise ring she'd made to celebrate the day her sales topped two grand.

"When he came back, we had a huge fight. He tried to paint this great picture of living off the grid. I told him I needed the Internet to sell my stuff. We were too far apart to even think about reconciling. I told him he could take Daz, but I expected half of the stud fees and a portion from the sale of Daz's get from Ross's mares."

"Sounds fair. But I'm guessing he didn't agree."

She'd expected hostility and name calling. Instead, he'd looked dumbfounded. He honestly didn't understand her at all. Somehow, that hurt worse. Had she really loved and married a man who didn't know her?

"He was upset. Worried about how he was going to swing the deal without my help, but he didn't argue with me. Instead, he went after our horse trailer that he'd lent to some guy hauling mustangs from Nevada. Something happened while Ross was there. Ross wouldn't talk about it, but he came back with a shiner and a bloody lip."

She'd spent nearly a dozen years tending his wounds.

"I gave him an ice pack...helped him get cleaned up. He offered to take me to dinner before he and Daz hit the road." She closed her eyes and sighed. "I thought—hoped—we might be able to be friends."

"But it was too soon," Paul supplied in a been-there-done-that tone.

"He tried using Daz against me. Said I was abandoning our *son*."

"Letting Daz go was like losing a piece of my heart. But I couldn't support us both at that point in my life, and I thought he'd be better off with Ross."

"You made the only decision you could given the circumstances," Paul said.

"Did I? Every day I wonder what would have happened if I'd said, 'Okay, Ross. I'll give Nevada a try.' Maybe I could have made B. Dazzled work if I drove to the closest town every few days to fill my orders. Maybe I would have liked living off the grid."

"Killing rattlesnakes with your bare hands."

She snickered softly, grateful for Paul's attempt at humor. "Exactly. Instead, I asked Ross to take me home. Ten miles. A stretch of Highway 99 I drove nearly every day. I know *what* happened because I've read the accident report. But, I can't remember *how* it happened. And that's what keeps me awake at night." An understatement.

"Trauma like that doesn't magically disappear, Bailey. My parents still talk about the night Neve Shepherd drowned."

Of course, Bailey remembered the tragedy that shook Marietta to its core. "It happened the end of my freshman year." Bailey hadn't known Neve, personally—only senior *boys* showed any interest in underclassmen girls, but she'd never forget the look on her father's face when he returned with the search party that found Neve's body.

"I think Ross jack-knifed the truck on purpose."

Paul's grip on her fingers intensified. "Why would he do that?"

The same question Maureen asked every time Bailey brought up the subject.

"To hurt me."

Paul started to speak, but she jerked her hand away and shook her head.

"Ross could be reckless. And impulsive. Even his friends called him a loose cannon. And he had a temper."

"Like OC?"

She swallowed hard. "Crazy, huh? I left Montana to get away from my father and wound up marrying someone just like him. How Freudian can you get?"

Paul scrambled to a sitting position and moved close enough to take her face between his hands. "OC is a hothead. I can't dispute the point. But people like OC Jenkins don't go around offing themselves and the people they love just to make a point. That would be the equivalent of giving up. Can you see your father ever giving up on anything?"

She pictured the tall, slightly stooped figure pushing the walker into the hospital a few hours earlier. Alone. Determined. The way Ross looked after she told him she wasn't going to Nevada with him.

Paul pulled her to him. "Accidents happen, Bailey. Ross had a lot on his mind, right? Distracted drivers make mistakes." He kissed the top of her head. "Just ask Austen. I borrowed his brand new Tiburon to impress a girl I'd asked out. On the way there, I somehow managed to clip a telephone pole—an old one, thank God. I rolled the car *and* landed crossways on the railroad tracks."

"Were you hurt?"

"Not a scratch. But the car was totaled. And Austen *wanted* to kill me. Mom wouldn't let him."

She brushed back a lock of hair that had fallen across his brow. "I'm glad."

Neither spoke for a heartbeat or two.

Bailey experienced the same sort of clarity she'd felt when she told Ross she wasn't going to Nevada with him. She knew her future would be changed by the decision she was about to make. Right or wrong, sometimes you had to go with your gut.

"This is probably a mistake, Paul, but it wouldn't be our first."

He brought his lips to within touching distance from hers. "Are you making a pass at me?"

"Pretty much."

She looped her arms around his neck and waited for him

to make up his mind. Her heart pounded so hard he could probably hear it. She moistened her lips in anticipation.

"Good," he said. "Because I want you worse than I ever did in high school. And we both know I couldn't keep my hands off you then."

He slipped his hands under the shirttails she'd pulled free when she removed her belt and unbuttoned the waistband of her jeans after eating too much Korean barbecue.

"The feeling was—is—mutual," she admitted. "But...we're not the same people we were in high school. What if the weight of all my baggage suffocates us both?"

The look in his eyes said he understood completely. "Mine will more than even out the load, Bailey."

The thought of them hidden by a wall of scarred old trunks and bags made her smile. She risked touching his arm. The skin of his forearm seemed a good deal more freckled than she remembered, the reddish gold hair wiry and thick.

"I can't promise you anything, Paul," she said. "So much is riding on OC's recovery and we both know how unreliable he is."

His hands settled at her waist. His fingers were warmer than they should have been, his touch sweeter and more penetrating that she wanted to admit.

"We're not kids any more, Bailey. We're two single adults who still have a thing for each other. People make love all the time without being in love. Why shouldn't we?"

She liked that point. Maybe his divorce had left him just as bruised and disenchanted as she felt. What was stopping them from taking advantage of this reunion?

She grabbed the hem of her shirt and tugged it up and

off in one single fluid movement. "I'm in."

She tossed it toward the nearby chair. Where it landed, she had no clue. Her gaze was locked on the delighted surprise she read in Paul's expression.

"For real?" he asked, his gaze dropping to her chest.

She looked down, too. She couldn't remember what bra she put on that morning. She certainly hadn't dressed for seduction. Luckily, she'd grabbed the pink lace. Her favorite. "For right now. Will that do?"

"Hell, yes. Everybody says focus on the now. I can do that. I can do that very well...when I'm looking at you."

She took a deep breath, fairly certain her breasts would swell against the sculpted pink lace.

"God, Bailey, you're even more beautiful than I remember."

"Do you know what I remember?"

His tongue flicked back and forth across his lower lip. "No. What?"

"I remember that stupid shift knob of your truck poking me in the most inconvenient places at the most inconvenient times."

He grinned and made a magnanimous gesture toward the bed. "No shift knobs in sight. But I could call Room Service if this is a sticking point."

The last vestige of hesitation left her. She scrambled to her knees and tackled him. "The only thing I'm calling Room Service for is Death By Chocolate. I saw it on the menu. But first we have to work up an appetite. Sound like a plan?"

He wrapped his arms around her and rolled to one side, taking her with him. "The best plan evva, as Chloe would say. Let's go for it."

His lips were within inches of hers but he didn't kiss her right away. First, he said, "I learned from our mistake, Bailey. I never travel without condoms."

They'd used protection back then, too. But they'd been impatient. Careless. Rushed.

"Good thinking."

She went off the pill when she and Ross got married, thinking they would start a family along with their new business. They'd tried but nothing took. For a period after his death, she'd beaten herself up about that, too. Now, she put the thought out of her mind.

Nothing was going to distract her from Paul's kiss.

The lips she remembered. The way he kissed? Not so much. The boy she'd kissed had segued into a man who knew what he wanted, what he liked and what he damn well planned to give her.

Paul could honestly say he hadn't seen 'sex with Bailey' as even a remote option when he fired up the Cessna. He'd figured the trip would involve a lot of pacing in hospital waiting rooms and ferrying OC back and forth from the hotel.

To wind up sharing a room with Bailey...a pleasant surprise. To be invited back into her life as a confidant of her worst fear, to hold her, kiss her...damn, he couldn't quite get his head around the bounty.

"I want you worse than when we were in high school," she'd said.

He knew exactly what she meant. He'd gone hard the moment she'd pulled off her T-shirt.

Every inch of her skin smelled like honey and roses. He wanted to go slow, remember every sensation, but Bailey had never been patient. Once she made up her mind to do something, it got done.

"Do you remember our first time?" he asked unbuttoning his shirt.

She brushed his fingers aside and took over. One, two, three, pull out shirt tails, four, five... "We came close so many times, but I think it was in my barn, right? The hayloft. Your Boy Scout sleeping bag."

He unbuckled his belt and unzipped while she pulled the belt through the loops. "The hay smelled good but the sleeping bag wasn't thick enough to keep the poking parts from poking you."

His belt joined her shirt on the floor. By wordless agreement, they both wiggled out of their jeans. Her panties didn't match her bra. Lime green bikinis with black polka dots. "Cute."

She touched the raised fabric of his navy blue stretch boxer briefs. "No more tighty whities."

His breath caught in his throat as her hand cupped his erection. "Not since college." Not since Jen started shopping for him.

She turned her attention to his bare chest. "Your muscles are so filled out. Chiseled, even. From swinging a hammer, I suppose. You're so manly, now." Her tone held a hint of teasing, but he thought he detected a bit of wistfulness, too. He felt the same.

"You're thinner *and* more voluptuous. How is that possible?"

She flexed her bare arm to show her well-defined biceps. "Exercise. For a while after the accident, I couldn't do anything. I felt like my body was melting into the sheets. As soon as I started physical therapy, I went gung-ho. One of my trainers, who also became my friend, called me Bailing Wired."

He squeezed the muscle. "Hey, that was my nickname for you."

"That's what I told her. Although I was never sure it was a compliment."

He locked fingers with her and leaned in close enough to nibble her neck. "It was. I admired your drive and fearlessness. Scared the bejesus out of me at times, but, man, you were something to watch."

She moved her head and shoulder in a way that told him she was enjoying his touch. He trailed his tongue to a pronounced bump on her clavicle. A broken collarbone from falling off a horse when she was ten. A scare like that might have stopped other kids, but not Bailey Jenkins. From what her mother told him, she was back in the saddle while her arm was in a sling.

She dropped back on her elbows. "This," she said, shifting to her right side to touch her collarbone, "was the first of many. Two cracked ribs. My kneecap is all screwed up. I broke my elbow, but it's stronger since I started lifting weights. A couple of toes. And fingers. And that's not even counting my ankle."

He slid off the bed so he could start at her feet. "Which toes?"

She wiggled her left foot. He kissed them all, which

made her laugh.

"And your right ankle."

"Obviously."

The scar wasn't as furious a red as when she first arrived in Marietta. He nuzzled his cheek against her wound, their gaze locked. "I'm sorry you were injured, but I've got a few war wounds of my own, you know."

He licked the inside of both her knees.

"You do?"

"Viral paper cuts. I give myself a yearly bonus to make up for the grievance."

He advanced to her mid-section, checking each rib with his lips. When he reached her bosom, he unsnapped the front-closure bra and separated the two halves of pink lace. Her small, perfect breasts greeted him, nipples erect. He had to taste them. He couldn't *not*.

She squirmed in a happy way that made conversation superfluous. Her hands moved to his bare back, stroking, finding her way again. She touched his hair. "Don't mention the gray," he said, glancing up.

"You have great hair. Always have. I used to dream about your hair."

"My *hair*?"

She laughed. "Don't sound so outraged. Maybe dream isn't the right word. There were times with Ross when we'd be making love and when I'd run my fingers through his hair, I'd think of you. Except in summer." He waited. "In summer, he shaved his head."

He didn't know what to make of that admission, but the thought disappeared when Bailey reached between them and worked her hands under the waistband of his shorts. She cupped his buttocks, squeezing. "You still have a pretty amazing butt."

Then she worked the fabric lower. It took both hands to free his erection. "Ah, there's my big Z." Her private name for his penis.

She petted and fondled until he feared he might shoot his wad the way he did the first time she touched him. Something that would have been mortifyingly embarrassing with anyone else.

"Are you sure you want to do this, Paul?"

"Positive. Are you having second thoughts?"

She blinked coquettishly. "I'm having naughty thoughts. Where are those condoms?"

He had to walk into the bathroom to his toiletries bag. When he returned, the bed was turned down, the lights lowered and pillows plumped...with Bailey naked and waiting, one hand touching her breast, the other lazily rubbing a spot between her legs.

"There's so much I want to do with you—"

"Later," she said, opening her legs for him. "I'm ready, if you are."

He sheathed himself then moved to the spot made for him. Wet heat beckoned, her womanly scent adding to his lust. One finger, then two, opening her to him. Her legs wrapped around him. She made a small peep but brushed aside his concern. "I need you inside me, now, Paul. Now."

He gratefully obliged.

They'd always fit together as if made from one whole. He'd always—well, after the first few times—been able to read her rhythm, feel the build inside her core.

Each thrust re-established their connection.

"Oh, yes," she cried, eyes closed. She sucked in her bottom lip as a wrinkle of concentration knit her brow.

Paul braced himself with one hand and slipped his finger between them, connecting with the tiny button they'd discovered through trial and error, with the help of some sex book he'd "borrowed" from his brother's room.

Her whimper jack-knifed through him, bringing him closer to the edge. Her ragged breathing matched his. He was close.

The moment her hips lifted off the mattress, he felt the life force inside him surge and catapult to completion. Aftershocks rocked them both as they panted hard in that most triumphant of ways.

"Better than a 10-K," he said.

"Better than a buckle run," she said. "And a lot more fun. Thank you, Paul."

He pulled back and gave her dry look. "Thanks? You never thanked me before. That's something our parents would have done."

She grinned. "You're right. OMG, we've become our parents."

He rolled off to dispose of the rubber. "Speak for yourself. I'm still young and vital, and after the movie I'll show you just how vital I really am."

He was kidding, of course. He'd be ready long before a two-hour movie was over.

She scooted off the bed and walked to the bathroom. "In that case, better order room service. I'm going to need

Death By Chocolate to keep up with you."

He flopped on the bed and reached for the menu. They were going to need more than chocolate for what he had in mind.

Bailey hadn't said this was a one-night stand, but who knew what would happen when they got back to Marietta? As she'd said, OC might be the deal breaker that sent her hightailing it back to California. He planned to make the most memories possible in the time they were given.

Chapter 15

THE SOUND OF a braying donkey woke Paul out of the warmest, sweetest rest he'd had since his children were born. He sat upright in bed, the covers pooling at his waist. A sliver of light through the curtains told him he was in a hotel room in Reno. A low female moan—one he'd heard in various incarnations the night before—told him who was in bed beside him.

Bailey Jenkins.

Holy shit, he almost said. A second braying sound stopped him.

"My phone. Damn. It's OC. I forgot I gave him that ringtone."

He snatched the phone off the bedside table. Bailey's snicker was a relief. At least, she wasn't offended. "Hello?"

"You can come and get me now. We're done here."

"Okay. Bailey and I will be there in..." He looked at Bailey who poked her messy head out from under the covers and gave him a Really? Look worthy of any pre-teen. "Give us half an hour. Have you had breakfast?"

"No appetite."

"We'll stop somewhere on our way to the plane, then."

OC didn't argue. He didn't say anything. Paul checked

the phone to see if they'd been disconnected. When he put it back to his ear, he heard OC say in a gruff, emotion-filled voice, "I need a drink, but Jack made me promise I wouldn't use what happened to him as an excuse to start again." He sighed heavily. "I'll be out front when you get here."

Paul hit the off button and looked at Bailey, who was sitting up, too. "Whoa. That was heavy."

"What? Oh, my God, don't tell me? Jack passed at midnight and Dad's been at a bar ever since?"

Paul pulled her into his arms. Her bare flesh was warm and fragrant. She smelled of sleep and sex and magic. Being with Bailey made all things possible. There might even be hope for OC.

"He sounded exhausted but okay. He promised Jack this wouldn't push him over the edge again." He gave her a squeeze, wishing with all his heart they'd had time to talk before life, families and work intruded.

Focusing on the moment worked great when you were making love for the third time, but they hadn't made any effort to discuss what came next. Were they dating? Did one night of beautiful sex make them a couple? A thing?

Bailey hugged him back then scrambled out of bed, as always favoring her right leg. She walked to her open overnight bag and picked out a pair of pink silk panties and a black and bronze Copper Mountain Chocolates T-shirt.

"I was hoping we could share a shower," she said, walking with the same grace she'd shown when she was crowned fair queen, only back then she'd been dressed in Wranglers, Ropers and a white, western shirt with pearl snaps and silver piping. "But I guess we'd better hurry."

She turned on the bathroom light then paused to add, "Poor guy lost his best friend. I know how that feels."

Did she mean me? He thought so. Or he tried to think, but watching Bailey Jenkins parade around naked deflected the majority of the blood flow to his brain in a completely different direction.

He bounded off the bed and crashed through the bathroom door. "We can be fast."

OC LOOKED AROUND the waiting room where they'd moved him after Jack stopped breathing. The honey brown walls reminded him of a spaniel he once owned. The framed posters were flowery and generic. Four long, narrow windows did little to provide either a view or sunlight.

The designated spot for a wheelchair fit snugly between a low table filled with dog-eared, germ-laced magazines and an empty chair. A nurse had offered him the use of a wheelchair after he'd awoken to a shrill, insistent alarm coming from Jack's monitor and lunged out of the makeshift bed without thinking.

He'd fallen, of course, adding to the chaos surrounding Jack's final moments on earth.

OC didn't know what he believed about death. He couldn't say what happened after you died. But he'd seen movies with ghosts hovering over their dead bodies. He wondered if Jack's soul had gotten a kick out of seeing OC being helped to his feet...foot...by two burly male orderlies.

He hoped so.

He glanced at the only other occupant in the room—a man in his early twenties, sprawled across three chairs.

I was that limber once, he thought. *Jack and I could sleep anywhere.*

They'd camped in places most humans didn't know existed. Places where you kept one ear open for wolves, the other for bears. When they were in the backcountry, they rarely drank. A sip or two from the flask one of them brought. But once they hit town...look out.

There was a time when they could drink any guy in the bar under the table. They'd had more than their share of laughs.

But OC wasn't laughing now. He'd stared reality in the face as Jack's breathing became more and more labored. The nurses visited every ten minutes or so from one o'clock on. They'd fiddle with the morphine drip, check his vitals, and smile sadly or encouragingly at OC, depending on their temperament.

The last thing Jack said that made any sense was, "Don't hate Marla, OC. Her thing with money is like us with booze. She bought shit because she couldn't *not* buy it."

OC wasn't sure he believed that, but Jack obviously did. And, despite everything, Jack still loved his wife. He'd called out her name several times—in pain or regret, OC didn't know.

Don't hate Marla.

OC understood hate. He'd lived off the emotion for many periods of his life. Hate made him strong enough to survive a childhood that would have killed a lesser man.

Hating young Paul Zabrinski for knocking-up his daughter made losing Bailey a whole lot easier. For a few years, he'd even managed to forget his role in her oft-expressed desire to leave Montana for good.

Hating minorities, foreigners, flatlanders and freaks kept him from looking too closely at his own mistakes.

"Mr. Jenkins?"

A white-haired woman wearing a long-sleeve pink uniform top and stretchy gray pants stood in the doorway. "Are you ready to go downstairs?"

"I told the nurse I could manage on my own but she wanted me to wait here."

The woman smiled broadly. "Thank goodness. Helping patients or their loved ones to the door is the only exercise I get."

"Given the size of her butt, she needs a mass exodus," OC swore he heard Jack whisper.

For a quiet man, Jack had a wicked sense of humor.

The woman fussed with OC's walker but finally managed to secure it to the wheelchair. Once in the elevator, she gabbed serenely the entire time it took to reach the main floor. She told him about Reno's housing boom—or bust, depending on which newspaper you read, and the importance of getting a flu shot each year.

"I lost a dear friend to pure stubbornness last winter," she told him as she set the brake on his chair. "Don't rob your loved ones of your presence simply because you think you're tougher than a little germ."

The old OC would have cussed her out until she scurried off in tears. The new and hopefully improved OC meekly nodded and smiled.

She wished him well and walked back inside.

The desert air made his nostrils crinkle. One of the nurses told him they were predicting temperatures over a hundred and five today. Another reason to get in the air as soon as possible.

That, and he needed to see his wife.

He fumbled with the phone in his shirt pocket, but after a couple of tries he managed to call Louise.

"Hello? OC? Is he gone? Has Jack passed?"

He'd planned to call her from the waiting room but he hadn't wanted to wake up the sleeping guy. "Yep. Just before dawn. I'm waiting for Bailey and Paul to come pick me up."

"I'm so sorry. I guess it's for the best if he had cancer, but it's still hard to believe we'll never see him again."

"He told me he was coming back to make things right between us. That's why she shot him." OC's throat squeezed tight. "He asked me not to hate Marla. How am I supposed to do that?"

"You could pray."

He shook his head. He didn't know where this sudden fascination with God and church was coming from, but he wasn't having anything to do with it. He saw God every day in the crystal clear water in the high mountain streams, in the flecks of dark gold in his beautiful daughter's hair, in his wife's generous smile. He didn't need to go to church or listen to a preacher tell him how to be a better man. Jack had given him the key, if OC was man enough to do it.

"Quit hiding in a bottle, OC. You're the best man I've ever known—my one true friend, but you act like the biggest horse's ass around most of the time. Stay sober. And every once in awhile, say something nice to the people who love you. From the heart. Even if it scares the shit out of you to take the risk."

"How 'bout I start by telling you I love you, Luly?"

Her voice sounded tearful. "I love you, too, dear heart."

"That doesn't mean I can forgive Marla for what she did to Jack, but I'm not going to let hating her eat me up inside. Okay?"

"That's a wonderful start, my love. I'll see you soon. I'm making pancakes for the children." Her voice turned light and happy. "I adore them both, OC. Do you think there's any chance Bailey and Paul might patch things up? I would love to be a grandma."

He looked toward the road and spotted a small silver rental car turning in. Bailey and Paul. He'd thought about the two of them a lot last night. He'd even conjured up the memory of his role in their break-up. "I don't know, dear, but I'll give it some thought. Bailey and Paul just pulled up. I'll see you in a few hours."

He pocketed his phone and sat up, making sure he had the bag of Jack's personal belongings the nurse had slipped over the handle. He hadn't looked through any of it, but he assumed Jack's billfold was there.

Paul jumped out of the driver's side, like a valet hoping for a big tip.

I got a tip for you, kid. Quit trying so hard. My girl loves you, and you're starting to grow on me.

Any worries Bailey had about trying to convince her father she and Paul were still the same dysfunctional couple they had been before making love three…no, four, times, counting the quickie this morning, disappeared the moment she saw him sitting him in a wheelchair outside the hospital. *He's aged ten years.*

She put aside her own worries and got out of the rental car to help Paul.

"Hey, Dad," she said, leaning over to give him an awkward hug.

When had his broad-as-the-mountain shoulders downscaled? "I'm really sorry about Jack. How are you doing?"

OC made his usual gruff mumble about being okay but then he surprised her by patting the hand she'd placed on the arm of the wheelchair for support. "Being here with him was the right thing to do. No man should die alone when he's got people who care about him."

His touch was warmer and more substantial than she expected it to be. He'd never been overly affectionate in the past.

"Do you need anything before we head back home? How are you on pills?"

He took a deep breath, as if just then noticing he was outside in the open. "I slept a little once it was clear Jack was past the point of talking. And one of the nurses showed me how to set the timer on your mom's phone. Every time it makes a ding-dong sound, I take a pill."

A second later, he reached across his body with his left hand and grabbed the handles of a large, heavy-gauge white plastic bag hanging down the back of his chair. "Jack wanted me to take his stuff. Said there was something for you in his wallet."

She carried the bag to the car as Paul stowed the walker in the trunk then pushed the wheelchair closer. She placed the bag on the floor of the backseat before stepping out of the way so OC could get in.

She couldn't imagine what sort of legacy Jack might have left her. He'd always been nice to her, but they were far from close. Marla wouldn't have allowed such fraternization, for one thing. Jack's wife seemed threatened by the fact OC had a child and she didn't. Somehow, that wound up being Bailey's fault.

"We're going to stop for breakfast, OC," Paul said, moving the chair out of the way of the door. "We could pick up some breakfast burritos to-go, if you prefer, but my father taught me never fly on an empty stomach."

OC, who seemed preoccupied with fastening his seatbelt, made a *whatever-you-want* gesture.

Paul used the chance to palm Bailey's behind and give her a lusty look that made her knees quiver. The mutual attraction between them would have been obvious to anyone looking.

She gave him a reprimanding scowl. Paul merely laughed, or, rather, started to laugh. Apparently realizing how inappropriate that might sound given their circumstances, he turned his chortle into a cough.

OC looked up. "You're not getting sick, are you? What'd you two do last night? Gamble till the wee hours?"

"Not me." Bailey put her hand to her heart. "I was in bed by nine."

Paul faked a yawn. She could tell it was fake because his eyes twinkled with humor. "I don't sleep well in hotels. I was up and down all night."

He started to push the wheelchair toward the hospital, but paused to call over his shoulder, "Don't worry, OC. I'll get you home in one piece. I promise."

"That's good. Lost all I intend to for awhile."

Bailey studied her father's haggard profile, trying to decipher any hidden meaning in his words. He looked exhausted. Too wiped out to care about what she and Paul had done the night before.

She closed the rear passenger door and got in.

Would OC have a problem with her getting it on with an old friend? Probably. She recalled him threatening to "castrate the little prick" when he found out she was pregnant. But a lot had changed since then.

She glanced sideways when Paul got behind the wheel. His aviator glasses hid his thoughts, but his grin was that of a happy, hopeful, satisfied man.

She knew the feeling. Little pieces of her old self had been mortared back in place. Who knew there was such restorative power in heat and passion?

"Everything okay? Are you ready to go home?" His warm hand settled on her bare forearm. Rock solid. Here and now.

But what awaited them in Marietta? His family...well, his brother, at least, hated her. "I'm fine...considering I'm a complete and utter mess."

OC leaned forward. "Jack told me something last night that got me thinking about you two. He said history only repeats itself if we don't learn something the first time around."

Bailey glanced at Paul. "That's...interesting."

"You're a good man, Paul. You two might have had a chance, if not for me pushing Bailey to have that abortion."

Bailey's jaw dropped. The A-word. Had OC ever spoken that word out loud in her presence? She didn't think so.

Paul killed the motor and turned sideways in the seat so he could look at father and daughter. "Go on."

"I bullied Bailey until she didn't have any choice," he told him. To Bailey, he said, "And I beat the snot out of Paul."

Bailey looked at Paul. "What?"

He held up his hand to let her father finish.

"I did it because I didn't want you trapped in Montana your whole damn life without a chance. 'Cause that's what happened to my mama, and it killed her. I killed her."

Bailey turned too quickly and bumped her ankle against her heavy leather purse. Tiny pin-pricks of pain danced across her vision but she kept her focus on her father. "What do you mean you killed her?"

"Ma was pregnant when she married my pa. In those days you didn't have options. She couldn't disgrace her family and she had no education, no skills to raise a child alone...so she got married, even though my pa was older, reckless and probably took advantage of her just because he could. He sure as hell didn't love her. She did the right thing...but being noble wasn't enough to make her want to live. She turned on the new gas oven and didn't light it one day when I was at school. She was dead by the time I got home."

"My grandmother committed suicide?" She looked at

Paul, trying to make sense of the idea. "But, you told me she died of influenza."

"Never told nobody the truth…except Jack. He said secrets undercut everything you build in life. No matter how strong the foundation, the whole thing will fall to shit if the ground under it caves in."

He looked at Bailey, first, then Paul. "I had no business sticking my nose in your business—even if I thought I was doing the right thing. I'm sorry."

He sat back without another word, eyes closed.

Paul looked at her, his expression reflecting her shock. "Maybe we'll pick up breakfast burritos on the way to the airport."

Bailey shrugged. She felt pummeled like a punching bag. Left hook followed by one to the gut. She looked over her shoulder. OC's silver hair hung lank and oily. The eggplant-toned bags under his eyes made his cheeks even more gaunt than usual.

She thought she'd excised the memory from her mind, but it came rushing back. As tough as it had been telling Paul her decision, nothing compared to the horror show at her house the night she told her parents she was pregnant.

OC grabbed her by the shoulders and shook until she fought back. Physical intimidation hadn't worked on her for years. His guilt-based mind games, though, did a number on her. He'd called her a selfish slut. Said she'd thrown away everything he and her mother had worked and sacrificed for.

She'd felt so mixed up she'd wound up believing the most selfish choice was to keep it, regardless of which of the subsequent options she picked: marry Paul, give it up for adoption or raise it herself.

In the end, she'd given in.

Only now did she realize not once in all those shouting matches had it occurred to her to ask why OC cared so much about something that was her decision, her life.

Would knowing the truth have made any difference, she wondered? Probably not at the time, but even a tiny bit of empathy might have pried loose a brick or two in the wall between them.

Maybe.

Chapter 16

"THE BARN? REALLY? This is your idea of a hot date?" Bailey asked the man lounging like a sexy western-wear cover model on a bale of hay—over which he'd spread a brand spanking new sleeping bag. "Did you leave the price tag on it for a reason?"

Paul grinned. "I was in a hurry. When you texted that you were on your way back from Bozeman, I did the math and figured out if I snuck out of Big Z's without telling anybody, we might be able to steal half an hour to ourselves. Here."

He tapped the puffy red, green and gold plaid material.

Bailey tried to act perturbed by the sudden booty call, but, honestly, she couldn't pull it off.

In the three weeks since their trip to Reno, she and Paul had had to scramble and plot to grab any time alone. His kids were here twenty-four/seven because their cousins were staying at Grandma and Grandpa Zabrinski's. Plus, Chloe was doing so well with Skipper her mother agreed to let her participate in several Western Show events at the fair. So, every morning—despite the fact Bailey didn't have a minute to spare—Bailey drove Chloe to this very barn to supervise her training.

She kicked off her sandals and hopped up beside him. "Works for me."

Paul pulled her close. "Unfortunately, we have to hurry because I'm meeting a potential renter here at three."

"You found a renter already? Wow."

Paul had offered her the place, but Bailey's money was invested in the infrastructure of her business at the moment. She couldn't begin to even think about moving out of her parents' house. Did her living arrangements compromise her sex life? Holy hell, yes. But if—the big *if*—she sold enough at her booth during the two weeks of the fair, she'd look into setting down some roots.

The big if. She didn't want to think about leaving. She wanted to think about staying forever. With Paul. Not that they'd talked about such things. Paul was too distracted and she was too nervous. What if her jewelry didn't sell? What if her prices were too high? Her designs too different? Or what if people remembered the stuck-up Fair Queen who left town as if it had cooties and wanted nothing to do with her?

She pushed away her fears and wrapped her arms around Paul's middle, burying her face in his neck. He'd been pushing her to go "all in." His optimism made anything seem possible. And he and his crew had pulled off the impossible, getting the fairgrounds ready for this two-week extravaganza.

"Aren't you burnt out? Did you sleep last night?" she asked, kissing his skin at the V of his Henley.

"Sleep is for sissies."

He kissed her, his tongue impetuous, taking advantage of her willingness to play. The barn was warmed from the sunlight that found its way through a cracked window here, an open stall there. She felt at home here—and in his arms, and she was eager to recapture the memory of their first time.

"How come we're not in the loft?"

"No hay. Can you imagine?" The mischievous glint in his true blue eyes made something elemental and pure take hold in her heart. "I hope the next renter shows better form than to let the hay mow run dry. Making love out in the open like this is dangerous. Anybody could walk in on us."

She threw a leg across his lap and positioned herself so she could unbutton his shirt. "Your brother, for instance. Didn't you say he lives next door?"

He worked his hands under the hem of her denim skirt, lifting it around her hips. "A mile or two away, but, yes, Austen could show up. I wouldn't put it past him."

She found the idea slightly titillating. She pulled his shirt up and off then took a playful bite of the corded muscle at the top of one shoulder. "Or your sister. I heard Mia's in town."

He squeezed her buttocks, rocking her forward to feel his hardness. "She is. With her kids. They're swimming at my house at the moment. So I think we're safe."

Safe. A funny word that had little bearing on what she was feeling right now. Being with Paul pushed her so far out of her comfort zone she wasn't sure she'd ever find her way back. But he made her want to come back for more.

She pulled off her tank top, with the built-in bra. "Being with you is never safe," she admitted. "But it's worth the risk. Always."

He kissed her breasts, teasing the nipples into perky points, then suckled. She wiggled and rocked against him, her body remembering what was coming. "I needed this so much."

"Me, too," Paul admitted. "You have no idea."

Was his tone as needy—desperate, really—as he thought it sounded? Did he care? Not a bit.

He thought about her a thousand times a day. Reached for his phone to call or text her every few minutes. He didn't make those calls because his life had been under a microscope since their return from Reno. His big nosy family wanted answers. What the hell was he doing dropping out of his life for a day to fly Bailey Jenkins to Reno? "I helped a dying man make peace. Exactly what any of you would have done if you were asked."

He'd kept his answer simple because he knew that was all they could handle...now. Eventually, he'd break the rest of the news: "I love Bailey. I've always loved her. The past is past. Get over it."

In the meantime, he worked his ass off trying to prove nothing had changed...when in fact, his very chemical makeup was rearranged, re-focused, elementally different.

He woke up to her scent every morning even though she wasn't in bed with him. But she would be someday. Sooner rather than later, he hoped.

He pressed his face to her chest and breathed in his fix, then stood, gently depositing her where he'd been sitting. "Skirt...works. Jeans...not so much."

"Good point, but, honey, promise me you won't start wearing a skirt to work. People would definitely talk."

He laughed. "It's a deal," he said, pulling a condom from his hip pocket. He bit down on the edge of the wrapper so he could use both hands to get out of his jeans.

After removing her skirt and panties, Bailey moved to her knees at the edge of the bale and took the foil package. She opened it and was ready when he stepped to her. "The best part of the barn is daylight. So I can see your beautiful body," she said, unrolling the condom.

"Hey. That's my line."

She put her arms around his neck and pulled his head down to kiss her as they fell backward. That she trusted him to make sure they landed softly was the highest of compliments. And a huge turn on. Luckily, she was ready when he entered her, confirming her pleasure with a long, low moan that nearly had him coming on the first thrust. Focus. Pleasure. Bailey. Me.

Each wiggle and grind sharpened the razor's edge of glory. Her shout of triumph took him straight over the edge. He poured the tangible part of him into her, even though he couldn't share his heart. Not yet. But soon. Please God.

Ever-practical Bailey managed to produce a purse-size package of tissues and tidied them both up, grinning the whole time. As they dressed, she asked about the new renter he was meeting in a few minutes.

"I can't remember her name, but it's written down in my notebook in the truck. She's from California. Raises llamas and alpacas and works part time for the school. She was buying a place near Livingston that fell through."

"Interesting. Did you tell her you were taken?"

He laughed. "No doubt she gathered that when I told

her my girlfriend and I would be here to greet her."

"Well, as much as I'd love to stay and stake my turf, I can't. Mom and the Dazzling Minions are waiting for me. I truly have to dash. If this was California, I could blame traffic, but…" She leaned in to kiss him. "No returning that sleeping bag. We might need it again."

GIRLFRIEND, THE WORD followed her all the way to the handicap-parking place closest to Exhibit Hall-A. The word both pleased and terrified her.

When she heard Paul's parents were back in town, she'd held her breath for two days expecting a confrontation. Nobody came. Then she overheard two of the Dazzling Minions talking about how Big Z's narrowly avoided a lawsuit from some unhappy customer. Bailey didn't know if their trip to Reno was partly to blame or the fact she was back in his life. She hadn't found the courage to ask.

She popped the trunk of her mother's car and got out. She'd needed to purchase a keyed cash box—to hold all the money she hoped to make—and three more Lucite earring displays. After four days of non-stop list-making and consecutive shopping trips to Bozeman, she was afraid to use her phone to check her credit card balance.

Today's run undoubtedly put her close to maxing out her limit. But she'd told herself she couldn't present the image she wanted using hand-me-down tables and her mother's mismatched tablecloths. So, she'd *invested* in half a dozen folding tables, new display racks, three sexy faux marble busts to display her big-ticket necklaces and a dozen turquoise, white and black linen tablecloths.

As the adage went, you have to spend money to make money, she told herself.

She hurried into the big hall, which was bustling with industrious people running every which way. She flashed a quick thumbs-up to her "neighbor," Sage Carrigan, who owned Copper Mountain Chocolates, then hurried to her booth.

"Oh, my gosh," she said, her step faltering.

B.Dazzled Western Bling glimmered like a freshly set diamond engagement ring beneath the fluorescent lights of the Fairgrounds Building-A.

"Doesn't it look great?" her mother said, looking up from adjusting a pair of dangling earrings on one of the four, barbless wire "trees" OC had twisted into surprisingly original shapes.

Thanks to her mother's addiction to Pinterest, they'd come up with several interesting and cheap ways to display her wares, including cowgirl boots they'd picked up at a thrift store then affixed to hunks of weathered wood to showcase her "Charming Boot Baubles."

"Fan-freakin'-tabulous," said Cynthia, normally the most reserved of the Dazzling Minions. "This is the best display in the whole building, Bailey. We're going to sell out."

The other three artisans chimed in.

Sharon, the other *homebody* minion, said, "I don't know who you had to sleep with to get a spot inside, but it was worth it. The sun gives me hives even if I'm under a tent. Maybe *because* I'm under a tent. Who knows?"

Bailey's cheeks were burning but, thankfully, nobody seemed to notice. Paul had called in a favor from Jane Weiss. Bailey knew because the woman had made a point of telling her. "You're lucky I owe Paul about a hundred thousand favors. This fair never would have happened without him. He's a good man to have on your side."

She knew that, but hearing the words from a woman Paul liked and admired...made Bailey want more from their fledgling relationship. Maybe, she told herself. Maybe they'd take it to the next level—like being seen in public together—after she knew how well her jewelry sold.

Tonya walked up to her, clipboard in hand. "Your dad volunteered to sub for us during our dinner hours or when our kids are showing animals, so I added him to my spreadsheet. He's our go-to sub."

Bailey doubted that would happen, but she didn't say anything. OC could disappoint them on his own...as he had most of her life.

She scanned the sheet, mentally tallying up the hours. "Looks great. Thanks so much. Did everybody get a copy?"

"Just about to pass them out."

The constant pool of acid in her stomach bubbled up like a cauldron in Yellowstone. If her jewelry didn't sell, she was going to be in payroll hell—even with Mom's help.

Louise, who hadn't been released to go back to work full time, insisted she was well enough to cover both her commitment to the Readathon and help at Bailey's booth.

Bailey was grateful, but ever since Reno something had changed between them. Not on Mom's part. Louise was as cheerful and positive as ever. But for Bailey, finding out about her grandmother's suicide had, in a way, explained—if not excused—OC's motivation behind pushing her to have an abortion.

Try as she might, Bailey couldn't come up with a justifiable explanation as to why Mom sided with him? Habit? Codependency? Fear? Or did Mom have so little faith in Bailey's ability to be a good mother?

After covering the displays and packing up the last bit of trash, the minions headed toward the main parking lot while Bailey and Louise slowly made their way toward Handicap Parking. Seeing an empty table in the picnic area, Bailey walked to a table and sat. "I need to catch my breath."

Louise chose a spot opposite her. "A momentary respite before the craziness. Good idea."

The breeze had warmed up but nothing like the heat of a Central Valley summer.

Bailey leaned forward, elbows on the molded plastic table. "Mom, Dad said something when we were in Reno that got me thinking, and I have to ask. When you found out I was pregnant, why didn't you support me when I tried to stand up to him? There were other options, you know."

Mom looked straight into Bailey's eyes for a good minute without answering. Then she took a breath and sat up a little straighter. "Now? You want to do this now?"

Bailey nodded.

"Fine. I let your father do the talking because he was speaking for both of us."

The conviction in her mother's voice shocked her. "Why? Would I have made such a terrible mother?"

Louise's expression softened. "Of course, not. You

would have—you will—make a wonderful mother someday. Watching you work with Chloe these past weeks has been sheer joy for me. But you weren't ready *then*. You needed to get away from Marietta…away from your father. And I know this sounds selfish, but I needed you to leave."

"Why?"

"Bailey, I've never been deaf, dumb or blind—even though I know you thought I was back then. I knew how much you loved your father. I saw how hard you fought to save him from himself. If you'd stayed here, married Paul and had your baby, you would have wound up just like me—OC Jenkins's pillar of support. I signed on for that job when I married him. I'm not complaining—even though there were times I wanted to give up. But I couldn't."

"Why?"

"Because I love him. Just like you do. Despite everything, you're here, aren't you?"

Bailey shook her head. "I came home for you."

"Did you?"

Didn't I?

Bailey sat unmoving, trying to make sense of her mother's words. "But it didn't work, did it?"

"What didn't work?"

"My sacrifice. I didn't accomplish anything. I never finished college. I lost my husband, my horse and my career. I'm living with my parents and starting over from scratch. I killed my baby for nothing."

Mom let out a sob and reached for Bailey's hand with both of her own. "I'm sorry you still have regrets, but I know—in my heart—what we asked you to do was the right choice at the time."

Bailey wiped her eyes. She *wanted* to believe her mother. Maybe someday...

Before she could bring up the subject of her grandmother, Mom's phone jingled.

"It's your dad."

Louise put the phone to her ear. "Now?" she asked after listening a moment. "Can't it wait? He's not going anywhere."

She looked at Bailey and sighed. "Are we done here, sweetheart? Jack's ashes arrived via courier." She gave a bemused sniff. "There's a career choice you don't hear about often."

Bailey couldn't face another drama at the moment. "Go ahead. I'm going to wander around the grounds and see what Paul's crew has accomplished."

As if saying his name had the power to conjure the man himself, a horn beeped and Paul pulled up to the table in a high-performance utility cart.

"Bailey Jenkins. Glad I caught you. Do you have minute?"

Bailey looked at her mother who stood and waved them off. "I'm taking off, too. Paul, thanks again for donating the book bags for the Readathon. With Bailey's bling on them, they're going to be a huge hit."

Bailey walked to the cart and got in. "How'd your meeting go with the new renter?"

"Great. Her name is Serena James. She loves the place. I gave her the same break on the rent I offered Jack and Marla because she's an animal lover and I think she'll actually look after my horses, unlike Jack and Marla."

"That's terrific. Is she pretty?"

She nearly clapped her hand over her mouth, shocked when the words she was thinking popped out of her mouth like a jealous shrew.

"Probably. I wasn't thinking about that. My buddy called while I was showing her around and wait till you see what he lent me. Finally. Some space of our own."

Bailey grabbed his thigh and held on tight.

Paul couldn't believe his good fortune. Things were finally starting to go right for him. He had a new renter for the ranch. The job he'd pulled his crew off to put out fires at the fairground nearly turned into a lawsuit, until Austen soothed over the homeowner's miffed feelings with a substantial break on the bill.

Bailey's work with Chloe had been a huge boon. He felt like they were in constant contact even though he'd only observed a few minutes of training the day his crew was cleaning up Jack and Marla's mess in preparation for showing a new renter. But seeing Chloe's proud smile that morning when she got Skipper to back up—a task she'd have to perform for the showmanship judges—made his feelings gel. Bailey belonged in his life. Period.

He just had to convince her—and his family. The fair provided the perfect venue. Neutral ground. Lots of kids around. People...Austen...would be on their best behavior. And, now, he had the perfect place to do that.

A minute later they reached the parking lot where horse trailers and cab-overs would remain for the duration of the fair. His pick-up sat adjacent to but not hooked up to a high-end stock trailer with living quarters included. "Chez Zabrinski for the next fourteen days."

"Nice," Bailey said. "Bigger than anything Ross and I owned when we were doing the circuit for a living. Is it yours?"

"Temporarily. I borrowed it from a friend who is taking a break from the circuit."

He hopped off the cart and hurried around to help her down. "Milady. Want to see the inside?"

"Is there a lock on the door?"

Her sexy little wink triggered a response worthy of his seventeen-year-old, hormone-enriched self. He opened the door and pointed to the automatic step that came out.

"Nice." She stepped inside and made a three-sixty, running her fingers across the faux-marble countertop with its mini-cooktop. "Does the couch pull out?"

He nodded. "I plan to put the kids up top and crash there myself."

"Speaking of kids…where are yours?"

"Shopping with their mother." He settled his arms around her. "They're headed to Disneyworld the day after the fair ends. So this was her last chance to get them packed."

She rose up on her toes and kissed him. "Chloe told me all about it. A bribe to get them to Atlanta where her step-dad is interviewing for a new job. She's not very happy about the idea."

She tasted of peppermint gum and cappuccino.

"I know. We had a long talk about the subject last night. Markie's okay with the idea, which irks his sister to no end."

"How do you feel about the move?"

"Shitty. Scared spitless. I get a little sick to my stomach whenever I think about them being so far away, but until recently I never felt capable of being a single dad. You changed that."

"Me? How? You're a great dad. I'm nobody's role model for anything."

"I know this is going to sound strange but…I think there was a part of me that believed the reason you chose an abortion over marrying me was because you didn't think I'd be a good father."

Her jaw dropped in obvious surprise. "That's almost exactly what I just said to my mother. I thought she supported OC's order because she didn't think I'd be a good mother."

He pulled her close and kissed her. "You're a natural, Bailey. I mean that. Chloe raves about how patient you are and you give her your full attention when you're with her…not texting or taking calls or planning for something coming up, like Jen and I both do."

"Horses require your full attention. I learned that the hard way. Plus, I love it when Chloe gets what I'm trying to teach her. It makes me happy."

"I think Jen's a little jealous, which has made her step up her game. She's been spending more time with the kids when they're at her house."

He took a deep breath. He'd debated about bringing up the subject but now seemed like the perfect time. "You know Mia's kids are here, right? They're staying with Mom and Dad. Mia's decided to move home, too. She's meeting with the movers today."

"Sounds familiar. I hope this move will be as good for her as it has been for me." She looked at him expectantly. "How are the kids taking the idea?"

"So-so. They're fourteen and eleven."

"Teenagers."

Paul lifted her hand to his lips. "Emilee is about the same age as our child would have been."

She would have jerked back her hand if he hadn't been holding it tight. "Oh."

The happy open look on her face shut down.

"Mia and Ed were in college when they got pregnant. Mia was determined that a pregnancy wasn't going to derail her goal of getting her law degree. She passed the bar five years after Ed. Juggling babies and childcare and college took a toll—on their marriage and on Mia, physically."

"You think the stress caused her cancer?"

"I don't know. But her life is completely f-ed up at the moment. And her kids are really, really unhappy." He raked a hand through his hair, frustrated that he couldn't make his words express exactly what he felt. "I guess what I'm saying is if Mia and Ed couldn't pull off an unplanned pregnancy when they were in college, what chance would we have had in high school?"

"Are you saying you think I made the right decision?" Tears pooled in her eyes like sparkling crystal drops.

He nodded. "Yes, but…"

"There's always a but."

He reached out and put his hand against her belly. "I'll probably always wish things could have been different. I am really sorry for the way I handled things, though. You didn't deserve all that crap."

"I wish things had been different, too."

He took her face between his hands and used his thumbs to wipe her tears. "Do you think it's possible for us to put the past behind us and start fresh?"

Bailey wanted with all her heart to say, "Yes." But something stopped her. She didn't know why. Paul seemed sincere in his apology. She appreciated the perspective time and his sister's situation had given him. But...could they ever completely let go of the past and move on...together?

He pulled her to him, two hearts pressed together, memories of heat and sex and wanting sweeping away the old pain.

Could they forget? Maybe not, but they could comfort each other in a way their bodies remembered. And maybe for now, that would be enough.

Chapter 17

BAILEY DIDN'T RECOGNIZE her first shopper of the morning, but she knew the type—bored, rich and looking to make a statement. Bailey's target market for big-ticket items.

B. Dazzled's bread and butter consisted of the under fifty bucks stuff—of which they'd sold a boatload in the past six days. Traffic had thinned out after the weekend, but Bailey was hoping the second weekend would draw new people from all over.

The lady studying Bailey's twenty-two-hundred dollar necklace was not from Marietta or Montana. L.A. by her tan and perfect, designer breasts. Bailey would have staked her profit on it.

"Good morning. How are you?" She picked up her polishing cloth and a pounded silver cuff. Mornings at the fair were Bailey's favorite time—especially on a morning after she'd spent the night with Paul. Chloe and Mark were staying with their cousins at grandma and grandpa's, which gave her and Paul some valuable together time. They'd even socialized with old friends and Mariettans. "If you have any questions about the stones, just let me know. Montana sapphire is quite unique."

The woman framed the faux marble bust in her cell phone camera and snapped a shot just as Sage Carrigan walked up. Although Sage and Bailey hadn't been close in high school, the two had a great deal in common now. Both businesswomen trying to make a living in their old hometown.

They'd caught up a few nights ago while the majority of fairgoers were watching Country and Western legend Alan Jennings, in the bandstand.

Sage had a permanent shop in town—and had even offered to display a few pieces of B.Dazzled jewelry if Bailey decided not to open her own store.

"That piece would really complement your skin tone," Bailey told her prospective customer.

"Do you think so? It's pretty, but quite a bit more than I usually pay for costume."

Bailey looked at Sage. They'd also discussed the knock-your-head-against-the-wall mentality that some people brought to the marketplace.

Both Copper Mountain Chocolates and B.Dazzled Western Bling sold unique, handcrafted products. If you wanted mass-made, you were better off shopping at the nearest big chain store.

"That piece is one-of-a-kind," Bailey told the woman. "The stones are Yogo sapphires we buy from a family-owned company that has been hunting and polishing this type of gem for four generations. The Yogo is almost always blue or purple, and they're not heat-treated. I guarantee you'll be the only person in the world with this exact necklace."

Sage subtly flashed her two thumbs up then cut out, dashing back to her counter when a young mother with three kids walked up. With novel flavors like papaya and chili pepper, her chocolates didn't generally appeal to children.

Sure enough, the woman took one look at the price tags and said, "How 'bout a corn dog?"

"What kind of metal is this?"

Bailey returned her focus to her customer. She explained about the quality of her silver. "Why don't you try it on? You'll love the feel of it against your skin. It's far lighter than it looks."

Ten minutes later, the lady walked out wearing her new necklace.

Sage applauded. "Great work, Bailey. Like reeling in an eighteen pounder. Your dad would be proud. Pretty soon we're going to be calling you the *big* fish whisperer."

Bailey surreptitiously took a bow.

Their camaraderie felt redemptive in ways Bailey hadn't expected. Until this week, Bailey hadn't realized how starved she was for contemporary female company.

In addition to Sage, Bailey had reconnected with several other Marietta classmates back in town for the fair. And the best part of all was realizing the Jenkins family drama she'd always felt separated her from others truly had passed under the bridge.

She jotted down the sale on the spreadsheet and was in the process of picking another piece to display when her parents came in.

Bailey didn't think she'd ever get used to seeing her father in a wheelchair, but OC's doctor had given strict orders not to walk more than a few yards on his new prosthetic until his stump was completely toughened up. Apparently Dad had set back his recovery a few weeks by pushing too hard, too fast.

"Hi, guys. Mom, I just sold the Yogo necklace."

"I know. I pointed it out to your dad as we were coming here. He complimented the lady on it."

"I had her preening like an old hen with peacock feathers," OC boasted.

"You were ogling her bosom."

"That, too. There was plenty of it."

She batted him playfully with her scarf. "I'm going to buy some chocolate. You'd better shape up, mister, or you won't get any."

"You know what I like. Don't come back without it or I'll turn you over my knee and paddle your behind." He winked at Bailey. "One of these days I'm going to do it just to see if she likes it."

Bailey reached for her purse to hide her blush. Ever since OC's return from Reno, her parents had been acting strangely flirtatious.

Although bemused—and a wee bit grossed out—did a child ever want to think of his or her parents as sexual beings?—Bailey thought she could see a light at the end of the tunnel. A flashing road sign saying: Move on.

She couldn't live with her parents forever. If she could find the right time to ask OC about giving up Jenkins's Fish and Game, she might suggest moving the retail part of her business to the front and making the back part into her home.

"Hey, Dad, I was wondering…would you consider—" Her question was cut off by a special ringtone.

Paul.

He started shouting before she could even say hello.

"Oh, my god, Bailey, what were you thinking?"

"Huh?"

"Chloe wasn't ready to do trick riding. You should have cleared it with me first. She's a novice, for God's sake. Someone saw her practicing this morning. She slipped and her foot got caught in the stirrup and she was dragged halfway across the arena. I'm following the ambulance to the ER right now."

Bailey had no idea what he was talking about. "How is she? What happened? Is she going to be okay? I don't know—"

He interrupted, his tone furious, afraid. "Not every kid is as fearless or graceful as you. She never should have tried that swoop. Especially not on Skipper. She could have been killed."

The swoop? Oh, God. "I did—"

"You didn't think. If you had, you would have asked me for permission and I would have said no. There's Jen. I have to go." He hung up without letting Bailey get word out in her own defense. He didn't need her. He had Jen—and the bond that even divorce didn't truly sever when the life of a child was at stake.

Her arm dropped limply to her side. She couldn't think. Her chest hurt as though she'd been dragged across an arena, which she had—twice, but never from trick riding on Charlie. And she never in a million years would have taught that trick to Chloe.

"Uh-oh," OC said, rolling closer. "What happened?"

"Chloe Zabrinski is on her way to the hospital. Apparently she tried to do the swoop from her horse and fell and was dragged. Paul is blaming me for teaching her the trick."

"But you didn't."

She shook her head. "How could I? I haven't been on a horse in a year. That's not the kind of trick you can talk someone through. She'd have to see it demonstrated."

OC groaned as if stabbed in the gut. "Your video."

"My what?"

He rubbed his forehead, his gaze not quite reaching hers. "Jack had a video camera back in the day. Big black thing. Cost a fortune. He filmed you practicing on Charlie. When they moved, he ran across his old videos and had them transferred to a DVD. That was his gift to you. I planned to give it to you as soon as the fair got over."

"That's nice, but if you've got the only copy, how would Chloe see it?"

"I don't know. He wasn't making a lot of sense. But he might have said something about YourTube."

"YouTube," she said, a cold wave flushing through her veins.

"He probably thought he was doing a good thing. You were really something back then. Fearless."

It was easy to be fearless when you didn't have anything to lose. Now, she'd lost everything—and, worse, Paul might lose his precious daughter all because of her. "I have to go."

"To the hospital?"

"No. Away. It's the curse. I'm a danger to myself and

others. Maybe I can find a deserted island with Wi-Fi and FedEx so I can stay in business, but..."

She grabbed her purse and spun around so fast, in such a panic, she nearly tumbled over her father. His hands closed tight on her upper arms. The more she fought to get free, the more fiercely he held.

"Let go, Dad."

"Never."

"I don't belong here."

"This wasn't your fault, Bailey. And I'm not going to let you run away in shame again. You are not to blame for all the bad things that happen in this town. Me? Maybe? But not you."

It's not your fault.

How long had she waited for someone to say those words? Her whole life?

A sob escaped, followed by a hurricane of grief. She wept in her father's arms until her mother, Sage and others rushed over to see what was wrong.

Between hiccups, she told them what she knew. Sage pulled up the video on her phone and showed them.

"My gosh, Bailey, I'd forgotten how amazing you were. No wonder you were crowned Fair Queen."

She put a hand on her Bailey's shoulder. "But you were an eighteen-year-old athlete who had trained for this for months, not a ten-year-old with an inexperienced horse trying the trick for the first time without any supervision or help. This is so not your fault."

Mom nodded. "Sage is right. Paul jumped to the wrong conclusion."

Because he still thinks of me as a self-centered, reckless girl who didn't take into account the consequences before she acted.

The truth hurt more than she could comprehend at the moment. It would take time...days...years to process. She'd get past this terrible sadness at some point—just like she had with her other losses, but she didn't know when. Or how.

She looked at her parents. Her friends. Her community.

Running away and trying to deal with life on her own hadn't worked out all that great. Maybe this time, she'd stay. She'd build her business, become an active part of Marietta and prove once and for all you couldn't keep the Jenkins down.

Hopefully, Chloe would be okay. Paul would apologize for blowing up at her when he learned the whole story. But did she want to give her love and trust to a man who yelled first and asked questions later?

The way her father did so often when she was growing up?

She would have liked a storybook ending. She'd almost let herself believe she and Paul deserved one. But one thing Bailey knew from losing Daz and Ross—and the Paul she'd loved in high school—nothing was a given.

Somehow, she had to figure out a way to move on again—without moving.

Chapter 18

PAUL RUBBED HIS face with both hands. His skin felt gritty from the dirt of the arena where he'd dropped to the ground beside his daughter's lifeless body.

The bile in his throat surged upward as it did every time he remembered Mark's panic-stricken cry. "Daddy. Dad. Come quick. Chloe fell. She's not moving."

Paul, his parents, brother and two friends from work had been sitting in camp chairs beside the trailer at the time. Paul had been considering breaking the news that he was seeing Bailey Jenkins again. Instead, he'd tossed his soda can to the ground and raced to pick up his panic-stricken son.

"Where? What happened?"

"The horse ring." Mark pointed, his skinny arm shaking like a branch in a high wind. "She was practicing trick riding. L...like Bailey. She fell off Skipper. On her head," he managed to get out between sobs.

"Dad, call 911."

Paul passed Mark to Mom. "Stay with Grandma. It's going to be okay."

Then he took off running—Austen at his side. "What did he mean trick riding? Has Bailey been teaching Chloe?"

"Every day for the past couple of weeks. Getting her

ready for the Western Showmanship."

"Trick riding is not a sanctioned event. Why would she do that?"

Paul's mouth went dry as he recalled some of the crazy, fearless stunts Bailey had pulled off when she rode Charlie.

By the time he reached Chloe, a crowd had gathered, including an off-duty paramedic who kept anyone from moving her.

"There's an ambulance on-site. It'll be here any minute," he told Paul. "She probably had the wind knocked out of her when she fell, but she's breathing now."

"Thank God she had a helmet on," Paul said, dropping to his knees beside her.

He'd reached out to touch her, but the paramedic stopped him. "The helmet will protect from a brain injury, but it won't help a broken neck. That's why we're not moving her until we get a back board."

A broken neck? The words echoed through his head the whole way to the hospital. Fear made him want to kick a hole in that perfectly innocent waiting room wall. His family kept their distance.

He had a vague memory of yelling at Bailey on the phone, blaming her for what happened. He'd owe her an apology no matter what happened, but he couldn't think about any of that until he knew for certain his little girl was going to be okay.

Jen came into the room. "I'm still waiting to hear how this happened? Where were you? Why was she alone? Why wasn't your old girlfriend with her? I knew this would happen when you bought her that goddamn horse, Paul.

You and your stupid horse fetish. You're not a cowboy, okay? You're never going to be a cowboy? When are you going to give up on that ridiculous dream and sell that stupid farm?"

Jen's questions and accusations pommeled him. For once he didn't mind. He deserved the blame. He was the one who bought Skipper. He was the one who brought Bailey back into their lives. If not for him, Chloe probably never would have gone online looking for images of Bailey. She never would have found a video of Bailey's stunt riding.

"From what Mark said, Chloe was trying to do trick riding."

"What kind of tricks?"

Paul shook his head. "I don't know. But I've seen riders lean sideways in the saddle and scoop a flag or ring from the ground. Mark said she watched a video on YouTube. I thought Bailey taught her the trick. I was wrong." He'd accused Bailey unfairly. Mark showed him the video on Chloe's phone once they reached the waiting room. "She wanted to show off for her friends and thought it would help seal her pick as the top Junior Princess."

"What is wrong with you people?" Jen screeched. "Who the fuck cares about some stupid fair so much you'd risk your life?" She crossed her arms. "I never understood why you bought that stupid ranch in the first place."

Because it was Bailey's home. Because my first time was in the hayloft of that barn. Because I loved her. I still love her.

"Mr. Zabrinski?" a voice said from the doorway. "Your daughter's back from the MRI. You can see her."

Paul grabbed Jen's hand and led her down the hallway to

the too-white room with a view of the fairgrounds. Jen elbowed him out of the way to get to her bedside first.

"Chloe? Baby? Are you okay?"

"Mommy?" Chloe's voice trembled. She appeared to be a little groggy, but at least she was moving. "What happened? The nurse said I fell on my head."

Paul touched her foot. "Good thing you were wearing a helmet. Can you feel this?"

She giggled and scooted her feet to one side under the thin cotton blanket. "Yes. It tickles. Is Skipper okay? I was leaning over and he stumbled. I let go so he wouldn't fall on me."

Jen tried to repress a cry of horror.

Chloe realized her mistake and reached up to reassure her mom. "He wouldn't have hurt me on purpose, Mommy. He's been really, really good since I started working with Bailey. She'd be so proud of him. Daddy, tell her this wasn't Skipper's fault, okay? I saw that video and had to try. It looked like so easy."

Paul felt sick again. First, he'd cursed her, and then he'd accused her of something she didn't do. He'd be damn lucky if she forgave him. Ever.

"Can I go back to the fair, now? I don't want to miss anything."

"Absolutely not," Jen cried. "You're coming home with me as soon as the hospital releases you."

Chloe started to cry. "Daddy. No. It was an accident. I'm fine. Tell Mommy I can go back to my horse and the fair. Please, Daddy. Please."

A part of him wanted Jen to take Chloe back to Bozeman with her to keep her safe. But Bailey was proof that bad things happened—it didn't matter what part of the country you live in or how careful you were.

"Relax, baby. Calm down. Your mom and I have to talk to the doctors. You're not going anywhere until they say you can. So, chill for a minute. Your grandma and grandpa and Mark are waiting to see you. Can I send them in?"

She nodded.

He motioned to Jen to follow him. When they were alone, he told her, "The fact is she could have fallen off her scooter in your driveway. Accidents happen. If the doctor gives her the okay, I'd like to take her back to the fair with me." He held up one hand when she started to protest. "She won't ride again. I promise. I'll tell her the doctor said so— and I sort of expect him to say the same thing. But she's leaving with you in a few days and her cousins are here…"

She frowned but gave in. "Fine. I have a million things to do before we leave. But no more horses. And I still think you should give up this crazy dream of being a cowboy. You're a businessman. Period."

He watched her walk away. *No wonder we didn't work as a couple. She doesn't know me at all.*

Yes, he was a businessman—he loved his family's store. But, deep down, in the quiet part of his soul nobody ever saw, he was sitting tall in the saddle, riding the open range with his cowgirl at his side. Bailey. Always Bailey.

And, now, he had to find her and try to convince her to trust him, to believe his sincere apology, to give him one more chance to prove he was worthy of being her cowboy.

Chapter 19

BAILEY'S HEART THUMPED as forcefully as when she was barrel racing. Her armpits felt sweaty. And the hand holding the old boot—one that didn't make the cut for B.Dazzled displays—trembled, making the white and yellow daisies it held dance.

"Are you sure about this?" she asked her mother before Louise could push the doorbell.

"You've asked me that ten times. Relax. We're here to see Chloe, who is undoubtedly bored and upset that she can't return to the fair."

The bell ding-donged in the distance.

Bailey had no idea who would open the door. Paul's mother? One of his sisters? She was pretty sure Paul was at the Fair, where Bailey and Louise had been until ten minutes ago.

Today was Bailey's morning to open the booth. Traffic was the slowest she'd seen. She'd have taken it personally if all the other booth-owners hadn't remarked on their lack of sales, as well.

"So, this isn't because people think I caused a little girl to get hurt?" she asked Sage.

"Don't be silly. People aren't stupid. They know you

didn't have anything to do with Chloe's accident. She's a kid. Kids do things without thinking. We're just lucky. It could have turned out much, much worse. Remember Neve Shepherd?"

Everyone of a certain age in Marietta remembered the drowning accident that took the life of the beautiful young teen.

The door opened, but the person greeting them wasn't Paul's mother. "Bailey. Mrs. Jenkins. What can I do for you?"

Austen Zabrinski hadn't changed from the arrogant jerk she'd encountered at the diner a few weeks earlier.

"Hello, Austen," her mother said pleasantly. "So good to see you. Thanks again for your contribution to the library Readathon. We're here to see Chloe." She held up a Readathon book bag. "I've brought her some new books. Is she awake?"

He didn't move. His broad shoulders and thick barrel chest blockaded the doorway as unwelcoming as a cement wall, until a small, freckled hand appeared on his sleeve.

"Of course, Louise. Please come in. Chloe will be over-joyed to see you. And, Bailey," Sarah Zabrinski said, her tone marginally less enthusiastic. *Because of Chloe's accident or our shared past?* "Chloe's been talking about you non-stop."

Austen turned and walked away without a word.

Bailey entered the foyer and looked around. The place looked about the same as she remembered. A big, rambling ranch-style with a cathedral ceiling and lots of windows.

"Mrs. Zabrinski, I'm so sorry Chloe was injured because of one of my old videos. I honestly didn't even know it was on YouTube until my dad told me. His friend, Jack—you heard about Jack and Marla Sawyer?—"

Sarah nodded, her expression grim.

"Apparently, Jack uploaded a couple of videos, thinking he was doing a good thing. A way for my dad and me to…"

Heal? Bond? Reach back for something lost? Bailey honestly didn't know.

Sarah Zabrinski closed the door.

"Chloe absolved you of any blame, Bailey. Luckily, this has turned into a teaching moment her parents are taking very seriously."

Louise nodded. "We saw them moving Skipper this morning."

Sarah sighed. "Yes. And Chloe's no longer a Junior Princess candidate."

Bailey approved—even though she had no say in the matter.

"That's all any parent can hope, isn't it?" Mom asked. "That your child learns from his or her mistakes…because we all make them."

The simple truth carried a weightier message given their history, but Sarah opted to keep things superficial. Maybe life for her had been difficult enough without revisiting old issues. "Indeed it is. Did I hear you say you have books? They will be most welcome because Paul took away her phone and iPad, too. Follow me."

She turned and led the way down the long hallway to the right.

To Paul's room?

Sure, enough. Paul and Bailey spent many an hour in this

DEBRA SALONEN

room—with the door open. Feet on the floor. House rules.

Still dark blue walls, but, now, classy, framed panorama shots of Montana vistas and wild flowers replaced the Santana, Backstreet Boys and Shania Twain posters. Paul's twin bed had been switched out for a queen, the comforter a modern pattern with bold silver, red and navy stripes. Chloe looked small and utterly out of place in it.

"Bailey," Chloe cried. "I told Uncle Austen you'd come. He said you were probably really, really mad at me for doing something so stupid."

Bailey detested that word. Her dad's favorite word when he was on a drunken rant. She carried the flowers to the bedside table and set them on a copy of Montana Rancher magazine. Hands on her hips, she leaned down and said, "I'm furious with you, actually."

Chloe's eyes went big. "You are?"

"I am. I nearly threw up when I heard you were hurt. And then somebody said you were trying to do one of my old stunts. I never would have forgiven myself if you'd been permanently injured, Chloe. My stomach is in knots just thinking about it."

She sat on the bed and pulled the little girl into a hug. "Promise me you'll never try anything like that again."

"I promise," Chloe said, her tone a squeaky peep.

"Good." She pressed a kiss to the little girl's head then sat back. "Do you know why I wasn't hurt or killed doing that trick?"

"Why?"

"Because my horse, Charlie, took care of me. He never would have let anything bad happen to me...if he could prevent it.

"I dislocated my shoulder in college because Charlie had a sore ligament and I had to borrow another horse to finish my heat. Until that moment I hadn't realized how truly special he was. How much he meant to me." She could name a few other instances that she'd minimized someone's importance to her, too.

"Are you saying Skipper isn't the horse Charlie was?" Sarah asked.

"He might be. Someday. If Chloe loves him and works with him and the two of them build an unbreakable bond."

Chloe's eye brightened. "If we do all that, will you teach me some tricks?"

"She might not be here, honey," Sarah said. "Once her dad is better, Bailey will be going back to California. Right, Bailey?"

Bailey hated that rumor. She had a hunch who started it.

She turned and looked Paul's mother in the eyes. "Actually, I've decided to stay in Marietta. Sage Carrigan told me the best way to establish a place in the market is through branding. My brand is Western Bling Montana-style, born and raised in Marietta."

Bailey couldn't read Sarah's expression. Not that it mattered whether Paul's mother believed her or not. Bailey had made up her mind to stay and that wasn't going to change—whether Paul hated her or not.

"I LOVE YOUR daughter."

OC gripped the handles of his walker a little tighter—glad for the support. His prosthetic felt like a dead weight keeping him rooted to the floor of Building-A, but Paul Zabrinski's forceful pronouncement nearly made him take a step back.

At least if we're going to have this out, I'm facing the man eye-to-eye, not sitting in a stinking wheelchair.

"You have a lousy way of showing it."

Louise and Bailey were due back any minute from visiting Chloe Zabrinski and here stood the little girl's father proclaiming his so-called *love* for OC's daughter. The old OC would have grabbed him by the scruff of his neck and marched the damn fool outside to have a go at it.

He looked down at the boot filled with its fake foot sticking out of his pant leg and almost laughed. His marching days were as long gone as his fighting days.

And the funny part was…he didn't care all that much. *Wouldn't Jack get a charge out of that?* He relaxed his grip on his walker.

"I know. But in my defense, I'm a dad. I reacted like a dad. I remember another dad reacting poorly when his daughter was in trouble and looking at something that might have changed—possibly ruined—her life."

OC hauled in a deep breath—*God, I miss cigarettes*—and let it out. "I blamed you back then. You blamed Bailey this time. Where does that leave us?"

"Both wrong. Bailey and I loved each other. We still do, although I may have made it impossible for her admit that. Which is why I need your help."

He took a step closer, his thigh bumping the table. One of the wire *trees* OC made to display jewelry wobbled back and forth but stayed upright. "And your blessing."

OC cleared the lump in his throat. "You're gonna ask her to marry you?"

"Tonight."

OC shook his head and let out a low whistle. "Don't you know anything about women, boy? It's going to take her months to forgive you. Years, mebbe."

Paul planted his hands on the table. "I know Bailey. She has the biggest heart of any person I've ever met. It's full of forgiveness. She forgave *you*, didn't she?"

The man had a point. Even at his worst, his daughter would pick his stinking, puke-covered body off the floor of the bar and take him home.

"She came home when you needed her even though her health wasn't a hundred percent. And back when she was…"

Even after all these years, he can't say the word. *I really underestimated the man.*

"She picked you over me that time, OC, but this time you're going to make sure she picks me."

OC's respect for Paul Zabrinski shot up into the rarified stratosphere reserved for a very few. And every point the man made rang true. If Bailey somehow managed to love the worst father in the world, she'd figure out a way to forgive Paul.

"What's our plan?"

Six hours later, OC's wheelchair rolled to a stop a foot from his daughter's booth. He'd exchanged his walker for the wheelchair at Paul's suggestion. A prop.

The big exhibit hall was nearly empty. Several shops had closed up early, he noticed. From the talk he'd heard this morning, most of the vendors were happy with the two-week length of the fair but all were exhausted—both physically and inventory-wise.

Louise stepped from behind his chair to walk to the rear table where Bailey was sitting, feet elevated on a tower of empty plastic bins.

What a trooper she is. For two weeks straight, she'd been unstoppable whether she was selling jewelry, schmoozing with the public, encouraging her staff or staying up late back at the Fish and Game making more jewelry. He'd never been more proud. And he planned to tell her that on their walk to the Midway.

Paul's plan required OC to persuade Bailey to take a few carnival rides together. A father-daughter thing.

"Stretch the truth. Tell her you regret never doing this kind of thing when you were drinking. Call it your last chance bucket list or something," Paul had suggested.

Not far from the truth, either. Since Jack's death, OC had been thinking a lot about all the shoulda, woulda and couldas in his life.

But seeing the look of exhaustion on his daughter's face made him wish he could call Paul to postpone. Unfortunately, tonight was the last night of the carnival. The carnies would be on the move tomorrow and Paul was adamant. "It has to be the Ferris wheel tonight, OC. You owe us this."

"Let's go, Queen Bee."

Bailey's head shot up. "Where?"

He held up the fistful of ride tickets Paul had given him.

"Last night for fun."

Bailey looked at her mother as though he'd spoken in tongues and she needed an interpreter.

"Let me close up, honey. Your dad is antsy. He insists this might be his last fair, and he wants you to go on some rides with him."

"His last? Why?" Bailey looked at him. "Now what, Dad? You've just learned you have a rare kind of cancer and only have a few weeks to live?"

Had he ever appreciated her snappy temper? Doubtful. "No. I'm healthy as a three-legged horse. But after what happened to Jack, I'm not taking anything for granted."

Her expression remained skeptical, so he added, "And I feel guilty. I never took you on rides when you were a little girl. It's not too late to make amends, is it?"

She took a deep breath and let it out. "I appreciate that, Dad, but I'm wiped out. Could we do it next year?"

He put on his best sad face. "I don't know. Can we? A lot can happen in a year."

She closed her eyes a moment, before reaching deep inside for the energy to give him what he wanted.

She righted her shoulders. "Okay. Let me wrap my ankle and get my boot on."

"Is your foot bothering you more than usual?" Louise asked, handing Bailey the flesh-tone elastic bandage.

"No. It's fine."

Even from a distance, OC could tell her ankle looked puffy and red.

Louise's expression came through crystal clear. "See? She's just like you. Always hiding her pain."

This afternoon, Louise had watched him like one of those hover-mothers she'd told him about who never let their children out of their sight. With good cause. She knew from experience that big emotional decisions triggered—or, at least, provided a convenient excuse—to over-indulge. And once he started down liquor's path, OC was powerless to make a detour.

She was smart to worry. Ever since Paul left here, the siren's call of drink had hummed through OC's mind like an old, familiar melody. But whenever his fingers itched to pick up a bottle, he'd picture the look on Bailey's face when she learned Chloe Zabrinski had fallen off her horse trying to replicate one of Bailey's tricks.

Guilt. Taking responsibility for something that wasn't her fault.

He'd seen that look before. When she drove him home from the bar on the nights he was blind drunk. When she stepped between him and Luly to keep their argument from getting out of hand. His girl blamed herself for a thousand things beyond her control—her father's alcoholism, her husband's actions, her mother's choices—and she'd learned that behavior from one person—him.

From talking with strangers on the online support group Bailey suggested he join, OC saw how he'd let guilt, anger and pain feed his self-destructive tendencies. For some reason, he'd blamed himself for his mother's suicide and his father's temper. He'd had the bad luck to grow up without any real love in his life and he hadn't trusted his wife and daughter to love him unconditionally.

"Just a ride or two," Louise said. "He's been as hepped

up as a kid all today. But none of the dangerous ones, OC. The Merry-Go-Round…and maybe the Ferris wheel."

Bailey pulled on a cowgirl hat adorned with sparkly rhinestones and peacock feathers. "Okay, Dad. Why not? I survived my first fair in fifteen years. That's got to be cause for celebration, right?"

Then she did something surprising. She reached out and took his hand.

Lucky for Paul, OC thought, Bailey never gives up on someone she loves. *Just like her mother.*

Chapter 20

THE LINE OF people at the Ferris wheel was about fifteen deep by the time Paul got there. Louise had texted him twenty minutes earlier to say: *B/OC on way to Merry-Go-Round then Wheel.*

He'd finished up the last minute touches in the camper and headed toward the Exhibitor Gate. Naturally, he'd bumped into a dozen people who'd heard about Chloe and wanted to make sure she was okay.

To have his grand scheme derailed by community spirit would have been the ultimate irony, he thought, breathing hard by the time he finally reached his goal.

"How long does it take to get on board?" he asked the teenager ahead of him.

"Five...ten minutes. Goes fast."

The kid had half a dozen piercings and about as many tattoos, reminding Paul again that he didn't want to be a single parent. He wanted a full-time, live-in partner to help him raise his children—and any others that came along.

He wanted what his parents had and he knew exactly who he needed at his side to make that ideal come true.

Bailey.

If she'd have him.

She might forgive him, but would she trust him to have her back when he'd failed both times the opportunity came up to put her first?

Maybe OC was right. Maybe I should have waited. Maybe she needs more time...

"Paul?"

He pivoted, nearly bumping into the kid ahead of him.

"Bailey." His cowgirl dream-come-true in skintight Wranglers, flashy red boots, and a sexy top made out of some pale aqua scarf-like material that nearly made him drool. Her natural straw cowboy hat sported peacock feathers and rhinestones to beat the band. "OC. What are you doing here?"

Bailey looked at her dad. "We're going to ride the Ferris wheel. Isn't that why you're in line?"

She pointed to the gap where piercing-boy had moved ahead.

Paul blushed. The smirk on OC's face made him feel seventeen.

He made an ushering motion and waited for her to push OC ahead of them. Managing a wheelchair on grass would have been impossible two weeks earlier when the fair started, but after fourteen days and hundreds of thousands of footsteps the grass had been flattered into a worn, if uneven, path.

"Are you using up tickets, too?" she asked, innocently. "Someone gave Dad a fistful and he doesn't want them to go to waste."

Paul could care less about buying a whole packet of tickets. He only needed enough to secure them a seat on the

Ferris wheel.

The cacophony of carnival sounds barely covered the thudding of his heart. His palms were so damp the construction paper tickets would probably be limp and disgusting by the time they reached the ticket taker.

Piercing-boy wrapped his arm around a girl Paul hadn't even noticed. She looked about twelve from the back, but as they turned to walk to the gaudy purple and teal colored "basket," he saw matching piercings and even more ink showing beneath her black lace tank top and leather bustier. Her boobs made her look older. Late teens, probably. About the age he and Bailey were the last time they took this ride.

"Did we look that young fifteen years ago?" She leaned in to whisper sotto voce. So close they nearly touched. Her sweet scent—rose, maybe—pulled him in even closer…until she noticed their proximity and jerked back.

"I was thinking the same thing," he said. "Shall we ride together? OC, would you mind? If I'm intruding, just say so."

"You'd be intruding if I was actually going to get on this contraption, but I'm not."

Bailey made a face—part disbelief, part confusion. "But, Dad, this was your idea."

"And it was a good one. I just ran out of steam." He reached down and massaged his thigh. "Getting on and off the merry go-round took more out of me than I thought it would."

Paul didn't know if OC was acting or telling the truth, but he appeared convincing.

"I'm sorry. I don't have to ride, either. We can go—"

"And waste these tickets? Hell, no. You two run along. I'll be over by the shooting game. Maybe I'll win you something."

"Next," the ticket taker barked.

Paul took her elbow and hurried them to the metal seat where another attendant held open the lap bar that would lock in place. The only technological improvement in the operation that Paul could see was the metal mesh side wings that apparently kept small hands from touching the greasy rocker arms that connected the basket to the framework.

"Are you sure about this?" Bailey asked, hesitating before stepping onto the footrest.

"Why the heck not? It's a gorgeous night. And I owe you an apology. What better place than the privacy of a Ferris wheel basket thirty feet in the air? If you tell me to go to hell, no one will hear."

"I'm not—"

"Let's move it, folks. People are waiting."

Bailey jumped as if prodded, and Paul hurried after her. The burly guy with biceps the size of Easter hams locked, checked and double-checked the mechanism before nodding okay.

The cart lunged backward the distance of one space, then shuddered and rocked back and forth.

Bailey's knuckles appeared white on the upper bar.

"Last time we rode this, you threatened to climb off at the top and scale your way to the bottom."

"A lot has changed since then."

"You've developed a phobia?"

She loosened her grip and turned slightly to look at him.

"Did you and my dad set me up?"

"Would you have met me here if I'd asked?"

"Probably not."

"I didn't think so."

She leaned forward, scanning the crowd below. "What did you use to bribe Dad? Tell me it wasn't a bottle."

Before he could answer, the ride whooshed backward and up, not stopping for three or four spots. "Of course, not." *I asked him for your hand—the old-fashioned way.* "I told him I was an ass. He agreed. Maybe he's got his phone aimed this way right now and hopes to get rich off the YouTube video when you dangle me over the side by the tips of my boots."

She rocked forward, making the cart swing back and forth. Paul gulped and grabbed the center bar. "Stop. You know I'm not crazy about heights."

"Which makes this whole thing even stranger. You could have called if you felt you owed me an apology, but you don't."

The ride started moving again, cresting the top then plunging with a stomach-goosing free-fall nearly brushing the landing before climbing upward again. They both laughed.

"I'd forgotten how fun this is." He thought a moment. "Maybe I've always associated the ride with getting dumped and hearing the worst news possible."

Bailey looked toward the moonlit outline of the mountains in the distance.

"Or so I thought at the time."

She glanced back.

"Hearing my daughter was hurt—possibly paralyzed—sort of put things in perspective."

Bailey's lips crooked upward. "I know exactly what you mean."

"I was wrong to curse you, Bailey. So wrong I can't even believe I said the words."

She took a breath and let it go, lifting her chin to look toward the sky. "Does that mean I'm curse-free now?"

The ride stopped at the three-o'clock position to let someone off.

"Not exactly. I asked my folks how to remove a curse, and Mom said as far as she knows Grandma Hilda's curses were irrevocable."

Bailey's posture stiffened. He quickly added, "Unless the curser kisses the cursee at the exact place and time of the original curse and can prove to the cursee how extremely sorry he is for cursing her in the first place."

He pointed upward.

Her body relaxed, her eyes softened. "A kiss, huh? How very Disney of Grandma Hilda."

The ride bounced and jiggled then arced upward. To Paul's good fortune—or maybe due to some witchy intervention—it stopped at the exact spot they'd been in fifteen years earlier.

The noise of the fair below fell away. The tattooed couple in the basket ahead of them was locked in a passionate embrace. The cart directly behind them was empty.

Paul's heart boomed against his chest wall. His fingers felt clumsy and thick as he reached into the pocket of his shirt for the ring he'd given his mother for safekeeping.

"Bailey Jenkins, I never stopped loving you. I tried to convince myself I hated you, but I think I hated myself more."

"Why?"

"For not supporting you. For making your decision tougher than it should have been. I know a lot of people—including some members of my family—who disagree, but they're not us. We were in this baby-making business together and I abandoned you when the road got bumpy. For that I am sorrier than you could ever know."

"Does that mean you forgive me?"

"I do. Can you forgive me?"

She didn't answer right away. But she reached out her hand and laid it along the curve of his jaw. "No."

His heart stopped beating until she leaned in and lightly pressed her lips to his. "There's nothing to forgive. We were kids. We both made mistakes. Fifteen years is a long time to pay. I'll always have regrets, but I can't change what happened—for you or anybody else. It's time to move on."

Move. The word he feared and dreaded. "Does that mean you're not staying in Marietta?"

"I didn't mean that *literally.* I'm done running, Paul. When Dad's finally ready to admit that his guide days are over, I'll convert the Fish and Game into a retail store. If B. Dazzled Bling continues to be successful, I've got my eyes on a spot in the Graff when I start working in precious gems. A girl can dream, right?"

"Dreams are good. Mine has a certain storybook kind of ending. You and me back together again."

He held the ring between them.

"Married...eventually, whenever you're ready...a kid or two...someday. Or not. I know you'll make a cool stepmom to Chloe and Mark."

The wheel reversed course and dropped a quarter of the distance to the ground without pause. His grip on the ring faltered and it slipped between them. Luckily, Bailey's reflexes were sharper than his. Her fingers closed around it and she pressed her fist to her chest.

"Are you proposing to me?"

"Yes."

"Is this the same ring you tried to give me that night?"

He nodded. "It's been in my folks' safe all these years."

She tried it on. A perfect fit because he'd borrowed one of her rings from her dressing table one day and taken it to the jeweler.

"It's...not a diamond," she exclaimed. "It's a sapphire."

"A Montana sapphire. If you want a diamond—"

She put her arms around his shoulders and kissed him. "The ring is beautiful. Perfect. And I love the symmetry of the gesture, but..."

Before she could complete the thought, the ride jerked to a stop. The burly carnie lifted the metal bar and motioned for them to exit.

"Wait," Paul cried, reaching into his pocket. "I have more tickets. Can we go again?"

The guy shook his head. "Not unless you go back to the end of the line. Other people are waiting."

He crossed his arms to make his point.

Paul could see Bailey's barely contained amusement when she got out then turned and held out her hand for him.

It wasn't a yes, but he could feel the ring on her finger and the sensation filled him with hope.

He mumbled "Thanks" as he followed her through the metal gate.

He looked around for a quiet spot where they could finish their conversation, but before he could pull her into the shadows, a voice said, "If it isn't Paul and Bailey. Riding rides. What are you? Seventeen again?"

Bailey tried to let go, but Paul tightened his grip. "Austen. Dad said you weren't coming tonight."

Austen shrugged. "Changed my mind." His gaze dropped to their hands. "So, did you two kiss and make up? I have to say that's pretty magnanimous on your part, little brother. She kills your first child before it has a chance to develop then nearly takes out your second with some stupid horse trick. Honestly, I don't think I could be that forgiving. You must be one helluva a lay, Bailey."

Bailey broke Paul's hold and stepped forward to face his brother. "So I've been told—by both of the men who loved me." She motioned him to lean closer and whispered something only he could hear before turning away. "Paul, I'll catch up with you later. I need to find my dad."

"Try the Beer Garden," Austen called in that smug, know-it-all tone Paul hated worse than anything.

Paul grabbed Austen's arm and swung him around, his right fist landing squarely against his cheekbone. The dull cracking sound made the crowd surge closer, sensing a skirmish of some kind. Austen went down, but his hands broke his fall. He rebounded, furious and ready to retaliate.

Paul couldn't feel his fingers and his wrist was on fire but he braced himself for a fight...until a cowgirl hat adorned with peacock feathers and rhinestones sailed between them, bounced off the waist-high fence and dropped like a Frisbee to the ground.

Bailey picked it up and put it on. "I changed my mind. I'm done running away from people's opinions." She put her hands on her hips and looked at Austen. "You love your brother. I get that. Me, too. I always have."

Paul stepped closer, ready to react to anything Austen might say or do.

"We both made mistakes back then. It's what kids do. If your family can't forgive me...well, I'll—"

"We'll—," Paul corrected. "We'll deal with whatever comes. Together."

She smiled at him then told Austen, "For the record, I don't know how to upload a video on YouTube. And I would never encourage any rider to try new tricks without a spotter and a lot of practice. I love Chloe and I would never—ever—do anything that put her at risk."

"Are we done here, Austen?"

Austen rubbed his cheek and shrugged.

"Good. Then, tell Mom I'll pick up the kids in the morning as planned."

"Oh," Bailey added, reaching into the Marietta Library book bag Paul had seen hanging from her father's wheelchair. "Will you give this to Chloe?" She pulled out a fuzzy pink bear with a bright yellow and purple bow. "OC won it for her at the shooting booth."

She looked at Paul and grinned. "Only cost him thirty bucks and the rest of his tickets."

He leaned in to plant a kiss on her lips then pulled her into the crook of his arm—right where she was meant to be. "See you later, brother. Get some ice on your cheek. Don't want a black eye when you're back in Helena, right?"

He didn't wait for an answer. He was still waiting for one from Bailey, and that was the only answer that counted.

OC CHUCKLED UNDER his breath.

He'd watched the whole confrontation from start to finish. He'd been on his way back from the game booth with his prize when he spotted Austen Zabrinski watching the Ferris wheel. The look on his face was one OC knew well—self-righteous indignation.

OC hadn't been able to catch everything said, but he'd heard enough to ache for his daughter. He knew she'd always regret her decision—even if he hadn't given her any choice in the matter at the time. The last thing she needed was some judgmental jerk butting in just when Paul was about to propose.

When she'd stormed away, OC had had to grip the arms of his wheelchair to keep from jumping to his feet to fight Austen. Luckily, Paul had taken a swing for him.

And a moment later, Bailey showed up. Breathless. Her eyes glittering with unshed tears.

He'd held out the bear and said, "This is for Chloe."

She'd looked over her shoulder then back.

"You're not going to let Austen Zabrinski dictate your future, are you? If you love the man, stand your ground, girl.

His family will adjust. People always do."

Her smile was the best he'd seen in days. Years, maybe.

Then she'd kissed his cheek and asked, "Want me to call Mom to help you get back to the exhibit hall?"

He'd waved her off. "I'll manage. Go. Do what needs to be done."

And she'd done him proud, standing up for herself—and Paul.

He waited until Bailey and Paul disappeared into the crowd then he hooked two fingers into the corners of his mouth and whistled—same as he'd taught his daughter at the ripe old age of five. People turned. A lot of people, but OC only cared about one—Austen Zabrinski.

When Paul's older brother looked his way, OC motioned him over.

"Mr. Jenkins," he said, surprisingly courteous given the disrespect and hostility he'd shown Bailey.

Misogyny stemmed from any number of different roots, OC knew. Austen's hang-ups only mattered where Bailey was concerned. "What can I do for you?"

"You can push this piece of shit wheelchair to Building-A."

"Why would I do that?"

"Because you're the kind of man who cares what people think."

"Unlike you."

"Damn right." He waited until Austen had his hands on the grips then he added, "I never gave a flying fig, but I care now that Bailey is back to stay."

Austen made a skeptical sound. "What makes you so

sure she won't take off again?"

"Cause she's pregnant with your brother's baby, and this time she isn't going to listen to anybody—especially not me—if we were foolish enough to try to talk her out of having it."

"Pregnant? How do you know?"

OC eased back in the chair and let out a sigh. "Same way I know where the fish are when I'm scouting a creek. It's a feeling. And I'm never wrong."

Last time, he'd known weeks before the test kit showed up in the garbage. Plenty of time to fret and stew about his daughter's future. And his conclusion set him on a three-day bender that culminated in a shouting match with Bailey where he used every kind of emotional blackmail he knew to convince her to do what he wanted—escape. The way he'd never had the balls to do.

This time, he'd do anything in his power to support her decision to stay. And that included coming clean with Austen Zabrinski.

Chapter 21

B AILEY FELT THE same type of after-buzz she normally experienced following a successful ride. She'd stood up to one judgmental asshole and felt empowered, excited and a little giddy.

"Are we really going to do this?" she asked, eyeing the open door of the camper. She wanted him. She did. And she wanted to say, "Yes. I'm ready to commit in a way I wasn't fifteen years ago. Ready to be the person I couldn't have been then."

But, what if they were rushing things? Was Paul prepared for the flack he'd get from his family? How would his kids handle the idea of a stepmother?

"By *this*, do you mean make love or get married?"

"Both."

She stepped into the trailer, drawn to the bear-hug size bouquet of stargazer lilies. Her favorite. *He remembered.*

He locked the door and pulled her into his arms. "Then, my answer is yes and...yes. I'd toss you over my shoulder and carry you to the Justice of the Peace if I thought I could get away with it, but I suppose we should let our families get used to the idea, huh?"

She wiggled her hips against his. "Guess what? I don't

care what anybody thinks."

His eyes narrowed with a look of lust and purpose. "No parents, kids, jobs, history or regrets?"

She shrugged out of her shirt, tossing it carelessly over the chair. "None."

She unbuckled her belt, unzipped and kicked off her boots, with no real grace. The only thing she needed right now was confirmation that he loved her.

He dropped to one knee and pressed a kiss to her bare belly. "I love you, Bailey. Will you marry me?"

She didn't hesitate this time. "Yes. My heart's always been here. With you, Paul. I finally feel like I'm home."

"Home to stay, I hope."

"And then some."

There was so much Paul wanted to say, but he decided to let his feelings do the talking. He kissed her the way a dying man welcomed light and hope back into his life.

He closed his eyes and experienced the feel, the taste, the heady aroma of the stargazer lilies he'd ordered off the Internet. "I feel like I'm home, too—even though I never left. Does that make sense?"

She worked his shirt over his shoulders. "Nope. But we never did. Maybe that's what makes us perfect for each other."

"Yin and yang?"

She moved back to unbuckle his belt. "Now, don't go all California on me."

Her low throaty chuckle shot straight to his groin. His jeans shrunk a size or two, which made getting out of them a team effort. Luckily, she was patient and very good with her hands.

They climbed into the elevated bed, ripping back the covers like two kids playing hide and seek. Only this game was for all the marbles.

They rolled together, naked limbs accommodating naked limbs. Desire obvious. "I brought protection."

"Better safe than sorry?"

"I would never be sorry if we got pregnant, Bailey. I want more kids. I want your kids. Tell me you feel the same."

He didn't have to hold his breath for long. "If we're that lucky, Paul, I will be over the moon for nine months. If...if we try and things don't work out..." Her voice dropped. "Will that be a deal-breaker?"

He squeezed her so tight she gave a little peep. "Never. But there would be some poetic justice if we *had* to get married, wouldn't it? How would you feel about trying right from the get-go?"

"Didn't we accidentally do that? In the shower in Reno?"

He blushed. "True. Do you think you're...?"

She frowned. "I've never been that lucky. We didn't use birth control the whole time Ross and I were married and...nothing."

"Maybe he was shooting blanks."

"Do you mean a vasectomy? Trust me, Ross had too much ego."

"I didn't mean that. He started bull riding pretty young, didn't he? Maybe he damaged his baby making parts."

"Oh. That never occurred to me. I blamed myself. I thought maybe something happened inside me when...you know."

He kissed her forehead, her eyes and the corner of her mouth. "If conceiving turns out to be a problem, we'll see a specialist. No worries. Okay?"

Her smile made his insides expand almost to the hurting point. "Sounds like a plan. In the meantime, how are *your* baby-making parts?"

She reached between them to fondle his junk. "I've heard jockeying a desk can be hazardous to your health, too." His anatomy answered. "No impediment here, I see."

They proceeded to take pleasure in each other, but more than that, they loved one another. With mouth and tongue, lips and body. Like alchemists, they took separate elements of need and desire and combined them in the most powerful aphrodisiac known to man—lust.

When he entered her, she moaned greedily. "Yes. You're finally mine, cowboy. I need to do this." She gently pushed him onto his back and threw a leg over. "Cliché, right? Cowgirl on top?"

He palmed her breasts, so captivated by her beauty and the blood pooling in his groin, he murmured the only answer possible. "Huh?"

She covered his hands with hers and laughed. "I love you, Paul Zabrinski." Then, she fell forward, hands on either side of his head, a look of intense focus on her face. "You...have... no...idea...how...much." Her hips ground in a tight circle, emphasizing each word.

His juices pulsed, lifting him off the bed.

They rode the wild, ageless tussle straight to a peak where earth and stars met in one fiery explosion. Bailey's cry of completion resonated in his ears, as sweet a sound as any he'd ever heard. He followed her to that point and beyond with a shout of utter triumph.

She dropped to his chest, spent and breathing hard.

"I love you, Bailey Jenkins," he said, stroking her hair, her bare back. "Thank you for loving me."

She nuzzled his neck. "You're welcome, stud."

They stayed locked in each other's arms, too content to move, until a faint chirping sound made Bailey lift her head. "Your phone or mine?"

"Yours. Mine is turned off."

She drew in a big breath. "Well, as much as I'd like to spend the night with you, I can't. I have to unload the boxes in the back of Dad's truck so I can finish packing up the tables and displays tomorrow. There's a deadline."

"Tell me about it." He groaned. "Big Z's outdoor adventure booth nearly killed me."

She scooted sideways until only one leg remained across him. "It was gorgeous. Dad was really impressed. Said the fake stream reminded him of Spring Creek."

He pulled back slightly so he could look her in the eye. "Really? I've been thinking about setting up the display in the store. Like you see in those big box Outdoor Rec stores. I even thought OC might consider coming to work for me. Maybe teach the basics of fly-fishing, making flies, stream fishing, hunting, and gun safety...you know, the kinds of things he could do in his sleep."

Bailey's mouth gaped in surprise.

"Having the Fish Whisperer on staff would be great for business, don't you agree?"

Bailey hugged him fiercely. "Paul, that's a fabulous idea. Mom and I have been wracking our brains trying to come up with something OC could do this winter besides sitting around feeling sorry for himself."

"Will you ask him or do you want me to?"

She blinked coyly. "Well, if you're serious about marrying me, you probably should—"

"Done," he said, "'Bout time.'"

"You asked him? When?"

"When I gave him the ride tickets and told him about my plan to propose on the Ferris wheel."

She slugged him playfully. "You sneak. Did Mom know?"

"Of course."

She flopped back, giggling. "Small towns. What have I done?"

He reversed positions, pinning her arms overhead. "Don't tell me you're already having regrets."

Her eyes sparkled with mischief and joy. "Never. But that doesn't mean I can't give you a hard time."

"True. You always have."

Her teeth worried her bottom lip. "Which is why I'm so good at it."

She squirmed, her naked breasts inches from his lips. "Among other things."

He licked one deliciously pointy tip. She arched into him with a soft moan. To his shock, he went hard and any chance of her leaving disappeared.

So much for good intentions, he thought. They had a lot to do—including planning a wedding, but all that could wait for tomorrow...after they broke the news to his family.

"YOU TOLD AUSTEN the truth about your mother?"

Louise's hands squeezed the plastic grips on the wheelchair so tight her arthritic knuckles started to pulse in pain. She consciously eased back and made herself take a deep breath.

"I took the blame. I told him I did what I was thought was right for Bailey *and* his brother."

"What did he say?"

"Not much. He's a lawyer. But, at least, the truth is out there."

The truth.

What was the truth? Had she failed her daughter by giving into Oscar's my-way-or-the-highway tough love tactic? The doubt ate her up inside for weeks after Bailey left. She'd nearly suffered a breakdown.

Oddly enough, Marla had been the one to reach out and pull Louise back to the world of the living. Marla had called Louise's blues "empty nest syndrome," and she'd cheerfully coerced Louise into going to Helena for a weekend of shopping, movies, spa treatments and one impulse buy.

Louise touched the tiny butterfly tattoo above her left breast. Her private memorial. "I want to call Marla. You can talk to people in prison, can't you?"

Oscar turned in his seat to look at her. "Why, for God's sake?"

"To tell her I don't hate her. Maybe if I'd been a better friend—if I'd paid more attention—things wouldn't have gotten so crazy."

He shrugged. "When are we going to take care of Jack's ashes? I want to get that done before you and Bailey start planning a wedding."

Louise's heart skipped a beat. "Do you think she'll say yes?"

Oscar reached over his shoulder and patted her hand. "Our daughter may be just as stubborn and pig-headed as her old man, but she's got her mother's brains. She'll say yes. I'd put money on it."

Louise pictured the cash box she'd tucked in her purse. "Speaking of money…I think our daughter is going to be very successful in her new career."

"Was there any doubt? Bailey Jenkins never does anything halfway. She's going to help put Marietta on the map."

They'd reached the car. The parking lot was three-quarters empty, but a continual stream of people hauling things to trucks made the area seem busy and alive.

Louise suddenly felt excited to be alive and facing a future primed with possibilities. Bailey was back to stay. Oscar's rebound was nothing short of miraculous.

Impulsively, she blocked the door when he reached for it.

"What? Did you forget something?"

She reached down and locked the brake then carefully sat on his lap. "Yes. I believe I did. I forgot to tell you how much I love you, Oscar Jenkins. And how proud I am of your recovery."

It was too dark to tell for certain if he blushed, but his smile looked embarrassed. He'd never handled praise well—

maybe because he experienced so little of it growing up.

"I'm not done, yet, you know. I plan to walk again."

"I know. And I think we should wait to spread Jack's ashes until you can walk to Spring Creek…even with a cane." Their foreheads touched, and she said softly, "I think he'd like to know you're back on your feet."

She felt his nod. "You've got a deal. Maybe I'll be able to walk Bailey down the aisle, too."

Louise had to blink away tears when they kissed. "You will, my love. I know you will."

Moments later, with the kind of impossible synchronicity that only happens in the movies, a loud boom, followed by a burst of fireworks that lit up the sky, marked the close of the Big Marietta Fair.

"This fair is one we'll never forget, huh?" Oscar asked, wrapping his arms around her as she settled against his chest to watch the show.

Louise nodded, too overwhelmed with emotion to speak. The best in fifteen long years. But, with luck and love, this fair would be one of many they'd enjoy with Bailey, Paul and the children. For the first time in too long to remember, Louise—book lover that she was—could see a storybook ending in her family's future. One she couldn't wait to watch unfold.

Epilogue

OCTOBER IN MONTANA was glory personified, Bailey thought, closing the gap of sweater at her throat. But nearly as chilly as a foggy winter morning in California's Central Valley.

The cold she could handle as long as it came with brilliant sunlight and a sky so big and blue it almost made a person weep.

Of course, she'd been an emotional mess ever since the plastic indicator showed a plus sign. Pregnant! The doctor confirmed: Reno. A shower neither she nor Paul would ever forget.

"How you doing, sweetheart? Too cold for you?"

Paul took his right hand off the steering wheel of the ATV to pat her knee. He'd traded in the tandem model for one that seated four, but since the children were with Jen this weekend, the backseat held her parents.

At long last, they were completing OC's promise to his best friend.

"I'm fine. Perfect. I only wish we were on horseback. Being outside like this makes me realize how much I miss riding." To be safe, she'd opted not to get back on a horse until after the baby was born.

Not that she'd had time to ride. The wedding was scheduled for the following Saturday. And even though they'd planned a simple, mostly family affair at the Graff Hotel, weddings were a lot of work, she'd discovered.

She was both excited and terrified. Between Paul's mother and hers, their low-key event was turning into something considerably more elegant—storybook, even. Far different from anything they could have pulled off fifteen years ago. And way more expensive. But with Paul's parents' support and the proceeds from the sale of Marla's junk, Bailey was fairly certain they weren't going into debt.

She glanced over her shoulder and smiled at her mother. Mom and Marla spoke once a week. Marla deeply regretted her actions. She'd gotten some help in prison and was taking some kind of medication to stabilize her mood swings. She'd insisted every penny Bailey made from the online sales of her *stuff* go into the wedding kitty, and to Bailey's surprise, she'd made enough to book to the Graff's luxurious honeymoon suite, too.

OC reached out and tapped Paul on the shoulder. "Just ahead on your left."

Paul shot Bailey an amused look.

Ever since Paul offered OC the job of Big Z's Community Relations Supervisor, her father had changed.

He taught himself how to use the computer and spent countless hours on the Internet, watching YouTube videos about fly-fishing, basically teaching himself how to teach.

To everyone's surprise, he'd turned into a single-minded, highly focused professional. Decisive, goal-oriented, driven.

Today's task had been on his To-Do list for months, but

he'd waited for his doctor's okay before asking Bailey and Paul for their help.

Paul slowed and made a gradual turn, allowing for rocks and ruts. Although the picnic area at Spring Creek was accessible by four-wheel drive vehicles, the place OC had picked out could only be reached on foot, by horseback or with all-terrain vehicles.

Paul had volunteered to drive them when he heard about the purpose of OC's mission.

"I want to get Jack off the shelf and out in the world again before winter sets in," OC said a few weeks earlier.

Paul had looked at Bailey and known intuitively she was thinking the same thing: they could use the opportunity for a little private good-bye of their own.

Thanks to working at her new shop every day, her ankle was nearly a hundred percent. She'd wrapped it that morning and put on a pair of hiking boots for extra support, but she'd promised Paul she could manage a short hike up river to the spot he'd visited so many years earlier.

"How's this, OC?" Paul asked, pulling as close to the embankment as he dared.

The water was much lower than it would be in spring, but thanks to recent rains the deep eddies looked bottomless and a few inches of water danced across the shallows.

"Just fine, Paul. Thank you."

Paul jumped out and waited while OC swung his legs over the side, his artificial prosthesis hidden by the heavy duck canvas of his Carhartts, his right boot the same as his left. Paul had seen OC's artificial limb when the man came into the store to formally apply for the job Paul was offering.

"You need full disclosure," OC said and pulled up his pant leg.

OC would always walk with a limp—and probably use a cane, but he'd come a long way since Bailey had returned. Most impressive of all, he hadn't had a drink in nine months.

"Do you plan to say a few words, Dad?" Bailey asked walking up to them.

OC looked at Louise, who remained on the bench seat. Paul saw the look of panic in his future father-in-law's eyes, which was surprising given how flawlessly OC handled the crowds at Big Z Hardware. Even in front of a crowd of a dozen or so who showed up for his first workshop, OC had been glib, ever the showman. Now, he swallowed hard and looked ready to bolt, which everyone knew was not possible.

Louise eased off the seat with her daughter's help then stuck her arm through her husband's and said, "I don't think Jack would expect anything formal. Why don't you two go for your hike and when you come back I'll have the picnic set out. We'll remember some of the good times and say our goodbyes privately."

Bailey looked hesitant. Paul noticed how she sometimes played mother hen to her parents. But now that both Louise and OC were back on their feet financially and health-wise, Paul planned to keep her too busy to worry.

He took Bailey's hand. "Good idea. We won't be long. I want to show Bailey a special spot I found."

The autumn sun cast a golden hue through the dying leaves. The path underfoot was slick in places so they took it slow. The nip in the air made his nostrils quiver. Winter would be here before they knew it and in late March they'd welcome a new child to the family.

"Are you okay?" he asked when her hand tightened on his.

"Fine. Just being careful."

Ironic, he thought, given the way they'd dashed carelessly through life in their youth. Reckless. Like typical teen-agers. "I remember stumbling here. Scraped the heck out of my hands."

She lifted their hands and kissed his palm. The gesture made him smile.

"You're going to be a great mother."

"Do you think so? Really?"

"Absolutely. Chloe and Mark are crazy about you."

She shrugged. "Seeing someone every other weekend isn't the same as living together, day in and day out. I know our relationship will have some ups and downs after the first of the year when Jen and Edward move and the kids are with us full time, but as long as they know I love their dad and won't do anything to come between you and them, I think we'll be okay."

He believed that with all his heart. Life had come full circle, and he'd never felt more hopeful.

He pushed aside some low branches and motioned her to go ahead into the small clearing. The conformation of rocks and trees created a private niche where he'd wailed over his loss and the vagaries of fate that ruined his dreams.

If we'd married and had our child, I wouldn't have Chloe and Mark.

The revelation was so obvious he'd probably said the words out loud a dozen times or more, but until that moment he hadn't felt the truth at his core.

Everything happens for a reason, Paul, he heard his grandmother say.

Impossible, given the fact he'd never met her. But the surety of the words made him stagger and reach out for a sapling.

Bailey stood without moving for several minutes, soaking in the beauty and peacefulness of the little glen. "I bet Grandma Hilda brought you here, Paul."

"I never thought of that. I suppose it's possible. She'd been on my mind ever since I called on her to curse you."

Bailey walked to a large boulder and sat. The sun had warmed the rock, as if preparing for her visit. "There's a peace here that feels very spiritual and connected. It's the right place to say goodbye."

He squatted beside her. "How do you say goodbye to someone who never was?"

She reached in her pocket and pulled out the beaded heart she'd finished last night. At the center was a small, perfect Montana sapphire.

She held it to the sun to watch it sparkle then kissed it and tossed it into the deepest part of the water. It made a tiny splash, but she swore the sound carried the hint of a child's laugh.

A warm rush of love and emotion swept through her from head to toe.

Sadness? Yes, but a beautiful peace she wanted to believe was forgiveness.

The last vestiges of guilt melted away. She'd made a choice she would always regret but she no longer hated herself for being young and pliable. She couldn't hate her father for doing what he thought was in her best interest. She didn't blame Paul for cursing her.

She turned to the man she loved and wept in his arms. He stroked her back and murmured soft words of comfort against her hair.

"It's okay. Everything's going to be fine. We're good, my love. It's all good." His comfort was a healing balm, too.

"That was beautiful, Bailey. I wish I'd put as much thought into this as you did, but I've been so busy."

She pulled back and put her finger to his lips. "I made that heart for me, Paul. A symbol of the gift I couldn't give before. Besides, you're not a look-back kind of guy. You're too busy looking forward. And I love that about you."

"You're right. I'm looking forward to all the possibilities a life with my soul mate has to offer. But I knew this closure was important to you. And I'm partly to blame for that. I'm the jerk who cursed you, remember?"

Before she could answer, he did something amazing.

He stepped back and looked at the sky and shouted, "Grandma Hilda, if you can hear me, I call on you to lift the curse. I want it to end. Now."

He looked around, head tilted as if listening for a voice, a sign. When nothing happened, he made an "I tried" gesture. "I guess it was worth a shot, huh?"

Bailey threw back her head and laughed, releasing an inexplicable rush of joy that bubbled up inside her. Happiness as rich and glorious as she'd ever known vibrated in every fiber of her being.

"The curse is gone, Paul. It worked."

He looked skeptical, as if she were humoring him.

"No, really. It's gone." She pressed his hand to her heart. "Wiped clean. I swear my heart isn't as heavy as it was."

"Wow. Who knew?"

He looked toward the sky again. "Thanks, Grandma."

Then his expression turned serious as he pulled her tight against him. "But do you know what I think? I think you lifted the curse, Bailey. By coming home and fixing things between us. By forgiving your father. That took a very brave person. And daring to trust me again, after I failed you twice…that kind of love heals everything."

His words were a balm to her soul.

"I love you, Bailey Jenkins."

She closed her eyes and kissed him with all the hope his words inspired in her.

But when the tug of responsibility reminded her of her parents waiting for their return, she pulled away. "We need to go now."

He took her hand started to lead the way. She glanced over her shoulder for one last look at this hallowed nook.

For a millisecond, she swore she saw two figures in the glimmering shadow. A grandmother holding the hand of a small child.

Her breath caught in her throat and tears clustered behind her eyes again, but she blinked them away. She joined Paul on the path, and together they walked side-by-side toward their wonderful, blessed future.

Look for book two in The Big Sky Maverick series

NOBODY'S COWBOY

Release August 2014

ABOUT THE AUTHOR

Former award-winning newspaper journalist Debra Salonen is a nationally bestselling author with 26 published novels for Harlequin's Superromance and American lines and one single title release for Harlequin Signature. Several of her titles were nominated for "Best Superromance," including *Until He Met Rachel*, which took home that honor in 2010.

In 2006, Debra was named Romantic Times Reviewer's Career Achievement "Series Storyteller of the Year".

Debra lives in the foothills near Yosemite National Park in California with her husband and two dogs. Luckily, her two children and three grandchildren live close by to keep Debra connected to the real world.

Visit her website at www.debrasalonen.com

Made in the USA
Columbia, SC
09 October 2022

68728096R00183